A LADY IN NEED
OF AN HEIR

Louise Allen

MILLS & BOON

First published in Great Britain 2018
by Mills & Boon, an imprint of HarperCollins*Publishers*
1 London Bridge Street, London, SE1 9GF

Large Print edition 2019

© 2018 Melanie Hilton

ISBN: 978-0-263-07878-7

MIX
Paper from
responsible sources
FSC C007454

This book is produced from independently certified
FSC™ paper to ensure responsible forest management. For
more information visit www.harpercollins.co.uk/green.

Printed and bound in Great Britain
by CPI Group (UK) Ltd, Croydon, CR0 4YY

Louise Allen loves immersing herself in history. She finds landscapes and places evoke the past powerfully. Venice, Burgundy and the Greek islands are favourite destinations. Louise lives on the Norfolk coast and spends her spare time gardening, researching family history or travelling in search of inspiration. Visit her at louiseallenregency.co.uk, @LouiseRegency and janeaustenslondon.com.

Also by Louise Allen

A Rose for Major Flint
Once Upon a Regency Christmas
Marrying His Cinderella Countess
The Earl's Practical Marriage

Lords of Disgrace miniseries

His Housekeeper's Christmas Wish
His Christmas Countess
The Many Sins of Cris de Feaux
The Unexpected Marriage of Gabriel Stone

The Herriard Family miniseries

Forbidden Jewel of India
Tarnished Amongst the Ton
Surrender to the Marquess

Discover more at millsandboon.co.uk.

For A J H. He knows why.

Chapter One

Early October 1815—Douro Valley, Portugal

It was the same as his memories, yet different as a dream. The river, tricky, pretending to be benign, ran wide here, below the gorges that lurked lethally upstream. The sky was blue, dotted with clouds, a roof over the valley with its tiers of intricate ancient terraces rising on either side. The harvest was over, the grapes stripped away, the leaves hinting at a change to the gold and crimson of autumn.

There were no sounds of shots or cannon fire, no victims of the fighting clogged the swirling brown waters. From the bushes on the bank a bird sang clear and pure and the scorching heat of summer was turning to something kinder.

The tranquillity was unsettling, dangerous. This was when the enemy struck, when you were lulled into relaxation, distracted by a moment's peace, a glimpse of beauty. Gray gave himself a mental shake. There was no enemy. He was no longer Colonel Nathaniel Graystone and the war was over. Twice over, with Bonaparte finally defeated scarcely four months ago on the bloody plains of Belgium.

Portugal was free from invaders and had been so for four years now. There were no ambushes here, no snipers behind rocks, no cavalry troops to lead into a hell of gunfire and smoke and blood. He was the Earl of Leybourne and he was a civilian now. And he was here on an inconvenient errand, the kind that assuming the title and the headship of his family seemed to involve.

The two men handling the *rabelo* shouted something in Portuguese as the sail flapped and Gray translated without having to think about it. He ducked low among the empty barrels as the boom swung over, then tossed a line to the man at the prow.

Doubtless it was beneath his new dignity to approach the Quinta do Falcão by working boat. He should have creaked for almost a hundred miles along the hilltop road from Porto to Pinhão in one of the lumbering old-fashioned carriages to be hired in the city, then held on to his nerve, his dignity and his hat as it negotiated the hairpin bends of the track leading down to the river. But this was the fast, efficient way to make the journey and twenty months had still not instilled in him the attitudes expected of a peer of the realm. At least, not according to his godmother, Lady Orford.

It was she, and his own uncomfortable sense of duty, that Gray could blame for his present situation. He was up to his ankles in bilge water and facing a situation that, in his opinion, called for either the skills of a diplomat or those of a kidnapper. And he was neither. It did very little for his mood and even less for the condition of his new boots.

The man managing the great steering paddle shouted something and jerked his head towards the bank. There were trees and a wide flat area about ten feet above the waterline and through the foliage he could see glimpses of red-tiled rooftops and the whitewashed walls of a low, sprawling house. As the boat steered nearer, fighting against the current, he saw gardens, then a landing stage.

'*É aquele Quinta do Falcão?*' he called.

'*Sim, senhor.*'

The house, the heart of the quinta or winemaking estate, came fully into sight. It was charming,

he thought, something of his edgy mood softening. It was gracious, beautifully kept, radiating
prosperity. A pleasant surprise, not the down-
at-heel place hanging on by a thread that he had
feared from his godmother's agitation. The boat
angled closer, the boatmen struggling to find
slack water nearer the bank. Through a grove of
trees Gray glimpsed what looked like gravestones
and a woman rising from her knees in the midst
of them, a flurry of garnet-red skirts against the
green. It was like a fashionable sentimental picture, he thought fancifully. *Beauty amidst the
Sorrows* or some such nonsense.

Then, with a sudden swoop, the boat was along-
side the long wooden dock. One man jumped
ashore, looped a rope around a bollard and gestured to Gray to throw across his baggage. Three
valises hit the dock, then Gray vaulted over beside them as the boatman freed the line and was
back on board with the boat slipping fast into the
current.

Gray waved and they waved back, gap-toothed
smiles splitting their faces under the broad-
brimmed black hats they both wore.

You may well grin, he thought. *The amount I
paid you.* But money was not the issue. Speed was.

'*Quem são você?*'

It was the woman from the graveyard demanding his identity. She made a vivid sight: garnet skirts above soft black ankle boots, a white loose shirt under a tight black waistcoat. Her hands were on her hips; her expression conveyed as little welcome as her tone.

'Good morning,' Gray said in English as he straightened up from his bags, ignoring her question as he studied her. The scrutiny brought up a flush of angry colour over her cheekbones and the wide brown eyes narrowed.

'This is the private landing stage for Quinta do Falcão.' She switched easily to unaccented English. Despite the costume and her dark hair, this was the mistress of the place, not one of the staff, he realised.

'Excellent, then I am where I intended to be. It would have been inconvenient to be dropped off ten miles adrift.' Gray looped the strap of one bag over his shoulder and picked up the others. 'Miss Frost, I presume?'

A narrowing of her eyes was all the confirmation she offered. 'I ask again, sir, who you are.'

'I am Leybourne. You should be expecting me. You should have had a letter informing you of my arrival. Your Aunt Henrietta, Lady Orford, wrote at least a month ago.'

One lock of dark brown hair slipped from its combs and fell against her cheek. Miss Frost tucked it back behind her ear without taking her hostile gaze from his face. 'In that case it went on the fire, as do most of her communications when she is in a managing mood. You are her godson, then, and if I remember rightly, Lord Leybourne. So you know what she is like.'

'Yes.' Gray held on to his temper with the same control he had used when faced with damn-fool orders from superior officers and offered no opinion on the Dowager. She was an imperious and tactless old bat, true enough, but she was doubtless right about what should be done with her niece.

'And you expect to stay here?' Miss Frost looked at the fast disappearing stern of the boat, her lips a tight line. A rhetorical question—unless she intended to refuse him hospitality. There were no other houses within sight and the nearest village was several miles away.

Doubtless Godmama Orford's intentions were correct, but he was beginning to wonder if marrying off this prickly female suitably was going to be as easy as she thought. Miss Frost might be lovely to look at, but her tongue had been dipped in vinegar, not honey. 'If that would not be inconvenient. I do not believe there is any other lodging nearby.'

'You can stay in the Gentlemen's House.' Miss Frost turned on her heel and walked away towards the buildings without waiting to see if he would follow. 'It is empty at this time of year,' she tossed back over her shoulder. 'We use it for visitors when buyers and officials come and there are none now, just after the harvest.'

Gray discovered that he was more amused than annoyed as he followed her. The performance was impressive, the rear view enticing and he found himself in some sympathy with anyone who consigned his godmother's missives to the flames. On the other hand, this was clearly not the life a single young woman of aristocratic family should be living.

A stocky, swarthy man in baggy breeches with a red sash around his substantial midriff hurried out of the house towards them. 'Senhora Gabrielle?'

'This gentleman is the Earl of Leybourne, Baltasar,' she said in English. 'He will spend tonight in the Casa dos Cavalheiros and take dinner with me. Please send one of the men over to make sure he has everything he needs until then.

He will require the carriage in the morning to take him back to Porto.'

'Thank you.' Gray arrived at her side and deposited the bags in a heap on the front step. 'However, I fear our business will take rather longer than one night, Miss Frost.'

'*Our* business?' Her eyebrows rose. Gray found himself admiring the curve of them, the length of her lashes as she gave him a very direct look. He could admire the entire effect, to be honest with himself. She had all the charm of an irritated hornet, true, but that temper brought rosy colour to her slightly olive complexion. The Frosts had married into the local gentry at some time in the past; that was clear. Then he reminded himself that he had to extract her from this place and endure the hornet stings all the way back to England, and her allure faded.

'I can assure you I have not returned to Portugal on my own account, Miss Frost.' He kept his voice pleasant, which appeared to make her more annoyed.

'You mean you travelled all this way simply as the messenger boy for my dear aunt? I had no idea that earls were so easily imposed upon. I cannot believe it will take me very long to say *no* to whatever it is she wants, but, please, make yourself at home, Lord Leybourne.' She made a sweeping gesture at the grounds. 'And stay for a week if that is what it takes to convince her that I want nothing whatsoever to do with her.'

Gaby watched the earl follow Baltasar along the winding path to the little lodge where they accommodated wine buyers, shippers and gentlemen calling to view the quinta. As an unmarried lady it was sensible to keep male house guests separate for the good of her reputation, although Gabrielle Frost of Quinta do Falcão was regarded almost as an honorary man in the neighbourhood, at least in her business dealings.

This man was definitely best kept at a distance. She had never encountered her aunt's godson that she was aware of, but then she had not been in England since she was seventeen. The war had seen to that. She turned away with a mutter of irritation when she realised she had watched him out of sight. The man was quite self-confident enough without having confirmation that his tall figure drew the female eye. He had been an officer, she recalled. That reference to *returning* must mean he'd been in Portugal during the war and he still moved like a soldier—upright, alert, fit. Dangerous in more ways than one. She should be on her guard.

The earl was probably well aware already that women looked at him, she thought, as she pushed open the kitchen door. He looked right back at them: she hadn't missed the leisurely assessment he had given her on the dock.

Maria—the cook and Baltasar's wife—looked up from the intricate pastry work she was creating at the kitchen table. 'Maria, *temos um convidado.*' She almost smiled at the word. *Convidado* sounded too much like *convivial* to translate *guest* in this particular case. 'An English earl, a connection of my family. Baltasar is taking him to the Gentlemen's House. Send over refreshments, please. He will join me for dinner.'

'*Sim, senhora.*' Maria gave a final flourish of the glaze brush over the pastry. She looked pleased, but then she enjoyed showing off her skills and Gabrielle, although appreciative, could only eat so much. As for Jane Moseley, her companion, she was a fussy eater who still, after almost ten years in Portugal, yearned for good plain English cooking.

Alfonso and Danilo were talking loudly in the scullery. From the sounds of splashing and clanking, they had been sent to fetch hot water for the earl's bath.

Everything was under control, as was to be expected. The household ran like clockwork with rarely change or challenge to distract her from growing grapes and making and selling port. The goodwill of the staff and the calm efficiency of Miss Moseley saw to that.

Which left Gaby free to get on with managing the quinta and the business of creating fine wine. And that was what she should be doing now— keeping the record books up to date in the precious lull after the hectic and exhausting harvest time and before the routines of the autumn and winter work. She let herself into her office and sat down at the desk, which had, of course, a good view of the Gentlemen's House to distract her.

She flipped open the inkwell, dipped her pen and continued with her notes about the terrace on the southern bank that needed clearing and replanting. Her father had once told her that in England there was a saying—you plant walnuts and pears for your heirs. It was not quite that bad with vines, but it would be many years before she saw a good return from the new planting, so best to get on with it at once.

She knew what Aunt Henrietta would ask about

that: What was the good of maintaining and improving the quinta for posterity when Gaby had no one to leave it to? She asked herself the same question often enough, and the answer was that, eventually, she would find someone she thought worthy of it, even though she was the last of the Frosts.

Four dozen grafted rootstocks...

She stopped in the middle of a sentence and nibbled the end of the quill meditatively. But that was why Leybourne was here, of course. He had come to nag her into returning to England, leaving the quinta and surrendering to her aunt's marriage plans. How her aunt had managed to persuade him to make the journey was a mystery, unless he had simply fled the country to escape her persistence, which was cowardly but understandable. Perhaps he was nostalgic for his war years in the Peninsula—she had caught his good Portuguese when he was talking to the boatmen and he had understood her first question.

Where were you in October five years ago, my lord? she wondered. Behind the lines of Torres Vedras, protecting Lisbon with Viscount Wellington, as Wellesley had just become, or skirmishing around as a riding officer seeking out intelligence on the advancing French? Perhaps he had been a friend of Major Andrew Norwood. No, best not to think of him, the shocking sounds that fists meeting flesh made, the lethal whisper of a knife blade through the twilight.

The violence that is in men's hearts...

Gaby bent her head over her ledgers. There was work to be done, a winery did not run itself. She could not allow herself to think about Norwood or the nightmares would begin again. He was gone, dead, and she was *not* going to allow him to haunt her.

The clock in the hall struck six as she finished her notes and lists. She put down her pen, blotted the ledger, assembled the papers and allowed herself to look out of the window at last. And there her uninvited guest was, strolling bareheaded through the cherry orchard as though he was surveying his own acres. He was heading directly for the burial plot.

She was probably overreacting, Gaby told herself as she ran down the stairs and out through the front door. There was no reason why he should not look around the grounds—they had been laid out as a pleasure garden, after all, and she was proud of them. It was perfectly natural that he should visit the burial enclosure and pay his respects, if he was so inclined. As for what he might find there… Well, that was not his business. He was a messenger passing through and would soon be gone. What he thought of her was not of the slightest importance.

She found him standing at the foot of her parents' graves, head slightly bowed, apparently deep in thought. She stood on just that spot almost every day, collecting her thoughts, asking questions, wrestling with difficult issues. She did not expect an answer from beyond, of course, but simply thinking about how her parents would handle any problem often gave her own ideas direction and validation. Her father had never given her firm instructions about the business, he taught by example and encouraged innovation. The only hard line either parent had laid down was, 'Follow your conscience, always. If you are uneasy in your mind, then listen and do the right thing.' It was a rule she attempted to live by.

'December 1807,' the earl said, looking up as she reached the headstone and faced him. 'The month the French took Porto for the first time.'

'Yes. There was an epidemic of the influenza, just to add to the general horror. I think the anxiety and stress of the invasion made my parents particularly vulnerable to the infection.' She could say it unemotionally now. Sometimes it even seemed like a dream, or a story she had read in a book, that time when she found herself orphaned with a fourteen-year-old brother and a quinta to, somehow, protect against the armies fighting to control a country in turmoil. She missed them all every day. The pain had become easier to live with, the sense of loss never seemed to diminish.

'And this is your brother.' Leybourne had moved on to the next headstone, reminding her just what a bad job she had done of protecting Thomas. He crouched down to read the inscription. 'September 1810. We were behind the lines of Torres Vedras, holding Lisbon by then. I remember those months.' Not with any pleasure, from the tone of his voice.

'The French killed Thomas. Not disease.' The French and treachery.

'Hell, I'm sorry.' He had bent down to read the inscription, but he looked up sharply at her words, then back to the stone. He reached out one long finger to trace the dates of birth and death. 'I had not realised he had been so young, only seventeen. What happened? Were they scavenging around here?'

'Only just seventeen.'

Old enough to be thinking about girls and so shy that he had no idea how to talk with them, let alone anything else. Old enough to be shaving off fluff and young enough to be proud of the fact. Young enough to still kiss his big sister without reserve when he came home and old enough to resent her worrying...

'He was with the *guerrilheiros*. Not all the time, only when your Major Norwood thought to…use him.' *Exploit him.*

Leybourne's head came up again at the tone of her voice. 'Andrew Norwood, the riding officer?'

'The spy, yes. He was happy to find an enthusiastic, idealistic lad who knew his way around the hills here.' An inexperienced boy. One who might well get himself killed—and then how useful that would be for Major Norwood, she had realised far too late. Gaby kept her voice studiedly neutral. Norwood might well have been a friend of the earl when he had been an officer here. He might be the kind of man Norwood had been.

'Could you not stop him?' Leybourne stood up. 'I'm sorry, no, of course you could not if he was bent on fighting the French, not without chaining him up. We had boys younger than that lying about their age to enlist.'

'If I had thought chaining him would work I would have tried it, believe me,' she said, heart-sick all over again at the remembered struggle, the arguments, the rows.

We are English and Portugal is our home, Thomas had thrown at her. *The French are our enemy and the enemy of Portugal. It is our duty to fight them.*

'I told him that we had a duty to try and keep the quinta going, to give work and shelter to our people, to have something to offer the economy when the fighting was over so the country could be rebuilt,' she said now. 'The French would go soon enough, I argued.'

While we skulk here, nothing but farmers and merchants. We are descended from earls, her brother had retorted, impassioned and idealistic. *We Frosts fight.*

Gaby came back to herself, furious to find her vision blurred. She blinked hard. 'I was so proud of him and so frightened for him. He was a boy who had the heart of a man and he was betrayed in the end.'

'By whom? Someone within the *guerrilheiros*? It was the same with the Spanish guerrillas, a few had been turned by the French for money or because their families were threatened.' The earl had his hand on the headstone, the strong fingers curled around the top as though he would protect it.

'No. But it doesn't matter now. The person responsible is dead.' Her voice was steady again and she had her voice and her emotions under control. She resisted the impulse to glance at the riverbank where two men had gone over, fighting to the death, into the rushing water. There was a wood stack there now, although no traces had been left to hide.

How had this man manged to lure her into revealing so much? So much emotion? Gaby found a smile and turned to lead him out of the plot, past the graves of her grandparents Thomas and Elizabeth and her great-grandparents Rufus and Maria Frost, who had first owned the quinta. Weathered now, that first stone bore the family crest the quinta was named for, a falcon grasping a vine branch, faint but defiant on the old stone.

'Lord Leybourne, if you come this way I will show you the rose garden.' The roses were virtually over, but it would serve to move him on to ground that held less power over her.

Or not, it seemed. 'Call me Gray, everyone does,' he said. The infuriating man was walking away from her towards the southern corner of the plot, not the gate. 'What is this?' He had stopped at the simple white slab that was tilted to face the rising sun.

L.M., he read. He glanced up, frowning at her as she came closer, then went back to the inscription. *March 25, 1811. Remember.* 'That is the date of the battle of Campo Maior. Who is this stone for?'

She smiled at him, amused, despite her feelings, by the way he frowned at her. It was clear that he resented not being in total command of the facts of any situation. The impulse to shock him was too strong to resist.

'My lover.'

Chapter Two

Gray straightened up, not at all certain he could believe what Gabrielle Frost had just said.

'Your *lover*? Your betrothed, you mean? Which regiment was he in?'

'No, you did hear me correctly, my lord. My lover. And, no, I am not discussing him with you.' She bent to brush a fallen leaf from the stone, then walked away from him, seemingly unconcerned that she had just dropped a shell into his hands, its fuse still hissing.

Lover? She was ruined. His godmother would have hysterics because no one, surely, except some bankrupt younger son, bribed to do it, would take Gabrielle Frost now. What the hell was she doing, admitting to it so brazenly?

Gray pulled himself together and strode after her out of the grave plot, letting the little wrought iron gate clang shut behind him. The garnet skirts swished through the grass ahead. Her legs must be long for her to have gained so much ground. He lengthened his stride for the dozen steps it took to bring him to her side.

'Miss Frost, stop, please.' It was more an order than a request and all the effect it had on her was to bring up her chin. As though he had not spoken she continued until she passed through an arch cut in a high evergreen hedge.

'Here is the rose garden. If you are going to rant at me, my lord, at least we are out of sight of the house here.' She made her way to a curving stone bench and sat down. It was a charming spot that overlooked a pool and fountain set in the middle of the curving rose beds, but Gray was in no mood to appreciate it.

He stopped beside her, his shoulder dislodging the petals of a late, deep red bloom the same colour as her skirts. The petals fell like blood-stained confetti on to her hair and he repressed a shudder at his own gruesome imagery. Thinking about that battle must have released memories he had buried for four years or more.

'Is this widely known?' he demanded. 'I heard no gossip, no whispers in Porto.'

'Of course it is not known. Do you think me a loose woman to brag of my…adventures?'

'Then why tell me, a total stranger?'

'Because you are the total stranger who has been sent to lure me back to England, I suspect, and now you know a very good reason why I should not go. You are also an English gentleman and you will not, I think, gossip, whatever you think of me.' She looked up at him, her head tipped slightly to one side like an inquisitive cat as she waited for his reaction.

'You shock me, Miss Frost.' Had the woman no shame?

'Then I am sorry you have had such an affront to your delicate sensibilities, my lord.'

'I do not have *sensibilities*, Miss Frost. Your aunt, however, does.' And they wouldn't have to be delicate to be outraged by this.

She shrugged, provoking a strong desire in him to give her a brisk shake. 'Yes, of course, I am sure she is all fine feelings. However, my aunt is a long way away and I do not care about her opinion.'

In the face of that brazen indifference there seemed little point in attempting to remonstrate with her. Besides, the horse was well and truly bolted and attempting to close the stable door was pointless.

Gray watched her face. Miss Frost was thinking, it seemed. Her eyes narrowed. 'Did you fight at Campo Maior, my lord?'

'I did. Why? And call me Gray.' There was no point in being at odds with her and he hated being *my lorded.*

'Why do I ask? You might have been close by when he was killed.' She said it without overt hostility, more, he thought, as though she was calculating carefully which of his ribs to slide a knife between for the tidiest extermination.

'Which regiment?' he asked.

'Infantry,' she unbent enough to admit.

'I was cavalry, probably on the opposite flank.'

'Then we have nothing to discuss, have we?' Gabrielle shifted her gaze from his face and looked out over the garden. Something, a frog perhaps, plopped into the pond, and a pair of magpies flew over, cackling wickedly. 'Gray,' she added, as though there had been no pause.

'We must talk,' Gray said after another silence that, peculiarly, seemed almost amiable. He found himself reluctant to break the tranquillity of the garden with speech.

'You must, I suppose,' she said with a sigh. 'Then you will consider your duty done to my aunt and can return to England. I do hope you have some other business in Portugal, because this is a long way to come just for a *talk*.'

'It is, however, the sole purpose of my journey.' A talk and a return with one young lady who was already proving ten times more tricky than he had imagined she would be. 'I could stock my cellars with port while I am here, I suppose.'

'Of course.' Gabrielle turned to him, something coming alight behind those mocking brown eyes. He had her serious attention at last and it felt like something alive, something vibrant. 'What do you hold at the moment? Is there a weakness in young growths to lay down, or perhaps you are running low on wines to drink at the moment? Or are you interested in investing in some fine old vintages? I can let you have good prices, although naturally you will want to do some tastings and see what is available elsewhere.'

She broke off, apparently lost in calculation. 'How long are you staying? I could take you to the Factory House, of course, make introductions and then go with you to the best lodges—not necessarily the biggest or best known.'

'The Factory House? That is some kind of club, isn't it? I had dinner there a few times when we retook Porto for the second time.'

'It is where all the growers from the English and

Scottish houses come together, along with own-
ers of the lodges and the shippers. It is a cross
between a club and a trading house and a mutual
support society, I suppose.'

'But you are not a member, surely? You are a
woman.'

Gabrielle stood up, forcing Gray to rise, too. Despite being shorter than he, she contrived to look
down her nose in disdain. 'This—' She waved
a hand to encompass the garden, the house, the
terraces rising above. 'This is Quinta do Falcão.
This is Frost's, one of the great estates, and I am
its owner. I would have to commit a far greater
sin than failing to possess a penis, or being suspected of somewhat loose morals, to be barred
from the Factory House.'

Gray took two long, slow breaths. He had faced
charging French cavalry and been bellowed at by
Wellington and had stood up to both. He was not
going to be reduced to fuming incoherence by one
young woman who said *penis* without blushing
and who admitted to taking a lover.

'Besides, there is the question of money,' she
added with what was suspiciously like a fleeting
smile. 'Ports are blended. This is not winemaking as in Burgundy or Bordeaux. We cooperate,
work with the others to create our wines. It would

be in the interests of no one to antagonise Gabrielle Frost of Quinta do Falcão.'

'I see. It is a matter of trade and profits.' He
sounded like a stuffed shirt to his own ears. A
pompous, disapproving outsider. Lord knew why
he could not seem to get a secure footing in deal-
ing with this woman. She was three years younger
than his own twenty-eight, he knew that. He was
an earl, he had been a colonel and yet there was
nothing in his experience to give him the slightest clue as to how to handle her.

His own marriage had hardly been one of perfect tranquillity, but Portia, when unhappy, had
sulked and brooded in a ladylike manner, not
fought back with sharp words and a complete
unconcern for propriety. But then, he reminded
himself bitterly, he had made a poor business of
marriage and he clearly understood nothing about
the female mind.

'Yes, trade,' Gabrielle agreed now, far too
sweetly. 'The sordid business of working to create something wonderful which you aristocrats
can enjoy and for which you may despise us, even
as you pay your inherited money to secure it. I
am in trade, *my lord*, just as surely as the tailor
who makes your very fine coats to fit your torso
to perfection or the bootmaker who moulds that

leather to your calves or the gunsmith who creates the perfect balance for your hand.'

'Are there any other parts of the male body you are going to enumerate this afternoon, Miss Frost?' Gray enquired, hoping for a tone of reproof and probably, he thought irritably, merely managing to sound pompous again.

'I will spare your blushes and refrain from mentioning breeches, my lord,' she said, with a comprehensive downward glance at his thighs.

Gray sent up a silent prayer that he was not blushing—and when was the last time he had feared that he was? Ten years ago?—and returned to the attack. 'You are from an aristocratic family yourself, Miss Frost, hardly in a position to sneer at my title.'

'I do not sneer at your title, Gray. I sneer at the nonsense of looking down on trade and industry and the creation of wealth.' She smiled suddenly and his breath hitched in his chest. 'You will join me for dinner, I hope, and sample our port.'

She was gone, her skirts whisking behind her with the rapidity of her steps, before he could reply. That was probably a very good thing because, he realised, he had been within a hair's breadth of lowering his head and kissing those full red mocking lips.

'Hell's teeth.' Gray sat down again, the better to swear in comfort. What the blazes had come over him? Barring lust, insanity and some sort of brain fever, that was. Gabrielle Frost was infuriatingly unlike any woman he had ever encountered and that included some very fast and dashing widows. She was independent, outspoken, immodest and outrageous. She was a damned nuisance to a man who had intended a rapid return to his own affairs, because he could not think of any way to extract her from her precious quinta short of kidnapping.

He had expected to find a lonely, struggling young woman bowed down by the burden of her inheritance and only too grateful to be whisked back to luxury and the glamour of the London Season. Gabrielle Frost appeared to be healthy, lively, prosperous and decidedly unbowed. She was no timorous innocent, but a woman of the world with an intense pride in what she did.

But he could not leave her here, not without making some effort to persuade her to do the right thing. He had promised his godmother to try to bring Gabrielle back with him and he could not break his word, not without a good reason. And he could see no reason other than her own stubborn inclinations—she was a young, single

Englishwoman of good family and she should be back in England under her aunt's protection until a suitable husband could be found for her. He was beginning to get an inkling of why no local gentleman had offered, he thought grimly.

She had already compromised herself thoroughly with this lover of hers, unless, of course, she was lying in an attempt to shock him so comprehensively that he left her here as a lost cause. But in that case, who was the memorial intended for? A friend? A man she had loved chastely?

Gray leaned back against the carved stone of the seat and attempted to think about the problem in military terms. If Miss Frost was the enemy entrenched in a fortress, how would he get her out? Starve her out? Bombard her defences until there was a breach in the walls and then storm in? Use an inside agent and have them unbar a gate? Use diplomatic means and negotiate a surrender?

He could not spend the time to sit on her doorstep for months until he wore her down, although what she was being so stubborn about he could not comprehend—surely she employed a competent manager who actually ran the place?

A siege would likely take years. Force was completely ineligible, which ruled out slinging her on to a boat and simply kidnapping her. An inside agent or diplomacy seemed the only feasible methods. He would begin with her lady companion, always assuming that the mature female his godmother had assured him was in residence hadn't been driven out—or driven distracted—already. He would not put either past Gabrielle Frost.

Gray closed his eyes and considered how to use whatever support an obviously ineffective, woolly-minded and careless chaperone might give him. He opened them a heartbeat later. The image on the inside of his eyelids was not some brow-beaten widow, but Miss Frost herself. And he could think about siege works and chaperones all he liked, but the honest truth was that he found the woman profoundly, inconveniently, embarrassingly arousing.

He moved, a frustrated jerk of his shoulders, and rose petals fell on to his hands. He touched one with his fingertip: soft, velvety, infinitely feminine.

This time he did not swear. Gray buried his head in his hands and groaned.

Well. That had been stimulating, in much the same way that a wasp sting was energising. Gaby swept in through the back door and went straight down the stone steps into the cellars. The door at the top had been open and there was a wash of lantern light at the far end, so she knew her cellarman was working.

'Jaime!' she called into the gloom.

'Sim, senhora?' He peered around a thick pillar, a dusty bottle in his hand, his wire-rimmed spectacles perched on the end of his nose.

'We have a guest for dinner this evening,' she said in rapid Portuguese as she joined him. 'An English aristocrat who needs port for his cellar.'

'Needs it?' Jaime queried with a grin.

'Every English lord needs our port,' she chided, returning the smile. 'Whether he knows it or not.'

'He is knowledgeable?'

'Probably not about the detail, or the business. I imagine he has a good palate.' Although how she knew that she was not certain. The fact that the man had the taste to dress well in a classic, understated style should have nothing to do with his appreciation of fine wine. 'He was here fighting during the war.'

Jaime grunted. 'You want to serve him the best, then?' He would approve of any Englishman who had fought against the French. He had been with the *guerrilheiros*. So had his son who had not come back.

'Yes.' Although not because she wanted to honour the earl's military service. 'And the new white.'

The cellarman's eyebrows rose, but he nodded and followed her as she walked along the racks of the unfortified wines, selecting bottles to accompany the food. One did not distract the palate from good port by eating at the same time. By the end of the evening, unless the Earl of Leybourne was a philistine, he would appreciate why she must stay here, comprehend the importance of her work.

And then he would go away and stop distracting her with thoughts that were absolutely nothing to do with vines and more about twining herself around that long, muscled, elegant body.

Laurent. Gaby bit her lower lip until the prickling behind her eyelids was under control. She had not been so naive as to think that the numbness of loss would last for ever. They had been lovers, friends, but not *in* love, after all. She was a young woman, and one day, she had supposed, there would be someone else who would stir her blood. She had not expected it to be an English officer.

But at least, she thought as she climbed the steps back into the daylight and dusted the cobwebs from her hands, it was only her body that was showing poor judgement, not her brain. That knew peril when it saw it.

She would listen to what he had to say after dinner, allow him to recite his message from Aunt Henrietta, then refuse whatever it was he was asking—presumably a demand that she move to England. She would say *no* politely this time. She should not have teased him in the rose garden. She had made him colour up, but she did not mistake that for anything but shock at her unmaidenly behaviour. This was no blushing youth, this was a mature, experienced, sophisticated man.

Lord Leybourne could hardly remove her by force—she would put a bullet in him first if he tried—but he had the power to disrupt her hardearned tranquillity and peace of mind and those she could not protect with her pistols.

'Lord Leybourne.' Baltasar wrapped his tongue efficiently around the awkward vowels as he opened the dining room door and ushered in her uninvited guest.

Add exceedingly elegant to sophisticated, experienced, mature, et cetera. Gaby fixed a polite social smile on her lips and rose. Beside her Jane placed a marker in her book and stood, too. *El-*

egant, but no fop, she added mentally, watching the way he moved.

'Lord Leybourne, may I introduce you to my companion, Miss Moseley. Jane, Lord Leybourne, who is making a short stay.' *Very short.*

Of *course* he had managed to pack evening clothes in those few portmanteaus and of *course* they had to emerge pristine, despite the fact he was not accompanied by a valet. And doubtless, those skintight formal breeches were at the pinnacle of whatever fashion was this month in London.

'Miss Frost, Miss Moseley.' He sat down when they did and smiled at Jane. 'Are you an enthusiast for port wine production as well, Miss Moseley?' Gaby gave him points for civility to a hired companion of middle years and no great looks. For many gentlemen Jane was, effectively, invisible. Not that she thrust herself forward to be noticed, and as a chaperone, she was indifferent to the point of neglect, which suited them both very well.

'No, I would not say that I am,' Jane replied, blunt as usual.

'That must make living in the midst of such intensive focus on the wine business somewhat dull for you.'

'Not at all. The effect of soil and rocks on the quality of the grapes and the effect of such a standardised form of agriculture along the valley is most interesting from a scientific point of view.'

'It must be.'

He really was making a very good job of sounding interested, yet unsurprised, Gaby thought. Most people were silenced by Jane in full flow. Many were intimidated or dismissive. She decided to take pity on him. 'Miss Moseley is a natural philosopher, my lord.'

'Gray,' he said, frowning at her. 'Please call me Gray, both of you.'

He should frown more, Gaby thought whimsically. It rather suited him with those severe features and dark brows.

Then he did smile and it was positively disconcerting how difficult it was not to smile back. 'I became so used to it in the army that I find myself looking round to see who this Leybourne fellow is.'

Now his attention had returned to Jane. 'Are you familiar with the map that William Smith produced this year, Miss Moseley? It delineates the stratigraphy of England and southern Scotland.'

A miracle, the man is as interested in rocks as Jane is.

Gaby settled back in her chair and let their con-versation wash over her. While he was talking about natural philosophy—and they had got on to the subject of Erasmus Darwin's strange ideas and his even odder poetry now—he was not thinking about ways to persuade her to go back to England.

'Madam, I have the wine.' Baltasar was back with the dusty bottle she had chosen earlier.

'An aperitif,' Gabrielle said and the other two stopped discussing fossils and looked across at Baltasar opening the bottle.

Again, as she had instructed him, Baltasar showed the label to Gray.

'A white port?'

'Yes, and a single quinta port, which is very rare.' She took the wine and poured it. 'Almost all port is blended so that we combine the grapes from different soils, different aspects, to give a richer, more complex result. I have experimented with using only our own grapes, but from both sides of the river and from different heights on the slope. I am really very excited with the result.'

Gray took the glass, sniffed, tasted and raised his eyebrows. 'That is very fine. I had never thought much of white ports before, but this is superb.'

'I think so.' She could say so without false modesty. It was essential to be critical of what she did, and this was, indeed, a triumph. 'Now we have to see how it matures, because I intend leaving it on the wood for another three years. Meanwhile we will begin again this year and treat twice as much the same way.'

'Three years?' Gray's assessing gaze moved from the wine glass to her face. He was not insensitive, he must have heard the commitment in her voice.

'Yes.' She met his gaze squarely. 'The satisfaction of personally developing and nurturing wine like this is what I live for.'

And you are not going to wrench me out of this place.

'That sounds very like passion to me, far more than satisfaction,' Gray said. His tone was neutral, as though he was making a commonplace observation, but there was something in his eyes, a glimmer of warmth, that made *passion* and *satisfaction* strike a shiver of erotic awareness down her spine. His gaze moved to her mouth and Gaby realised she was biting her bottom lip. Perhaps it had not been her imagination back there in the garden when she had thought for a fleeting moment that he was about to kiss her.

'*Jantar está servido, senhora.*' Baltasar had given up on English.

Gabrielle finished her wine. 'Shall we go through?'

Gray offered his arm to Jane, which earned him a look of grudging approval. Jane might be used to dismissive bad manners, but that did not mean she enjoyed them. Not that she allowed any annoyance to show. When subjected to such neglect Jane was more than capable of producing a book and reading, ignoring the visitors in her turn.

Dinner was surprisingly enjoyable. Gray showed an intelligent appreciation of the unfortified local wine she served with the food and made flattering comments on the various dishes. His words would make their way down to the kitchens and please Maria, as he clearly intended. And he kept strictly off the subject of England and her aunt, much to Gaby's relief.

When the meal was over, she rose and he politely came to his feet. 'Will you join me for a glass of port in the drawing room, Gray? We do not drink it in the dining room, where the smell of food dulls our palates.'

If he was surprised at not being left to enjoy the

decanters by himself, he managed not to show it, but followed her and Jane out. He did look somewhat taken aback when Jane bade him goodnight and turned to the stairs.

'Miss Frost, your chaperone has abandoned you.' He stood at the door, holding it open.

'My companion has clearly decided that you are not bent on seduction this evening. Do come in and close the door. You are quite safe, you know.'

'*I* am? That is hardly the point in question. You should not be alone with me, Miss Frost.'

'As we are the only occupants of the house except for my very loyal servants, I hardly think we are going to cause a scandal, Gray. Now, come in, sit down, try this very excellent tawny port and listen while I tell you that whatever you have to say I am not going to England. Not now. Not ever.'

Chapter Three

'And do, please, call me Gabrielle,' Miss Frost added with a smile so sweet it set his teeth on edge. She poured two glasses of amber liquid from the decanter on a side table, handed him one and sank down gracefully into an armchair.

Gray would have had money on it that the exaggerated grace was as much a calculated provocation as the sweet smile. He took the glass with a smile at least as false as hers and settled into the chair opposite. 'Very well, Gabrielle. Tell me why you refuse to countenance whatever your aunt's request might be?'

'I assumed rightly, did I not? She wants me to go to England and has sent you to fetch me.'

'Yes,' he agreed. Gray crossed his legs, lifted the glass, inhaled and almost closed his eyes in pleasure. The wine could not possibly taste as good as the nose promised. 'It seems a perfectly reasonable suggestion to me.' It had actually been rather more of an order, but saying so was hardly likely to help and he had to agree with his god-mother. Gabrielle Frost was too young, too well bred and too lovely to be alone and running a business in a foreign country with only a blue-stocking as an exceedingly careless chaperone.

'If I go to London, she will insist that I marry George.' Gabrielle's lips tightened into a straight line. 'I will not, of course, but arguing about it is a crashing bore.'

'I understand your objection to a first-cousin marriage,' Gray said. 'But Lord Welford is your aunt's stepson, not a blood relation in any way.' He took an incautious mouthful of the tawny port, choked and stared at the glass. It was every bit as good as the aroma had promised. 'This is superb.'

'It is indeed, whereas George is a spoilt, dim, selfish, pompous little lordling.' Gabrielle took a sip from her own glass and allowed her lips to relax.

Gray crossed his legs. 'Not so little. He's my height now.' Still spoilt, still inclined to be pomp-ous. Selfish? Gray had no idea, although it was to be expected that the indulged heir to an earldom would have a well-developed sense of entitle-ment. For himself the army had knocked any self-importance that he'd had out of him, but George, Viscount Welford, had never been allowed near anything as dangerous as a militia exercise, let alone a battlefield. 'I have to admit, he is not exactly the sharpest knife in the box, but he is not an idiot and it is a good match.' He took a more restrained sip of the port. He deserved it. 'And she cannot force you to the altar.'

'She will nag and cajole and lecture and hector and make my visit an absolute misery. But let us assume that I am foolish enough to do as you ask and weak enough to give way to my aunt's matchmaking. Let me calculate who gains what.' Gabrielle, whose wits were clearly as sharp as any boning knife, began to mark off points on her fingers. 'I gain the heir to an earldom, the expectation of becoming a countess one day and the opportunity to enjoy the English climate—I understand that rain is supposed to be good for the complexion. In return I give up my inheritance, cease the work I love, subjugate myself to the dictates of a man less intelligent than myself and who would run the business into the ground and surrender to being bullied by my aunt. Somehow I do not think that a title and clear skin weigh more heavily in the scales.

'George, on the other hand, gains a very valuable wine estate and me. With all due modesty, I believe I am wealthier, more intelligent and better-looking than he is. Of course, there is a something on the negative side for him, too—I would make his life a living hell in every way I could think of.'

Put like that, Gray could sympathise. In her shoes he would not want to marry Lord Welford either. 'Leaving aside Lord Welford—'

'By all means, please let us do that.' She was positively smiling now. One glossy lock of brown hair slid out of the combs that she wore in it, Spanish-style, and slithered down to her shoulder. Gabrielle moved her head at the touch on her neck and the curling strand settled on the curve of her breast, chocolate against warm cream.

He could not keep crossing his legs. Gray ground his wine glass rather vigorously in his lap, refrained from wincing and ploughed on. If he had wanted to spend his life negotiating with hostile powers, he would have joined the diplomatic corps, not the army. 'Leaving him aside, you clearly cannot remain here.'

'Why ever not?'

'You are single.'

'Portugal is full of single women.'

'You are inadequately chaperoned.'

'Fiddlesticks.'

'Fiddlesticks? You admit to having had a lover—what kind of chaperonage does that argue?'

'The kind I want. I am very glad I had a lover. That lover.' Her chin came up, but there was a sparkle in her eyes that hinted at tears suppressed. Or anger.

'Very well.' Clearly he couldn't shame her into doing the right thing. 'Who are you going to leave this quinta to? I hope you have a long and healthy life, but one day, you will need an heir.'

'To leave it to my own child would be ideal. Unfortunately that requires a marriage.' She shrugged. 'Back to the problem with husbands.'

He tried for a lighter note. 'They are really such a problem?'

'If I marry a local man, the quinta will vanish into a larger holding and lose its identity. If I was fool enough to marry in England, what husband is going to want the trouble of an asset so far away? He will sell it or hand it over to some impersonal manager. It will no longer be Frost's, either way. *"By marriage, the husband and wife are one person in law: that is, the very being or legal existence of the woman is suspended during the marriage."* That is William Blackstone, the legal writer. Believe me, I have read all round this. How would you like your very being suspended? More port?'

'Thank you. And, no, I would not like it. But then, I am a man.' Gray got to his feet, glass in hand as she glared, tight-lipped. He needed to move before he gave in to the urge to shake the infuriating female. Or kiss her. That combination of temper and intelligence and sensual beauty was intoxicating and he was tired after a virtually sleepless, uncomfortable river journey, exasperated and, totally against his will, aroused.

If he had not been concentrating on the sideboard and the decanters, he would have seen her rise, too. As it was, they collided, her forehead fetching him a painful rap on the chin. Gabrielle clutched at him one-handed. He did the same to her and they swayed together off balance, breast to breast.

She smelled of roses and rosemary and something else herbal he could not identify. Her breath was hot through the thin linen of his shirt and her body was soft and supple against his, which was as hard as iron. Gray steadied them both, set her back a safe six inches and took the glass from her hand. 'I'll get the wine.'

From the grip that she had on her glass, and the second or two it took for her to relax it, that collision had shaken her as much as it had him. Gray made something of a business of pouring the port, careful about drips, precise in replacing the stopper in the decanter, anything to give them both time to compose themselves from whatever that had been. Other than lust.

'Thank you.' When he turned back, Gabrielle was seated again, fingers laced demurely in her lap. She took the wine from him, her hand as steady as his was, and he wondered again at her composure. Or, at least, the appearance of it.

'What are your plans for tomorrow?' she asked. 'Please, feel free to rise at any time that suits you. If you could look in at the kitchen on your way past as you leave this evening and tell them when you would like hot water brought over and breakfast prepared, that would be helpful for the staff.'

Gray wrenched his thoughts away from speculation about how her skin would taste. Plans? Was there any point in staying here other than to torture himself? Gabrielle's answer to his godmother's demand that she travel to England was clear enough and he couldn't blame any woman with a choice in the matter for not wanting to marry George.

On the other hand he had promised to try. A good night's sleep might present him with an idea and more time might show him a lever to use against that strong will of hers. After all, she did not have to marry George: London was full of eligible young men whom any sensible lady would be happy to marry. After such plain speaking, surely even his godmother would realise that a match with her stepson was a lost cause and would focus her attention on finding her niece an acceptable partner.

Gabrielle was attractive. She had a flourishing vineyard and port business as a dowry. Her connections were good and no one needed know about the lover unless she had an inconvenient conscience and decided to confess. She could make a highly respectable match if she would only control her devastating frankness. He should make some effort to persuade her, he told himself. She might be set against marriage now but, surely, all it would take would be to find the right man.

As a gentleman he could not, with a clear conscience, leave her alone out here even though she showed every sign of being completely in control of her world. As a gentleman, he reminded himself, he should not be thinking about her in the way he was.

Gabrielle cleared her throat and he recalled that she had asked him a question. 'Plans? I would like to see your vineyards, if that is possible. Learn a little about the production of this elixir.' He toasted her with a lift of his glass and she inclined her head in acknowledgement. The curl slid across the swell of her breast, and another, he was certain, was about to slip free. *Breathe.* 'And this is far better than anything I have. You are right, I should see about adding some to my cellar. I will rely on your advice.'

Gabrielle did not seem too disturbed by his intention to stay a few more days. Perhaps the opportunity to sell him an expensive cellarful of wine counterbalanced the irritation his presence caused her. Perhaps she had failed to notice that he was fighting arousal with all of his willpower. Probably every man she came into contact with simply seethed with desire around her and she ignored them all.

'Stay, then,' she said, her voice indifferent, holding neither confusion over that…*moment* just a few minutes before, nor resentment over an uninvited guest. If she had noticed that his breathing was tightly controlled, then apparently it did not disconcert her in the slightest.

'I will be taking a boat down to Porto in a few days' time on business. You could come with me,' she suggested. 'I can recommend places to stay until you find a ship to give you passage home, which will not be difficult.'

'Thank you. That would suit me very well.' Possibly by tomorrow he would have recovered the use of his brain and could produce some arguments for her returning with him.

'I am sorry you have had a wasted journey,' she said as he put down the glass and got to his feet.

'It is not over yet. Who is to say whether it will be wasted or not? Goodnight, Miss Frost.'

Chapter Four

'Goodnight.' Gaby looked at the closing door, then down at the dregs of her port, then back at the door. Neither glass nor wooden panels gave her any insight into why she had made that idiotic suggestion. What was she thinking of, giving Gray the opening to stay for five more days? And then to commit to his company for a day on the river and perhaps another day in Porto was madness.

He was a threat. Not that she believed for a moment that he would succeed in persuading her to go to England against her better judgement. But that was hardly the problem, was it? The problem was that she found herself strongly attracted to him and, it seemed, that feeling was reciprocated. He hid it well because he was a sophisticated, experienced man, but she had recognised the signs. It was merely a physical attraction, obviously, but even so…

She found she was on her feet and pacing. It was really insufferably hot indoors. No, *she* was insufferably hot. It was a long time since she had lain with a man and, apparently, the hard, distracting work was no longer enough to keep any yearnings at bay.

Gaby rehearsed a string of the riper Portuguese oaths that she had heard at the height of the harvest when everyone was hot, tired and at the end of their tether. They did not help. Why couldn't she desire one of the numerous charming gentlemen who came her way both in local society and among the English and Scottish merchants and shippers in Porto?

There were enough of them, for goodness' sake. Intelligent men, handsome men, amusing men. Men she could probably marry if she got to know them better, if marriage was not such an impossible trap. Marry and she lost control of everything, became a chattel of her husband's, surrendered Frost's totally to his mercies.

It was cooler out on the terrace with the breeze from the river rustling the creepers on the walls of the house. She closed the double glass doors behind her and walked up and down, smelling the night-perfumed flowers, watching the bats harrying the moths, willing her nerves to calm.

It was time to move on. She had sensed that for a few months now in the restlessness of her body, the way the sharpness of grief had mellowed somehow into sadness and regret. *Betrayal* was no longer the word if she found another man to…love? No, *desire*. She had been close to loving Laurent and perhaps, if they had had longer together, then their feelings would have become even deeper, more intense, but she thought not.

If I did find a man I could like and we had a child, but without marrying…

Gaby stopped dead in her tracks. That had never occurred to her as a solution. What was the Portuguese legal position on illegitimate children inheriting? Possibly it was the same as in England and they would have no claims by right, but she could will her property to whomever she wished if she was not married, she was sure of that.

Why hadn't she thought of it before? It would take a great deal of working out, of course. Gaby paced more slowly. The position of a child born out of wedlock in this conservative country would be at least as difficult as in England, if not worse. She would have to seem to be married and yet without the legal burden of a husband controlling everything. A widow, in fact.

Now, how—short of marriage and murder—did one achieve that?

'*O senhor está fora,*' Baltasar informed her as he brought in her breakfast.

'He is outside? Since when?'

'He has been there since early. He asked for his hot water and his breakfast for six o'clock and he was already awake when Danilo took them over. I think he has been walking. Now he is sitting on the dock, watching the river.' Baltasar rolled his eyes. 'I do not understand these English gentlemen. He is a lord. He does not have to rise so early. He has no work to do. Why does he not sleep?'

'I think he is a restless man, if he has nothing to occupy him,' Gaby suggested. 'He is a man used to action, to having a purpose.' And that purpose, that sense of duty, however misguided, had driven him here. He had failed in his mission and now he had an enforced holiday.

How dreadful for him, to have to try to relax and enjoy himself, to be a tourist.

She finished her breakfast and went to the window. Yes, there was that dark head, just visible through the screen of bushes. She poured another cup of coffee, filled up her own and went out across the terrace, carrying them in steady hands to the steps down to the dock, just above where he was watching the Douro's relentless flow.

Gray was sitting on the boards, left leg drawn up, supporting his weight on his right arm, the other resting casually on his knee. She felt a fleeting regret that she could not draw. All it would take would be a few economical lines to catch that long, supple, relaxed body.

'Good morning.' He did not turn his head and she was certain she had made no sound.

'You have sharp ears.'

'I can smell the coffee.'

She came down the steps, set the cups down and sat beside them, an arm's length away from him. 'It might have been Baltasar.'

'Not walking so softly.' He turned his head, then smiled faintly. The lines bracketing his mouth deepened, and his eyes narrowed as he looked at her and then he went back to studying the water. 'Thank you.'

'You have shaving soap on the angle of your jaw.' She extended one finger, almost close enough to touch, then he turned his head and the tip of her finger made contact with smooth skin. Gaby jerked her hand back.

He was freshly shaven, his hair slicked down with water, but the rest of him was casual, relaxed. He put up his free hand, scrubbed along his jaw.

'That has got it.' Her voice was quite steady, considering that she felt as though she had been stung.

She leaned back on both hands, her legs dangling over the water as she watched him from the corner of her eye. A loose linen shirt, a sleeveless waistcoat, a spotted kerchief tied at his neck like a coachman, loose coarse cotton trousers tucked into a battered pair of boots, a broad-brimmed hat discarded on the planks by his side. He was dressed like a man who understood the heat of this valley in summer, one who had fought through the dust and the baking sun while wearing uniform. Now, in the milder warmth of October, the costume was still practical for wandering about the countryside.

'Is it strange being back here in peacetime?' she asked, following through her train of thought.

Gray was silent and she wondered if she had been tactless and he would not answer her. She had no idea what his experience of war in this country had been like. For some, she knew, it had been hell. For others, luckily placed, a jaunt. But he was simply marshalling his thoughts, it seemed.

'It is a pleasure to see the country tranquil, to watch children playing, people working, young men flirting without having one hand on a weapon,' he said. 'But it feels like a dream. There are moments when I hear gunfire and have to remind myself that it is hunters, when I smell smoke and tell myself it is a farmer burning rubbish, when the birds stop singing for a moment and I have to stop myself looking around for the ambush. It is hard to spend nine years fighting and then shrug off the habits and the reflexes that have kept you alive all that time. I look at this river—' He broke off with a shake of his head.

Ah. So he has seen the hell, ridden through it.

'And watch for the bodies being carried down,' she finished for him, repressing the shudder. There had been too many to retrieve for a decent burial. Many must have found their graves in the sea. Certainly no one had ever reported finding the body of Major Norwood that she knew of.

'Yes. One of the things I like about England is the absence of vultures.'

Gray picked up his cup and looked directly

at her over the rim. *Dark grey eyes like water-washed steel.*

'I should not be speaking of such things to a lady.'

Gaby looked away from those compelling eyes. They saw too much. She shrugged. 'I lived through it, too, I saw the bodies, the wounds, the hunger. Most times it is better not to remember, but sometimes it is hard when you need to talk and you cannot, because other people cannot bear to listen.'

Gray made a soft sound. A grunt of agreement. He understood, perhaps, although he would have fellow officers to talk to, men who had been through it and knew, men he could be silent with and yet feel their support and empathy. She had no one she could speak to about the things that had happened. But that was probably the burden that most women who had been through war carried: no one wanted to admit that shocking things had happened to them, had been witnessed by them. It was much easier to pretend nothing had sullied their sight, nothing had disturbed their ladylike lives.

Gray had been married. She recalled Aunt mentioning it in a letter in the days when she did not simply toss them aside unopened. A good marriage, apparently, by Aunt's definition of *good*. But his wife had died some years ago. A tactful woman would not refer to it, but then, she wanted to understand him for some reason and that was more important than tact.

'Did your wife ask you about it? Or did she want to pretend that it was all beautiful uniforms and parades and glory?'

'We were married for three years. We were together for, perhaps, six months in that time. I was home wounded for three months after Talavera. She noticed it was not all parades then.' His hand went to his left shoulder as he spoke. Gaby doubted he realised he did it. She had seen no awkwardness in the way he moved that arm; it must simply be the memory of old pain.

'Was it serious, the wound?' The way he spoke about his wife—or, rather, the way he did not—made her wonder what kind of marriage it had been.

'Bad enough to send me home. Not bad enough to prevent me getting her with child while I was convalescing.' Now he sounded positively cold.

'You have a child?'

'Twins. A boy and a girl. James and Joanna.' He was looking out over the river again, his profile stark and expressionless and she suddenly understood. Twins, but his wife dead, presumably in bearing those children. What must the guilt be like for a man who had left a pregnant wife behind to bear his children and die doing so? A wife, it seemed, he hardly knew and, she suspected, had not loved at all.

'So they are about five now. Where do they live?'

'Winfell, my house in Yorkshire.' He lifted the cup to his lips and drank deeply.

'You must miss them.'

'They have my mother. But, yes, I miss them. They have got used to me being home this past year and I have not yet become blasé about the novelty of watching small children grow.'

Charmed despite herself, Gaby felt a twinge of guilt. 'You left them behind to perform this errand for your godmother.'

'I thought it my duty.' The severe lines that had softened when he spoke of his children were set again. 'I did not—*do not*—like to think of an English gentlewoman alone and unprotected in a foreign country.'

'It is not foreign to me. This is my home,' she pointed out. 'No one thought to bring me to England when the war was on.'

'I did not know you were without your parents then.'

But my aunt did. I was not an heiress until Thomas was killed, though. No benefit in taking all that trouble with me before then.

'And if you had?'

'I would have done my best to get you to Lisbon. You and your brother.'

'We would not have gone. We would not have abandoned the quinta and our people. You had your duty. We had ours.' He made a noise suspiciously like a grunt. 'If an enemy invaded England, would you expect your mother to abandon Winfell, your staff and tenants, your inheritance?'

This time the grunt was nearer a smothered laugh. 'I would expect her to have the Civil War cannon refurbished and to settle in for a siege. Woe betide any enemy who attacks what is hers.'

Gaby did not make the mistake of pushing the point. She finished her coffee, flicked the dregs into the river and watched as fish rose hopefully to investigate. 'How do you intend spending the day?'

'What are your plans?'

'To walk the terraces. Now the harvest is finished, it all needs checking over.'

'Don't you have people to do that?'

'Of course. And I have their reports, but I still see for myself. I must prioritise the work, think about the more long-term planning. Do you leave your estate in Yorkshire in the hands of your steward and never check on what he tells you? No, I thought not.'

'Might I come with you?'

'If you wish.' She glanced at his boots. They certainly looked sturdy, but she felt the temptation to needle him. 'Can you walk far in those?'

'You think a cavalryman cannot march?' Gray got to his feet in a sudden, fluid movement and held out his left hand to pull her to her feet.

His fingers were dry and warm as they fastened over hers and he lifted her easily towards him. The shoulder wound had healed cleanly, it seemed. 'I have no idea. Can you?' She led the way back to the house.

'For miles if we have to. But do you not ride?'

'No, not to inspect the terraces. It is such a bother mounting and dismounting endlessly.' She opened the kitchen door. 'Maria, food for his lordship as well, please.'

Her own capacious leather satchel was already waiting, bulging with water bottle, notebooks and packets of food. Maria bustled out of the pantry with another in her hands and offered it to Gray with a twinkling smile. His compliments on dinner had obviously reached her ears and even now, despite several years of peace, she still believed in feeding everyone as though there would be famine tomorrow.

Gaby looped the strap of her own satchel over her shoulder, shook her head at Gray's attempt to take it from her and led the way out past the winery and on to the track. 'I will check this side of the river today and the other bank tomorrow. I looked at the more distant areas the day before you arrived.'

She strode up the slope and turned on to the first terrace. Jorge, her manager, had noted nothing at this level, but she never took anything for granted. Gray paced along behind her as she shook posts, checked the wires, peered at the terrace walls, then followed her back and up to the next level.

A miracle, a man who does not have to talk about himself the entire time.

These support posts were looking worn. Gaby dug out her notebook, made an annotation, moved on.

Gray's silent presence was oddly companionable and she could check the vines without having to think what she was doing, which left her free to brood about yesterday's insane scheme. But was it insane?

She needed an heir—or an heiress, she wasn't fussed which—and the child needed to be legitimate or, rather, to appear so. She could not afford the risk of marrying because the man would take everything by law so... *I need a convincing husband to kill off.*

'*What* did you say?'

'Hmm?' Oh, Lord. Had she been thinking aloud?

Gray was staring at her. 'You said something about killing someone off.'

'Scale insects.' Gaby flipped over a badly mottled leaf to show him the tiny dark brown lumps. 'They are the very devil to kill off because they have a sort of shell, a bit like limpets. But they suck the goodness out of the leaves and spread diseases, so we have to try.'

They carried on.

Supposing I find a suitable man, one I can bear to lie with, one with intelligence.

She was thinking along the same lines as breeding livestock, she realised with a little inward shudder, but brains appeared to be something that were inherited and this child was going to need their wits about them.

'Can you hold that wire taut?' she asked. Gray took a firm hold on the one she indicated and she went to the other end of the row and gave it a twang. As she thought, loose. 'Thank you,' she called and made a note.

So, find the right man, think of a way of ensuring that when I come back here as a pregnant sorrowing widow people will believe in the marriage.

A hawk screeched overhead, a lonely sound in the vastness of the sky. Gaby tipped back her head to watch it and met Gray's gaze as he looked up to do the same thing. He grinned and pushed the broad-brimmed straw hat further back on his head.

Something was niggling at her. Could she use a man like that and then simply vanish with his child? Wouldn't he have the right to know he was a father? Would she want anything to do with a man who did not care if he was? This scheme was full of pitfalls. So, to square her conscience she would have to discuss it with him, make certain he had no scruples. Was it even ethical to use a man as a stud in this way, even if he was perfectly willing, or was she being absurdly overscrupulous? Men married to breed heirs every day of the year. Her wretched conscience. How much easier to simply not care about how her actions affected anyone else…

'This banking looks unstable to me,' Gray called and Gaby went over to where he was crouched down at the foot of the terrace wall. 'Something has been digging.'

'A fox, I expect.' Another note. She carried on along the foot of the terrace wall.

'Rights?' Gray had come up close at her shoulder without her even realising. 'The rights of man? Rights of way?'

Hell, I must be thinking out loud again.

'Water rights.' Gaby improvised as he strolled off to look at a clump of late orchids. 'We can cut up to the next level from the end here. We do not need to walk right back along the terrace.'

She had to find an intelligent man who would happily give up his rights in his child and who would not turn round and blackmail her. She clambered up the stones at the far end and walked slowly back until she found she was standing above Gray. He had leaned back against the stone wall, hat in hand, and was looking up, watching the hawk and its mate circling high above them. His hair was thick, curling slightly at the crown, thick and virile and temptingly touchable.

There was a fig tree at the back of the flat area

and Gaby went and sat under it, took a long drink from her flask and checked her notes against Jorge's. That was better than thinking about how a man's hair would feel between her fingers, how his weight would be over her, how those broad shoulders would…

Stop it.

She made a few annotations, but the sun was in her eyes and Gray was still somewhere below. She tipped her hat down over her nose and closed her eyes against the glare, the better to think.

Chapter Five

Gray wandered across the short grass beside the row of vines looking for Gabrielle. She was very quiet—he couldn't even hear the occasional muttering that seemed to signify deep thought.

He was impressed by her work here, as he knew she intended him to be. She was proud of her quinta and she had every reason for that. If Gabrielle had been a man and his godmother was agitating for a return he would have told her, in no uncertain terms, to leave well alone. But she was not a man. How she had escaped the war unscathed he could not guess, although obviously the loss of both her brother and her lover must have left emotional scars.

Luck could last only so long. Sooner or later if she stayed here, she was going to need help and support, the strength only a husband could give her, but she seemed to cling to her independence and her control of the quinta, as a mother clung to a child, terrified to let it walk off on its own. If she chose her husband well he would surely place the estate in the hands of competent managers, although, given the distance from England, he supposed selling would be prudent.

A splash of colour under the angular arms of a fig tree betrayed her presence. Deep blue skirts today, with a similar linen undershirt and black waistcoat to yesterday. It seemed to be her working uniform, practical but feminine. And she was asleep, he realised. Only her chin, firm and decided, and her mouth were visible beneath the tilted straw hat. The lower lip was full and sensual, the upper curled a little as though she dreamed of something pleasant.

Gray moved silently across the parched grass, avoiding dry leaves, a twig, until he could fold down cross-legged, facing Gabrielle. Her note-book had fallen from her hands and lay open in her lap and he squinted at the pencilled notes, trying to read upside down.

3 ps on 2 rotten
3 wires?
5 wall—fox?
Blackmail

He blinked and looked again. The cryptic notes obviously referred to different terraces and *ps* probably meant *posts*, but *blackmail*? It was hardly an ambiguous word. Was someone trying to extort money from her, or did she believe her aunt was blackmailing her in some way to return? Perhaps she was marshalling more arguments to throw at him if he tried to persuade her again.

Arguments were not all she might throw, he thought whimsically. She had a knife in a slim sheath attached to her belt. It lay beside her now, a workmanlike blade that she had used to probe rot in a post and lop off a broken trail of vine.

The erratic shape of the fig threw a comfortable patch of shade just where he sat, but the October sunshine was warm on his back and he felt his muscles ease, his shoulders drop. Had he really been this tense? He supposed he must, because he could not recall feeling consciously relaxed since he had heard of his father's death and had left the familiar army life for one of ancient obligations, new duties, half-understood roles.

Home had held the children, yes, but they had been upset and confused because their beloved Gran'papa was no longer there, only Gran'mama and she was sad. And he had felt himself struggle to feel at home in a house that held memories of his own marriage and his singular failures as a husband.

He thought he had left everything better than he had found it. Jamie and Joanna ran to him now when they saw him, smiled at him, held up their arms to be lifted. His mother was slowly coming to terms with her loss and he was throwing himself at all he had to learn as though the outcome of a battle depended on it.

But when he got back to England again he was going straight home and paying no heed to any demands but those of his immediate family and the estates. He was going to live for the present and the future. He'd had enough of guilt and regrets.

Meanwhile he could practise living in the moment by basking in the sun and looking at a lovely, if maddening, woman and listening to the birds and the rush of the river far below.

She had been asleep, Gaby realised. She felt too limp and comfortable to do much about waking up, not for a minute or two, although she opened her eyes just a little. The weave of her straw hat was a light open work and through it she could see Gray sitting cross-legged in front of her, shoulders in a comfortable slump. For the first time he did not look like an ex-officer, just a big, rather weary, distractingly attractive man.

And he was looking at her mouth. She licked her lips and his gaze sharpened, fixed and, in the moment, she was hot and there was a disturbing, throbbing ache low down. Then Gray moved, swivelled the satchel on his hip and took out the water flask and the heat ebbed, leaving only a distracting tingle.

He is the first new, interesting man who has come into your life since you have begun to recover from losing Laurent, she told herself.

One had to be practical and recognise this for what it was: a rather inconvenient attack of lust. To which the *interesting* man in question was contributing by tipping back his head to drink and showing off a long bare throat with a gleam of sweat and the slightest hint of dark chest hair escaping at the point where his neckcloth was pushed aside.

Gaby sat up rather too fast, pushed her hat back on her head and reached for her own water. 'Have I been asleep long?'

Her voice sounded surprisingly normal without, to her ears, any hint of 'let me bite your neck and discover what you taste like.'

'Ten minutes.' Gray pushed the cork back into

the flask. 'A catnap.' He got to his feet, casually letting the satchel swing down in front of him, but not before Gaby was aware that she had not been the only one becoming a trifle…heated.

Mischief made her reach up to him in an invitation to pull her to her feet. His hand was big and hard with rider's calluses and she had a sudden desire to see him on horseback.

'This is almost the top terrace.' She released his hand with a nod of thanks. One could tease a man too far and she had no intention of provoking anything. At least, she hoped she had not. 'We can eat up there. The view is excellent.'

They climbed in silence, checked the final terrace, then walked along to where the shell of a stone pigeon tower gave both shade and a support for their backs. Gaby checked for ants and scorpions, kicked aside a few pebbles and settled down on a flat stone that had fallen from the parapet. Above their heads wild rock doves flew out in a noisy clatter of alarm.

'I remember these towers.' Gray eyed it, staying on his feet. 'They were perfect for snipers.'

'And they make good watchtowers. I think centuries ago they were both dovecotes and lookouts.' She tried to keep her voice neutral. One could not, after all, go around flinching from a feature that was scattered throughout the length of the valley.

'Yes.' He sat almost reluctantly, as though he could feel the sights of a rifle trained on his chest. 'I can see three more from up here.' He pointed across the river and eastward. The furthest was the most tumbledown, a haunt for owls and jackdaws now.

When she did not answer Gray looked at her sharply. 'What is wrong?'

'That one.' She pointed to the furthest, the half ruin. 'That was where the French found Thomas. They had sent a scouting party down, and he was watching for them. He would have seen them, crept out intending to make his way down to the river, taken his small boat and let the current carry him swiftly down to Régua, where there were still Allied troops. You had not all fallen back on Lisbon then.'

'But he didn't make it?'

'They must have known he was there. Someone had circled round behind him and they caught him as he left the tower. They beat him, shot him, left him for dead.' She said it calmly, clinically, so she did not have to think about the reality behind those bland words, her brother's battered, bleeding, abused body.

'How do you know this? Were there others with him?'

'He was alone. I know it because my lover brought him to me. He found him barely conscious and brought him home. He did not approve of treating idealistic boys as though they were hardened *guerrilheiros*.'

Gray would work it out in a moment, he was not stupid or slow.

'Your lover was *French*?'

'Yes, he was a French officer, although he was not my lover until later. I did not know him then.' Gaby let her head fall back against the warm stones, closed her eyes. She did not particularly want to see the expression in his, just at that moment. 'He found Thomas, gave him water, bandaged the gunshot wound, asked him where home was and Thomas trusted him enough to tell him.'

'An honourable man, your French officer.'

That she had not expected. Gaby twisted round to look at him. 'Yes, he was.' For a moment she thought she saw sympathy, understanding even, before she realised that the very direct look held questions and suspicions. 'And I am an honourable woman. An *Englishwoman*. I had nothing to tell him, no intelligence to give him, no safe harbour for him or his comrades and I would have given none of those things if I had. We were two people who came together in the middle of an… an earthquake. There was no politics, no war for us. It lasted a few nights over many weeks, that was all.' She turned away again, hunched her shoulder in rejection. What did it matter what he thought of her?

'How did you know of his death?'

'I gave Laurent a locket. It had the crest of Quinta do Falcão on it and a lock of my hair. Six months after the battle, it reached me with a note inside. My hair was missing but there were a few strands of Laurent's blond hair and a scrap of paper with the name of the battle and the date. He must have confided in a friend, told him what to do if he was killed.'

'Did you love him?' Any trace of sympathy, softness, had left his voice.

'Do you think me wanton?' She watched the sunlight on the water below. She had no need to read whatever his thoughts were in those steely eyes, she could guess. 'That I would sleep with any man who happened by?'

Had I loved Laurent?

She would never know whether that potent

mixture of attraction, gratitude, liking—*need*—
would ever have amounted to love because she
was never going to become emotionally entangled
with another man, ever again. *Thank goodness.*
There would be nothing to compare. But there
might be the love for a child if she could only find
her way through the maze of problems, actual
and moral, that her insane idea was throwing up.

'Are you going to report all this back to my
aunt?' That would certainly put the cat among
the pigeons.

'Hell, no,' Gray said. He sounded properly
outraged. 'What do you think I am? A spy for
her? She should have sent one of her moralising
friends if that is what she wanted. She is correct.
You should not be here, alone. You should come
back to England, make a proper marriage. I promised her I would try to persuade you of that and
give you escort, but I undertook nothing else.
Certainly not to critique your morals.'

'Thank you for that, at least.'

There was silence, strangely companionable.
Gaby let out a sigh she had not realised she had
been holding and let her shoulders relax back
against the rough stones.

This was becoming all too comfortable. Confession was clearly a weakening indulgence. She

sat upright again, opened her satchel and began to take out the food. 'Would you like to come with me to a dinner party tomorrow night?'

Gray had found a chicken leg and paused in midgnaw. *He really does have a fine set of teeth...* A sudden flash of where those teeth might be employed made her grab for a bread roll.

'Yes, very much, thank you. But will your hosts not mind an uninvited stranger?'

'Not at all. I will write a note when I get home. It is only up there, see? To the left of that big rock on the shore? The next quinta along. Their house is close to our boundary and the estate stretches away to the east. They are another Anglo-Scottish-Portuguese family, the MacFarlanes, and they have been here as long as the Frosts.' Gaby stuffed the roll with cheese and found a tomato. 'I like him a lot. She is a terrible snob, so she will be delighted to have an earl at her table, but other than that and the fact that she wears pink too much, she is tolerable.' She bit into the tomato, then sprinkled salt on the exposed flesh and decided she had been fair to Lucy MacFarlane. 'Her husband, Hector, has been like an uncle to me. They throw big dinner parties so there will probably be at least a dozen other guests.'

'Will they not have invited a gentleman to balance you?'

Gaby shook her head, her mouth full, and swallowed. She never tired of the sweet tang of the tomato juices on her tongue, the warm pungency of the cheese, the springy resistance of the fresh-baked crust of the bread. Here in the sunlight, with the scent of herbs and the distant sound of the river, was a kind of sensual little heaven.

'There are so many spare gentlemen around, what with visiting buyers and partners and officials from the government making inspections,' she explained as she split another roll. 'The ladies are always outnumbered.'

'Stops the gentlemen becoming complacent.' Gray reached for another chicken leg.

She was *not* going to watch him eat it. Her imagination was doing a perfectly good job of visualising those muscles moving in his neck as he chewed and swallowed, his tongue coming out to lick his lips and savour the herb-infused oils it had been cooked in.

'The gentlemen are much more concerned with discussing the harvest, debating whether or not to declare a vintage, garnering information and downright gossip about rival quintas, rival lodges.

The ladies are so much ornamentation as far as they are concerned.'

'Except you.' He said it seriously, not as though he was mocking her, which was a pleasant surprise.

Gaby risked a look. The chicken leg was nothing but a bone now, dangling from long, lax fingers. 'Except me,' she agreed. 'I spend the evenings carefully not flirting, not gossiping, not discussing the things the men consider feminine concerns. Then when the ladies withdraw I stay put and they simply pretend I am not female. Obviously I must put something of a crimp in the conversation if they are dying to discuss mistresses or boast of their sexual performance or relieve themselves, but they can always take their cigarillos out on to the terrace and do all of those things.'

Gray gave a snort of amusement. 'I do not think your aunt has the remotest idea just who she is expecting me to bring back to London. I look forward to watching you. Do you scandalise the other ladies?'

Gaby shrugged. 'They are used to me. This will be a social evening only, I think.' Some of the other women she even thought of as friends, although she had little in common with their day-to-day lives. 'Wine?' She passed him the flask of red.

'Good. Yours?' Gray wiped the neck with one of the napkins Maria had wrapped the food in before passing it back to Gaby, then ruined the civilised effect by scrubbing the back of his hand across his lips.

The soldier, not the society gentleman, Gaby thought, repressing a smile.

'No. This is a MacFarlane vintage. They make more table wine than I do. You'll have to talk to them at dinner tomorrow—I'm sure Hector Mac-Farlane would be delighted to sell you—'

She broke off as a flicker of darkness scuttled out from a boulder beside Gray's left boot. The knife was in her hand ready to throw, then she realised that he had slid his own blade from his boot and had it poised in his hand. They both watched the scorpion, then it skittered off over the edge of the terrace and they relaxed in unison, shoulders touching as they leaned back.

'These days I don't like killing anything I don't have to, even those wicked little devils,' Gray said as he slid his knife back out of sight.

'Neither do I,' Gaby agreed. There was a mark on her blade, a smear of sap, and she rubbed it clean with her thumb.

'How well can you throw that?' Gray asked.

'Very well. Old Pedro, my father's steward, taught me when I was only ten. See that dead plant over there?' A large, desiccated thistle was silhouetted against a post on the edge of the terrace.

'You can hit that from here?' He sounded politely sceptical.

Gaby shifted the knife into a throwing grip and sat up. Beside her Gray stood and out of the corner of her eye she saw him draw his own knife again. His throw followed hers in a fraction of a second. Hers skewered the head of the thistle to the post, his cut the stem beneath the head.

'I'm impressed.' He walked across to retrieve both knives.

'So am I. Shall we go back down again now? Now, what was I saying? Oh, yes, Uncle Hector is sure to offer to sell you wine.'

She thought she heard him mutter, 'Everyone in this damn valley wants to sell me something,' but when she looked at him he grinned back.

Really, the man was all too easy to like—she couldn't recall now why she had found him so severe, so difficult, when he had first arrived. Perhaps she could survive a week of his company, after all. Provided she could stop looking at his mouth. Or those shoulders.

Chapter Six

It was early, the light was thin, weak. Nothing stirred inside the house or out. Gaby turned, squashed up the pillow and burrowed into it. *Far too early to be awake.* She turned to the other side. But something had woken her, a soft thud and a crunching sound that had somehow become part of a dream about cracking walnuts.

She sat up, listened. Nothing, just her imagination, but it was impossible to go back to sleep now. She lay and thought about Gray instead.

Last night at dinner she had thought him subdued, somehow. Polite, careful to involve Jane in the conversation, observant about what they had seen on their walk up through the terraces. And yet it was as though someone had turned down the wick on a lamp. Perhaps he was tired or missing his children, or he regretted committing to stay for a few days and travel down to Porto with her. He had excused himself after the meal and gone back to the Gentlemen's House. No intimate conversations last night, which was doubtless a good thing.

Sunlight was penetrating the shutters now. When she slipped out of bed and went to look the morning was perfect: cool, clear, filled only with the sounds of nature. The river, early birds, a distant dog barking. The water would be cold, but the bathing place would be beautiful and she could paddle her feet and watch fish rise and the kingfisher hunting.

It took minutes to pull an old gown over her head, find some rope-soled shoes and a towel and let herself out into the garden. A blackbird flew off, making its usual overdramatic fuss about nothing. The ginger kitchen cat sauntered out of the wood store, inspected her, sneered in a feline manner and strolled off, tail up, in search of a breakfast mouse.

Dew-soaked grass brushed her ankles. The air, not yet warmed by the sun, sent goosebumps up her arms and she threw the linen towel around her shoulders as a makeshift shawl. Foolish to even think of wading at this time of year when the river was chill with the very last of the melt water from the mountains, but she was restless.

The Douro was not a safe river to take risks with, except where it had carved little bays and deposited shingle to protect them. There it was possible to find pools with slow-moving water, deep enough to swim in, safe enough to relax. There was one just upstream of the house, beyond the edge of the lawn, through a thicket of willow. Gaby trod softly, hoping to see the kingfisher on his favourite dead branch overlooking the pool.

Something was splashing about beyond the screen of low-hanging branches. She moved warily. It might be a stray farm animal taking a drink or it might be a pack of the semiwild dogs that roamed the foothills and were best avoided. She eased the leaves apart and caught her breath.

Gray was standing thigh-deep in the pool, stark naked. His back was to her, his arms raised as he ran both hands through his wet hair. He had just stood up, she realised, as the water sheeted down from his shoulders.

His skin below the neck was pale, the muscular definition of his shoulders and back a pattern of light and shade as the sunlight hit him. She followed the dip of his spine down to the narrow waist, the tight, neat buttocks, the horseman's strong thighs where water droplets clung to dark hairs.

A river god, magnificent, male. Gaby's mouth was dry, she could have no more closed her eyes than levitated. Then the kingfisher flew past the mouth of the bay, a flicker of iridescent blue, and Gray's head snapped up, his arms dropped to his sides. For a moment the man watched the bird and Gaby watched the man, then he turned and she took two hasty steps back among the low-hanging leaves.

Her foot came down on a dry branch with a crack like a pistol shot. There would be no mistaking it for anything but a footfall. She almost fled, then realised that would betray the fact that she had been watching.

She cursed in Portuguese, loudly enough to be heard, and pushed on through the wall of greenery, unfurling the towel from her shoulders as she came, as though preparing to stop and undress.

In the water Gray moved and she looked up. The flapping towel half obscured her vision, but not before she saw the diamond of dark hair on his chest between his nipples, the trail downward to his navel, downward to the junction of his thighs and—

Gabrielle gave a startled shriek and spun around, the towel like a banner behind her.

Hell. Gray took two strides out of the water, grabbed his own towel and slung it around his hips. 'I apologise. I did not realise that anyone else would be swimming. I asked last night and they said there was this bay, but that it would be cold.' And thank heavens for chill river water or she would have had even more of an eyeful.

Gabrielle made a vague gesture with her hand, her back still turned. Her neck was pink below the pinned-up plait of dark hair. 'Not at all. I probably wouldn't have swum, and anyway I should have made more noise in case anyone was here, but I was hoping to see the kingfisher.'

'It flew past just before you came. If you stay there a moment, I will put on my trousers.' That was thoroughly uncomfortable, pulling them on over chilly, damp flesh, but he tugged them up, fastened the falls. 'I'm more or less decent now.' It wasn't as though she was a virgin. She must have seen a man's chest before. Seen all of a man. Even so, he draped the damp towel over his shoulder and down across his torso.

Gabrielle turned, the movement swirling the thin cotton of the faded gown over her curves, and he realised that she was probably naked under it, ready to swim if she had felt brave enough to face a brisk dip. Now he was on the shore they were close enough for him to see that her pupils were dilated just a little, her breathing rapid enough to lift her breasts distractingly.

She had seen enough to excite her, just as the realisation excited him. Gray wondered if the more intelligent thing to have done would have been to sit down in the river and wait for her to go away. He'd have frozen his parts off, of course, it was far too cold to sit about in, but...

'*What* did you say?'

'Death before dishonour,' he muttered. 'I should simply have gone under the water.'

'Gentlemanly, but idiotic,' Gabrielle observed. 'But then, so many of the things that gentlemen consider necessary are. I'll leave you to...' With a flap of her towel she vanished into the willows.

Gray carried on drying himself. The fact that his thawing anatomy was beginning to take a decided interest in proceedings was a distraction he tried to ignore although, as that was the crux of the problem, it wasn't easy. He had thought yesterday that the attraction he felt was probably mutual, now he was certain. He had taken care not to be alone with Gabrielle last night, but an intimate chat over a glass of port was hardly in the same league as face-to-face confrontation with him naked and her as good as.

It was nothing more than a physical reaction, of course, but he was not going to accompany her on her tour of the remaining terraces, that was certain. His shirt tails refused to tuck in smoothly between the loose linen trousers and his still-damp skin and he pulled them out again impatiently and left them hanging, flipped the towel over his shoulder and walked barefoot back towards the Gentlemen's House.

Gabrielle was an attractive young woman. He had been celibate since... Since when? Gray stopped halfway across the lawn and thought. Hell, six months. His father's death, everything that followed, had swallowed up both time and emotional energy. But that explained why he was feeling decidedly edgy now. Being alone so casually with Gabrielle, who was not a virgin and would be quite well aware of what her feelings and reactions meant, was going to reveal any stirrings of desire.

As he stripped off again in his room and stood in the shallow bathtub, pouring blessedly hot water over himself, Gray wondered whether he should say he had changed his mind, would be leaving the next day.

But that would be to acknowledge that he was aware of that flare of attraction on the riverbank and that awareness was much better left unacknowledged. Besides, he was finding this insight into another world, one he had seen during the fighting but had been ignorant of, fascinating. They were adults, neither of them wanted an entanglement or complications, surely? It would be easy enough to manage his feelings for a few more days.

It could have been very awkward. Gaby wrinkled her nose at herself in the looking glass as she prepared for the dinner party. *Awkward? Downright embarrassing.* They had both felt that flash of desire, she was certain, and it had only been superior acting skills on both sides that had dampened it down. Or, rather, banked it behind masks of indifferent politeness. *Flash?* It had been more like a lightning strike.

Over breakfast she had braced herself to extend the invitation to climb the terraces on the far side of the river as they had discussed the previous day. Gray had clearly rehearsed a story of letters to write first. Then, he said, he had realised that he was close to some point of particular interest to him from the time he had passed through the area in August 1810. He asked for the loan of a horse for later in the morning so he could ride out and see if he could locate the French position he remembered.

Gaby had agreed with a definite sense of relief and reminded him about the evening's dinner party. 'We will leave at six if you could be ready by then,' she said before she stepped down into the boat and Jorge skulled her across the river.

Gray had walked towards the house without a backwards glance. She, of course, only saw what he was doing because she happened to be facing backwards, not that she would dream of looking otherwise.

Now she held up one of a pair of earrings to her left ear and another from a different set on the other side and made herself concentrate on choosing. Yes, definitely the silver-and-pearl drops. Her hair was up in an elaborate knot secured with a silver comb, and they went well with that. She hesitated over the jewellery tray that Paula, her maid, had fetched from the safe and finally settled on the intricately worked silver chain with one large pearl suspended from it. With the chain twisted round her neck three times the pearl lay perfectly, just at her cleavage.

Her gown had been made in Lisbon two months before and was unworn. She had seen an illustration in one of the Paris fashion magazines that were imported in large numbers now and had sent it off to the dressmaker who had been holding fabric for her from the last time she had been in the capital. Gaby stood up, smoothed down the deep garnet silk and stepped into her evening slippers.

Yes, that would do very well. She did not want an affaire with Gray, but she did want him to realise that she was not some poor little provincial chit stranded abroad who needed to be brought back to England and London society in order to bloom. He could tell Aunt Henrietta that she had fashionable gowns and good jewellery and a lively social life and that would certainly annoy her, even if it did not discourage her from her efforts to dislodge Gaby from Portugal.

Gray was waiting in the hall, a handsome, most civilised, gentleman in his immaculate evening clothes. A red cabochon stone in his neckcloth echoed the gleam of the signet on his left hand, the finishing touch.

And I know what is under those clothes now.

Gaby kept that tantalising thought hidden under a polite smile as he came to the foot of the staircase and held out his hand to assist her down the last few steps. 'Thank you.' She rested her fingers on his arm when he offered it. *Very formal tonight, aren't we?* Probably Gray was using that formality as armour, just as she was.

'You look beautiful, Gabrielle.'

It was the first time he had used her given name without her asking. Deliberate or a slip? 'Thank you, Gray.' Baltasar opened the front door as Gray settled his hat on his head and Gaby looked out, past the lanterns that had just been lit against the gathering shadows. 'Oh, good, the carriage is prompt. The distance is very short,' she explained, 'but it is not a road one wants to walk over at night—not in evening shoes, at any rate.' She was determined on polite small talk this evening while the thoughts of that morning still made her feel warm and flustered.

Gray handed her in and took his place facing her. The hood of the barouche was down still, but the coachman would raise it before they came home. Now the fresh evening air was pleasant and the lack of intimacy felt...safer.

'Did you find the location you were looking for?'

'Yes, and with less trouble than I had expected.' Gray took off his hat and laid it on the seat beside him. The breeze ruffled his hair slightly and she thought that she preferred that to the smoothly combed effect. 'It was a place where a party of French snipers ambushed our forward column. I was puzzled at the time at how they had arrived there unseen, but once I was able to look about freely I could see there is a gully behind the rock that would have given them cover.'

'Was it a bad skirmish? Did you lose many men?'

'No, fortunately. Three wounded and those not seriously. It was a delaying tactic on their part and they didn't press their advantage once they'd diverted us.' He stared out over the darkening landscape. 'Interesting how one views the countryside when one isn't expecting to be shot at from every patch of cover.'

'Are you glad now that you came back and can see Portugal in peacetime?'

The other day when she had asked for his impressions, Gray had said that it was a pleasure to see the country at peace and she was expecting a similar response this time. Which was why she had asked, she supposed. It was a safe subject for conversation.

* * *

Am I glad? Gray frowned at the passing terraces and tugged at the lobe of his left ear, an old habit while he was thinking. *And I must stop doing that*, he thought with a sudden burst of irritability. Portia had complained about it, saying he would end up with one lobe longer than the other. Strange how now the only clear memories he had of her were of complaints, or of weeping or sulking. *I can hardly blame her, I must have been a most unsatisfactory husband.*

Gabrielle cleared her throat and he remembered that she had asked him a question. 'I am not sure that *glad* is the right word. It has made me think not of the war, but of the fact I was away from home. It has reminded me that I was a poor husband and that I could have been thinking a lot more deeply about what I was doing and why.'

'A poor husband because you were away so much? But every man who was fighting was in the same position, surely?' When he simply shrugged she had the tact not to pursue it. 'You were fighting your country's enemy, *Europe's* enemy. Doing your duty, helping win the war.'

He had joined the army because it was a family tradition and because he was running away. Running from the mess he and Giles, his closest friend, had got themselves into. Running from the woman they had accidentally hurt and who his conscience had eventually driven him to marry.

'Yes, I was doing my duty,' Gray agreed, conscious that he had fallen silent for too long again. The carriage lurched over a rut and began to descend the slope again. 'And I was enjoying myself. Most of the time. But I was the only son, the heir. My father supported me, but he must have been deeply uneasy.' But had the army needed *him*? Would he have done better to have stayed in England? He could have gone into politics or increased the wheat yields on the family estates or joined a branch of government service as Giles, now Marquess of Revesby, had done for a while.

Instead, even after he had returned to England and married Portia out of a poisonous mix of pity and duty, he had left again and spent nine years fighting his way up and down the Peninsula. And he *had* enjoyed it, that had not been a cynical remark just then. No one in their right mind found pleasure in a battle, let alone its aftermath, of course. He had not liked being wounded, or suffering dysentery or narrowly escaping frostbite in the Pyrenees, but he had found just about everything else stimulating, satisfying. Addictive.

Now, seeing Portugal at peace, he knew he

should be glad that he had contributed to that and to the freeing of Spain. He should have been glad of a marriage that had given him Jamie and Joanna. And, he supposed, freed him from the necessity to marry again. He was a fortunate man, healthy, wealthy, privileged. His duty revolved around the Yorkshire estates and London and that should be enough for any man. So why was he so damnably restless?

Chapter Seven

'We have arrived.' Gabrielle made no reference to his lapse into silent thought as the carriage came to a halt.

Gray pulled himself together. 'I apologise. I had not realised how many layers of memory this has stirred up. I should have asked you more about our hosts this evening.'

'Hector MacFarlane; his wife, Lucy; their son, Angus, twenty; and their daughter, Annabelle, eighteen. I've known them all my life. I do not know who else they will have invited, I'm afraid.'

The carriage came to a halt in front of another low whitewashed house, roofed like the Quinta do Falcão with red pantiles. This one was differentiated by a vast panel of the blue-and-white *azulejo* tiles on either side of the double front doors. During the war Gray had become familiar with the tiles, a style that could be found all across the

Peninsula, and he made a mental note to comment on them if conversation became sticky.

'Handsome house,' he remarked as Gabrielle began to gather up her reticule and fan and twitch her shawl into order. 'Not such a fine garden as yours, though.'

Gabrielle smiled. 'You must say that to Jane. She is responsible for most of it.'

A pair of big—very big—sandy-haired men came out on to the front steps as the groom opened the carriage door. Gray handed Gabrielle down and turned to look at them. They had to be father and son—one greying now, his waist thickening, the other not yet in his prime, but both of them imposing. Hector and Angus MacFarlane, he assumed, resisting the instinct to square his shoulders in a show of primitive masculine rivalry. They looked as though they spent their leisure time tossing the caber or throwing the boulder or some other kind of Highland sport.

Gabrielle seemed not to find them in the slightest bit intimidating. She waved and called out, 'Good evening!' Then she abandoned him to run and kiss the older man on the cheek as though greeting a favourite relative. 'Here is my guest, Nathaniel Graystone, Earl of Leybourne. You must sell him several cases of port while you have him at your mercy—I have been indoctrinating him on the subject. Gray, I must tell you that Mr MacFarlane has been like an uncle to me for as long as I can recall.'

Gray strode up the path, smiled and held out his hand. 'MacFarlane, thank you for accepting such a last-minute intrusion on your evening.'

'Our pleasure, my lord.' The light blue eyes were assessing and, Gray thought, not quite as warm as the welcoming words. The pressure of the big hand on his was not subtle. 'Allow me to present my son, Angus.'

The younger man's expression was definitely wary. Then he saw Angus's gaze move to Gabrielle and understood the underlying coolness.

Now, is that sexual possessiveness or neighbourly protectiveness?

'Gray, please.' He smiled warmly, allowed no speculation or reserve to show in his expression as he shook hands with Angus, managed not to flex his well-crushed fingers and then was swept through the door on Gabrielle's heels, into a crowd of people clustered in the wide hallway.

'We were all admiring the portrait of my wife that has just arrived from Lisbon,' MacFarlane explained, gesturing to a full-length oil in an elaborate frame. The frame was not all that was elaborate. Gray schooled his expression into one of polite admiration as he regarded the ornate gown, the complex hairstyle, the abundance of jewels, all painted with considerably more skill than the wooden features of the lady in question.

She did not seem displeased with it, he thought as his host guided him to her where she stood beside the painting, holding court. 'Gray, allow me to introduce Mrs MacFarlane. Lucy, my dear, the Earl of Leybourne, Gabrielle's guest.'

Gray shook hands, commented politely on the portrait and observed that, fine as it was, it could not do justice to the sitter, which was true. Lucy MacFarlane was considerably more vibrant in the flesh than on canvas. Wearisomely so, he decided after five minutes of her sprightly conversation. And she, too, was putting on a bright social manner over considerable reserve.

They want Gabrielle for their son—and who could be surprised at that with such a fine estate located next door to their own? But they haven't made their move yet, she is completely unselfconscious around Angus.

Gabrielle certainly did not seem inclined to flirtation with her neighbour, whom she appeared to regard in the light of a brother. *He's younger than her in years and in experience*, Gray decided, watching covertly as he was introduced to the other guests. There were several neighbouring wine producers and their wives, the owner to the biggest cask-making business in the area with his two daughters and a Portuguese gentleman who appeared to hold some government position in the nearby town.

He was perfectly capable of keeping up social chit-chat while thinking of two other things at the same time and Gray circulated, keeping one eye on Gabrielle as he did so. Yes, she was far more mature than the MacFarlane son and he doubted she had ever given young Angus a second thought as a potential husband. His father was clearly playing a long game and he certainly would not want her lured back to England and the many marriage prospects there.

The meal was pleasant enough, he found. The food was excellent, the wines, of course, superlative. Gray was seated next to Mrs MacFarlane with the wife of one of the wine producers on his other side and was kept busy attempting to describe the latest London fashions to the ladies. He invented details without a qualm and wondered if in a few weeks the ladies of the Douro valley would be flaunting braided trims on their hems, lavender muslin with yellow dots for daywear and high puffed sleeves with crimson ribbon bows for evening. Pastel colours, he declared, were positively passé for all but the youngest girls.

Best to change the subject before he gave his ignorance away entirely. 'I had not realised that there were Scots so involved in the port business,' Gray remarked to Mrs MacFarlane.

'Oh, yes.' Her lips tightened. 'Since the events of last century many Scottish younger sons found the Continent, and Portugal, healthier politically. And the gentlemen of Edinburgh enjoy their port wine.'

By *events* he assumed she was referring to the Jacobite uprisings. Perhaps he was in the house of Stuart supporters and a health to King George might not be tactful. Gray turned the subject yet again.

Gabrielle was partnered by Angus but, from what he could see, she was ignoring him in favour of an energetic discussion with the husband of Gray's own dinner partner. Comments about *grafted root stocks* and *declaring a vintage* and *ridiculous duties* floated down the table. Miss Frost was most certainly not engaged in flirtation. He caught her eye as he thought it and smiled. Gabrielle smiled back and he was conscious of Mrs MacFarlane beside him stiffening.

The ladies, including Gabrielle, departed after the dessert course, leaving the gentlemen to their port and nuts. MacFarlane did not resume his seat as most of the men did once the ladies were out of the room, but strolled down to Gray.

'Did you develop a liking for cigarillos when you were in the Peninsula, Lord Leybourne?'

'I did. Not enough to seek them out in London, though, I must confess. Finding a reliable supplier is tricky. Too many seem dry.'

'Shall we go out on to the terrace and blow a cloud? I can recommend an importer if you like this sort.'

Not the subtlest of approaches, Gray thought, picking up his glass and taking a sip as he followed his host outside on to the stone-flagged platform that appeared to run right around the house. *But if he wants to sell me some of this port, I'll not put up too much of a fight.*

MacFarlane struck a light, then leaned against the balustrade, drawing slowly on his cigarillo. 'You are a relation of Gabrielle's, I believe.'

So, this is not about port, after all. 'No, not at all. My godmother, Lady Orford, is her aunt. There is no blood tie.' He blew a cloud of fragrant smoke, recalling evenings by the campfire when coarse cigarillos were smoked more as insect repellent than anything.

'Ah. I had assumed you were here on family business.'

'My godmother wishes Miss Frost to spend a Season in London and I am both messenger and, should she decide to accept the invitation, escort.' Telling his host to mind his own business was tempting, but ill-mannered. Gabrielle thought of him as an uncle, after all.

'Lady Orford intends to thrust Gabrielle into the London Marriage Mart, then?' There was no humour in the query, and in the spill of light from the dining room Gray could see that the older man's colour was up over his cheekbones.

'I am not given to questioning a lady's motives,' Gray said, regretting his good manners a moment before. 'Although Lady Orford certainly made a most advantageous match herself when her family sent her to London as a young lady to make her come-out. Her aunt is very concerned for Gabrielle's welfare, as one might expect.' There was someone behind him in the shadows, he realised, his awareness of their presence suddenly uncomfortable. Instinctively he shifted, putting his back to the balustrade, balancing his weight.

For goodness' sake, he chided himself. *This is a dinner party, not the start of a brawl.*

'Or perhaps you have hopes of pre-empting that visit?' MacFarlane's tone was forced, but he put just enough jocularity into the remark for Gray to choose to shrug it off as misplaced levity following too much wine, rather than insulting curiosity. If he chose. He decided that he did not wish to.

'Nor am I in the habit of bandying a lady's name about in speculation on such matters.' The presence in the darkness moved out and revealed itself to be Angus MacFarlane. Father and son together made a formidable bulwark in the fading light.

Oh, for... He was not going to stand up straight, start facing off with these two like a trio of stags on the rutting ground, but if they thought he was going to be intimidated into scuttling back to Porto, they could think again. There was the sound of voices further along the terrace, chatter and a feminine trill of amusement. Gray took a long drag on his cigarillo, slumped comfortably against the balustrade and blew smoke gently into Angus's face.

'You cannot have her. Gabrielle is not so foolish as to be dazzled by a title. She belongs here, with me.' Angus drew back his impressive shoulders and Gray contemplated his options if the pair of them decided to try dumping him over the side into the bushes below.

It really did not do to engage in fisticuffs with one's host, but knocking some manners into young MacFarlane was tempting. 'Fustian,' he remarked so mildly that it was a provocation in itself.

Angus took an abrupt step forward and Gray pushed himself to his feet. Nonchalance was one thing, finding himself pinned against the stonework with his nose in the other man's neckcloth quite another.

'I am marrying Gabrielle Frost and you have nothing to say to the matter.'

Really, it would be too easy. A fist in the stomach, sweep his legs out from under him and the young idiot would go down like a felled oak—

'Certainly Lord Leybourne has nothing to say about my marriage.' Gabrielle stepped out from the shrubbery. 'Angus, what nonsense is this?' From her tone he might have been a scrubby schoolboy who had brought a bucket of frogs into the drawing room.

'I... We...'

'Angus is being a trifle previous, that's all, lass.' MacFarlane moved forward, giving his son a none-too-gentle shove to the side. 'Of course your father and I had planned this for years, but I wanted Angus to finish at Oxford and then come back here, get a grip on things.'

'Then let me assure you both, Quinta do Falcão is not something Angus will be getting a grip on. Not by marriage, not by purchase. I had no idea you were labouring under this misapprehension, *Uncle Hector*, but I hope I have cleared it up. Now, I find I have a headache. Perhaps you would be so kind as to call for my carriage? Gray, will you give me your escort?'

'Of course, Miss Frost.' Well, that was more effective than a fist in the gut. More like a knee in the groin, if he was any judge.

'Thank you so much for a delightful and informative evening, Uncle Hector,' Gabrielle said sweetly. 'Will you be very kind and make my excuses to Aunt Lucy, Angus? Gray, if you are ready?'

'Goodnight, gentlemen. Excellent port and cigarillos, by the way.' He followed Gabrielle along the terrace. 'Ouch,' he remarked once they were out of earshot. 'Do give me a moment while I check my clothing for blood splatters.'

'I apologise,' she retorted. 'That was insufferable of them. You are my guest—how dare they attempt to intimidate you like that?' When Gray did not reply she glanced up, the candlelight making her eyes glint. 'They didn't do a very good job of it, did they?'

'Young Angus needs to realise that he cannot rely on his size and a pair of broad shoulders to win his fights for him,' Gray said, amused. 'He'll find himself laid low by smaller, faster, opponents a few times. Then, if he's got any sense, he'll find himself whatever is the Lisbon equivalent of Gentleman Jackson's salon and learn some self-defence.'

They arrived at the front door as the butler came out, Gabrielle's shawl over one arm, Gray's hat and gloves in his hand. 'Miss Frost, I understand you require your carriage. The word has gone out to the stables. It should not be long.' He bowed himself back inside.

'Did Uncle Hector ever find out about your French...er...friend?' Gray asked as he helped her arrange the shawl more closely around her shoulders.

'No. We were very discreet.'

The carriage drew up before Gray could reply. The hood had been raised and the interior was dark as he handed Gabrielle in. 'That was an embarrassingly frank revelation of their intentions. What will you do now?' he asked as they started off. He wished he could see her face. How upset was she to have fallen out with such old friends?

'Nothing, I suppose.' From the rustling of silks and the sudden waft of jasmine scent he supposed she had shrugged. 'It would be foolish in the extreme to fall out with a neighbour, one of the community. We all rely on each other. If they have any sense they will pretend nothing happened and so will I, unless Angus is foolish enough to try to push the issue next time we are alone.'

'Is it wise to be so relaxed about it? A forced marriage is not outside the bounds of probability.' He wouldn't put it past the MacFarlanes, they had ample motive.

'Let them try. Being compromised would never force me to agree.' Gabrielle made a sound that was somewhere between a sob and a growl. 'I *hate* this. All I want to do is to run the business, make good wine, employ skilled local people and carry on the family tradition. Yet, simply because I am a woman, it is a problem. *I* am a problem. An object to be traded. I cannot trust anyone, it seems.'

'You can trust me.' Gray reached for the shadowy form next to him and pulled her gently against his shoulder. It was disconcerting, finding the prickly, confident woman so affected by that betrayal. 'I do not lie to you, Gabrielle, and I do not try to trick you. But I cannot change the marriage and property laws for you here, nor in England.' He was not at all sure he would if he could because it went right against all his learning, all his protective instincts. Surely few women had the capacity to manage their own finances as Gabrielle did? Or perhaps they could, if they only had the training. It made him wonder about the education of his own daughter…

In the circle of his arm Gabrielle stiffened, jerking his mind back to the woman here in the darkness with him.

Gaby froze, then relaxed. Gray's hands were still as he held her, he was not groping or fumbling—not that she could ever imagine him doing either thing—and it seemed he was simply offering her comfort.

It was not his fault that this was not at all comforting. What would he do if she kissed him? She could not quite believe that all he was feeling was a friendly wish to console her. Under her cheek she could hear his heart beating, could tell that his breathing was not quite steady, could smell the subtle musk of warm man beneath the traces of smoke and port and cologne. Warm, aroused man?

It would not be fair. In fact, she told herself, it would be as dishonourable as a man taking advantage of a woman to try to seduce him. Gray was not here for dalliance, he was here because his misplaced sense of family responsibility and natural chivalry had forced him to do her aunt's bidding. And, she suspected, he genuinely believed she would be better off marrying a *suitable* English gentleman. She could not blame him for the attempt at carrying out her aunt's wishes.

Now—finding himself with an armful of willing young woman, one who he knew was not a virgin—he was exhibiting a self-control that was positively saintly.

Or perhaps not. She could feel his lips moving against her hair and the big body so firm against hers was tense… Gaby twisted within the circle of his arms and tipped back her head to look up at him. His face was a pale oval in the gloom, but his breath was warm on her cheek. 'Kiss me, Gray?'

'Why?'

That was a very good question, damn him.

Then she felt, more than heard, his breath hitch. 'Because we both want to? Because we are both adult, single people?'

He did not reply in words, simply bent his head and found her lips, teasing along the seam. She opened to him with a sigh, accepted his tongue into her mouth with the touch of her own, tasted him and hungered for more. Gray kissed like a dream: firm, gentle yet assertive, devastatingly thorough. And like a dream, the kiss ended all too soon, leaving her dazed and wondering.

Her fingers were in his hair and it took her a moment to free them, to stroke down to the nape of his neck and away. She felt him shiver under the caress. 'That was...good.'

'Yes,' he agreed, settling her back against his chest. Somehow she had moved—*or been moved?*—from his side to sitting across his thighs. 'It was. And unwise.'

Ah. Sitting like this, there was no mistaking the fact that he was aroused. Gaby's memory presented her with a perfect picture of what was under those elegant evening clothes, which did not help her own control in the slightest.

'Probably very unwise,' she agreed equably and shifted to the seat opposite him. It was hard to tell in such poor light, but he did not appear to be greatly relieved that she had moved. If she went back... *No.* 'But thank you. I needed...something.'

'I am happy to provide a distraction.' There was a smile in his voice, which was a relief. Many men would have been offended at the suggestion that they were simply a comfort.

'I did not require distracting.' Mercifully her pulse rate was calming from thunderous to merely rapid. 'But a human touch from someone I can trust, that has steadied the ground under my feet a little.' Which was true. Whatever turmoil that kiss had thrown her into, it had also calmed something inside her, soothed a loss even as it had awoken desires and longings she did not want to examine.

'It did not do a great deal for my equilibrium,' Gray confessed. 'Perhaps I should take a midnight swim.'

'Not after a rich meal and wine, it would not be safe,' Gaby said hastily, then laughed a little when she realised she was being teased. How strange, to laugh with someone at their gentle teasing, to be held with passion and yet without demand. What a long time it seemed since she had experienced either. Jane was a sensible, loyal companion, but she did not have a ready sense of humour and she most definitely was not given to spontaneous demonstrations of affection. If Gaby had hugged her she would probably have sent for the doctor.

The carriage was descending now, and they were almost home. What would happen if she took Gray by the hand and led him inside, up the stairs to her bedchamber? Would he go with her? She wanted to make love with him, whatever the risks… And then she thought of another risk of lovemaking: if she wanted a father for her heir, she could not do better.

And I must not. I cannot use *this man like that and even if I did, I cannot bring up a child here with everyone knowing it was born out of wedlock. I must not.*

The temptation was awful. The carriage pulled up, one of the grooms let down the step and opened the door and Gray handed her out, but did not release her hand as the man swung back up behind the coach. It clattered off to the stables leaving them standing at the edge of the wash of light from the lanterns by the front steps.

'I wish I could ask you in, but—'

'I wish you would, but—' Gray lifted her fingers to his lips. '*But* we should not, must not.' The trace of laughter was back in his voice. 'Will not.'

'You are right, although I find it difficult to remind myself why not,' Gaby confessed. Her pulse had kicked up again and a disturbing, long-ignored, intimate pulse was beating, hot, demanding.

'You are upset, you feel betrayed and you seek

comfort. But comfort is not what we would bring each other, I think,' he said, serious once more, her hand still in his enveloping grasp. 'And I remind myself that you are a lady and that I am not a marrying man, not any longer.' Gray turned and walked towards the door, opened it for her. 'Goodnight, Gabrielle.'

'Goodnight, Gray.' She reached up, touched his cheek with her gloved fingers and felt a little prickle of evening beard through the fine silk. A man who shaved twice a day, she imagined, recalling the dark curls on his chest, the line leading downward… 'No swimming, now.'

His chuckle was cut off as she closed the door. Gaby stood just inside, peeled off her gloves, twisted them in her hands, then, finding her legs singularly unwilling to walk towards the stairs, leaned back against the carved panels and closed her eyes with a sigh. Gray's body had felt as solid, as invincible as these old chestnut planks, she thought.

Against her back the door shifted, just a little, as though someone had leaned on the other side. Was he there, thinking about her, wanting her?

Chapter Eight

'Senhora Gabrielle?'

'Oh, Baltasar, you made me jump.'

'I am sorry, *senhora*, that I was not here to open the door. I was not expecting you home yet.'

'That is quite all right.' It was necessary to speak calmly, maintain her composure, pretend that she was somehow in control of the emotions tearing through her. 'I have a headache so we came away early. Send Paula up to my room, would you, please?'

She only wanted to be alone to think and she would have managed without her maid, but the gown was impossible to get out of alone. Even better would be to lie in Gray's arms and not have to think at all.

In her chamber Gaby smiled at her maid and submitted to being unbuttoned. She agreed that it was a stuffy evening with a storm brewing, perhaps, which would account for her headache. She managed not to snap when Paula made her usual slow examination of each piece of jewellery before she locked it away and dismissed her, saying her head was too sore to permit the usual lengthy business of hair brushing.

In reality her head was not aching at all, but her insides felt decidedly peculiar. Part was unsatisfied arousal, she decided. The rest of the discomfort was anger over the MacFarlanes' scheming, disappointment to have lost an old friendship and apprehension over how she was to go on now.

The best thing would be to pretend nothing had happened, as she had told Gray she would. She should dismiss Angus's pretensions and his parents' ambitions and treat them as she did any of the other families along the river. If they were prepared to play the same, unspoken game, then in time the awkwardness would be smoothed over.

But Angus was not a mature young man who would put aside his humiliation easily. Between them she and Gray had administered a serious snub and he might well be difficult to deal with the next time they met. Nor would his mother take her rejection well. Angus was the apple of her eye

and she would find it impossible to comprehend
Gaby's unwillingness to marry him.

She took pins from her hair and shook out the
carefully arranged curls. A coolness between the
neighbouring quintas would be noted and commented upon up and down the Douro and there
was the making of some tricky social and business situations if that happened.

The brush slid through her hair and she began
to count under her breath. *'One, two, three...'*

On the other hand, if she was away for a while,
then a slight change in the relationship might well
go unnoticed. It would certainly give Angus time
to recover his wounded pride and his parents the
opportunity to look around for another bride for
him.

And this was the best time of the year to be
away. The harvest was in, the experienced workers were busy on familiar routine tasks. Her team
was strong and reliable, perfectly capable of carrying on without her for a while, especially if she
was somewhere that the post could reach within
a week or so in case of any unexpected problems.

'...ninety-nine, one hundred...' She had talked
herself into going to London, Gaby realised as
she put down the brush.

Which left the small matter of that kiss. If

she announced that she was, after all she had said, planning to travel to London with him, then Gray—and any man with an ounce of self-preservation—would run a mile. Or assume he had been skilfully entrapped. As it was he had made the point of stating that he was not intending to marry again. *Oh, dear.* There was nothing for it but some very plain speaking. Thank heavens Jane was such a late riser…

'Baltasar, will you please go over to the Gentlemen's House and ask Lord Leybourne if he would join me for breakfast?'

Gaby poured coffee, spread apricot jam on one of Maria's pastries, warm from the oven, and practised looking businesslike. She had dressed with great care, exactly as she did every morning, had her hair in a simple braid and did not think she could look any less like a woman attempting to exercise her seductive wiles on a man. What Gray would think was another matter.

Baltasar opened the door to him, produced another place setting and went out.

'Good morning, Gabrielle.' Gray sat down, held out his cup for coffee and took two pastries. He looked faintly wary.

'Good morning.' This was beginning to feel

awkward. Gaby cleared her throat. 'You must be wondering why I asked you over for breakfast.'

'I am a trifle curious, I confess.'

'You must not think that what I am about to say means that I am asking you to— Oh, thank you, Baltasar. Cheese flan. Lovely. No, I do not think there is anything else just at the moment.'

Gray waited until the door closed behind the major-domo. 'Ask me? Or not ask me?'

'Yes. I mean, no.' The pastry chose that moment to disintegrate, showering her bodice in a shower of flakes. 'Oh, *blast.*' She stood up and brushed them off. Gray silently handed her the platter and she took another. 'Thank you.'

He helped himself to a slice of the flan and began to eat. Perfectly composed, the irritating man.

'Yes. That is, I am not asking you to marry me.'

Gray dropped his fork.

Not so composed, after all, she thought with fleeting, short-lived satisfaction. 'What I mean is—'

'That I am not to assume you have expectations because of one kiss in a carriage?' He sounded very dry indeed and not remotely amused.

'If you will just allow me to finish?' *Don't snap. It won't help.* 'What I mean is that I have decided to return to London with you. With your escort, that is. Not *with* you.' *And stop twittering.* 'What I do not want is for you to assume that I have read far too much into a simple moment of…desire and have set my cap at you.' Now he *was* looking amused, damn him. 'I had thought that if I simply announced my change of mind, my intention to travel with you, you might feel uncertain of my motives and that would be awkward. I decided that frankness was the best option—and do not dare laugh at me!'

'I am not. I am delighted to encounter such a very straightforward and frank approach. It is exceedingly refreshing after the hints and sighs and manoeuvrings of most of the unmarried ladies I encounter.'

'You have a high opinion of your desirability on the Marriage Mart,' she said coldly, still not too sure he was taking her seriously.

'I am an earl, single, under forty, with all my own teeth. I am not in debt, not flaunting mistresses and not given to wearing corsets,' Gray pointed out. 'One learns to be very nimble on one's feet.'

'Do you not *want* to remarry?' Gaby asked, startled into open curiosity.

'No. Why should I? I have my heir.'

'I would have thought there were other benefits to marriage.' He raised one eyebrow. 'Not *that*. Well, as well as that. A domestic life, a hostess, a mother to your children…'

'My mother acts as my hostess, raises my children.'

'And will not, if you will forgive me, be able to do that for ever.'

'Wives do not live for ever, either.' Gray was not smiling now.

'I beg your pardon. Of course, that was thoughtless of me. You are still mourning your wife—' *Of all the insensitive, thoughtless things to have said.*

'I am not still mourning. Portia died five years ago.'

Well, yes, but if you loved her, it would still hurt in fifty years. Gaby swallowed a gulp of coffee in the hope of drowning the queasy sense that she had blundered. *I don't know. I can't guess and I shouldn't try.*

'I was not so enamoured of the state of marriage to feel any desire to re-engage with it and besides, I am not good husband material,' Gray said with the certainty of a man informing her that the sky was up and the earth was, most definitely, down.

It was on the tip of her tongue to ask why he would not be a good husband. Gaby bit back the question.

Stop it. You like him, you desire him and you have to travel with him without it becoming hideously embarrassing for both of you, she lectured herself silently.

'We are straying from the point,' she said severely. 'I intend travelling with you to London, accompanied by Miss Moseley. I trust, as this was presumably your intention in coming here, that this is acceptable to you?'

'Perfectly.' Gray reached for the coffee pot and refilled his cup, contemplated the sugar and, with some deliberation, added one very small lump. 'You are running away, then? I had not expected that of you.'

'No, I am not and you are trying to provoke me again.' And why that should be Gaby was not sure she wanted to investigate. 'What happened last night with the MacFarlanes was awkward and it could make for a difficult situation. A coldness between the two houses could lead to gossip and all the businesses are too intertwined for that to be healthy. No one will think anything of it if I go to London for a month or two. This is the quiet season and I can leave things in the hands of a good manager. It is hardly as though I am off to Brazil, letters will arrive within a week or so.'

She watched him drink his coffee, his good humour, it seemed, restored. That flash of darkness when he had spoken of his marriage had vanished behind what she was beginning to suspect was a carefully maintained mask. Perhaps an officer, someone who must lead men day after day through the most numbing routine and into the most terrible danger, needed such a mask.

'A strategic retreat in order to regroup,' she said and thought his smile was genuine.

'You will stay with Lady Orford, of course.'

'Stay in Aunt Henrietta's London house and have George thrust at me morning, noon and night?' Gaby rang for more coffee. 'No, I will hire a house for the duration of my stay. What objection can there be to a lady setting up home with her chaperone in a respectable location? I am certain you can advise me on how to find a suitable agent and which areas are most eligible.'

Gray resisted the temptation to sink his head in his hands or ring for brandy and drink himself into oblivion. Probably drinking brandy was a capital crime in this part of the world...

Gabrielle Frost was rapidly driving him to distraction. The pull he felt towards her, physically, was hardly a surprise. He was not a monk. He was perfectly capable of finding himself aroused by a wide variety of attractive women—and was equally capable of either acting on that if it was returned and appropriate, or not. Gabrielle had him tossing and turning in his bed like a randy youth.

And it was not simply the sexual connection. He liked her, too, when she was not forcing him to confront memories and issues he had been quite effectively ignoring. How long would it take to get back to London? Less than two weeks. Three if they were unlucky. Then he would either have to deliver her—kicking and screaming, most likely—to his godmother or he must install her in an hotel, find her a house agent and reputable staff—and be berated by Lady Orford for doing what Gabrielle wanted, not what her ladyship ordained.

Life would be very much simpler if he left Gabrielle here, returned to England, wrote to his godmother apologising for failing to persuade her niece to visit and then retreated to Winfell, a safe two hundred and fifty miles away.

Coward, his conscience whispered. *She is quite right. Leaving her neighbours to recover from the*

ruin of their dynastic plans is sensible. She is ma-
ture, intelligent and wealthy enough to cope with
London, even demonstrating a degree of eccen-
tricity. She needs you—and not in the way you
need her. You're a colonel of cavalry, a hard-
ened veteran. Are you going to be routed by one
young female?

Hopefully not, but those fine brown eyes and
that lithe figure and his overheated imagination
would be his undoing if he did not keep a firm
hold on his willpower. It did not help that she
made him smile. The fantasy picture of her laughing up as she lay beneath him naked, those long,
long legs curled around his hips, that thick brown
hair spilling over the pillows, those lovely breasts
against his chest—that was almost irresistible.
And it must be resisted. He needed a mistress,
a practical arrangement. He did not want a wife
and most certainly not a passing affaire with a
young lady under his protection.

'Of course. It will be my pleasure.' He thought
his tone conveyed nothing but willing agreement.
'I do not envisage any difficulty finding something suitable—the Season has not started. You
will require a suite in a reputable hotel for perhaps a week while we find the right house. The
Pulteney is the most prestigious, but noisy, being

right on Piccadilly, so I would recommend Grillon's on Albemarle Street—just as well located and rather quieter. When do you want to travel?'

'In three days, I think. That will give me plenty of time to make arrangements here.' Gabrielle got up, stopped beside him on her way to the door. Gray stood and for a moment they were close enough for him to see the few freckles that dusted the bridge of her nose. 'Thank you, Gray.' She laid her hand on his shoulder, stood on tiptoe and dropped a kiss on his cheek, then she was gone and he could hear her calling to Baltasar from the hallway.

He thought he would probably be spending a great deal of time on deck when they sailed. He would walk up and down in the wind. The nice, cold wind.

Gray lounged on the colourful cushions in the cabin of the *rabelo* and contemplated the toes of his boots. They were dry, he was comfortable and they were making rapid progress downstream. It was all very different from his journey upstream. This was no working boat, but the quinta's water-borne equivalent of a carriage with a small cabin amidships, comfortable benches, a tiny fold-down table and glazed windows. The steersman still stood on his high platform at the stern, wielding the long oar that kept them on course, but instead of looking over a load of barrels and pipes of port, the man was sighting across the roof of the cabin.

He was beginning to develop an eye for the wine-growing countryside, Gray realised. The terraces were subtly different as they moved downstream, the slopes less steep. 'There are fewer vines planted here,' he remarked as they passed the small town of Ermida.

'And soon, none, or only patches for table wine.' Gabrielle looked up from the paperwork she had been bent over for more than an hour. 'There is more agricultural land and orchards, the closer we get to Porto.' She signed a document, flapped it about to dry the ink, folded it and took a stub of candle and some sealing wax from her bag, struck a spark with a tinderbox and began to seal the pile of documents that she had been working on.

Gray watched, despite himself, as she sat carefully tilting the stick of red wax and the candle, pressing her signet ring into each puddle before it set. Her concentration was total, her fingers, deft. Finally she slid the heavy ring back on her left thumb, shuffled the letters and sat back. She looked up and caught his gaze. 'There, all done.'

'That is an old ring.'

'It is the original seal of the quinta. Made for a man's hand, of course. I usually wear it on a chain around my neck, but I will be doing business in Porto and I make a point of wearing it when I am there.' She smiled ruefully. 'The first time I was in a meeting and drew it out on the chain in order to seal an agreement I realised that every man around the table was staring at my—' She waved her hand vaguely at her breasts. 'That was a lesson learned, believe me.'

Miss Moseley gave a genteel snort. 'They should not have been looking.' She frowned at Gray, who had been keeping his eyes, and his imagination, well under control, and turned back to her contemplation of the riverbank, occasionally jotting a note in the book on her lap. Perhaps she was a more effective chaperone than he had thought.

'There is a small hotel I use when I visit Porto,' Gabrielle said as she corked her ink bottle and began to fit her writing implements back into the small wooden box she had produced from another of her capacious satchels. He was developing a grudging respect for her approach to business— focused, efficient, fast. It was grudging because she was a woman, for heaven's sake. A lady. She shouldn't have to know about business, let alone work at it. The fact that she was good at it and showed every sign of enjoying the process was neither here nor there, it was as wrong as setting a blood mare to pull a dung cart.

'I am sorry, I was wool-gathering. You were saying?'

'A hotel,' Gabrielle repeated patiently. 'It is small, but clean and comfortable. I suggest we try for rooms there. Then tomorrow, while I make my calls, you can find us berths on the next ship bound for London.' When he nodded agreement— at least she was not proposing to march down to the docks and haggle with seamen herself—she added, 'What were you daydreaming about, Gray?'

'The Godolphin Arabian, one of the founding stallions of the thoroughbred line. He was a gift from the Sultan to the King of France and some-how ended up as a carthorse before Lord Godol-phin found him.'

'And men say that the workings of the female mind are mysterious,' she teased. 'Whatever made you think about racehorses as you sail down the Douro?'

'I cannot imagine,' he lied, averting his gaze from the lovely lines of the thoroughbred in front of him.

Chapter Nine

'There is Spain.' Gaby leaned on the ship's rail next to Gray and nudged his elbow companionably with hers. 'The entrance to the harbour of Vigo.' She had been below since they had reached the open sea, organising the cabin to her liking and making sure that Jane, not the best traveller, would be comfortable in the cabin they were sharing.

'Is the accommodation satisfactory?' Gray asked. 'It seemed so, but what would suit me might well not be to the liking of two ladies.'

'It is well fitted out and has more space than I feared. You found us a good ship, I think. The captain was very obliging about stowing the port I have brought for you. We will see how it is handled at the other end, but I may well use him again.'

'What port?' Gray half turned, one elbow still

on the rail. The freshening breeze whipped his hair across his eyes and he pushed it back with an impatient gesture.

'I did promise to see to replenishing your cellars. You do not have to buy it, of course. I can easily sell it in London through my usual agents, but I thought you might like first choice.'

'You, Miss Frost, are a merchant to your fingertips.' There was a hint of admiration there, not the condemnation she half expected.

'I have to buy all the smart new clothes I will need for London somehow.' She could easily afford an entire new wardrobe, but it did not do to boast of her wealth, even to Gray. The thought brought her up short.

Why do I think, even to Gray? Do I trust him so much then?

Gaby tucked the puzzle away to think about later. 'Does my aunt have good taste? I can't recall and anyway, I was too young to be much interested in gowns when I saw her last. Now I find myself reluctant to put myself in her hands to any extent.'

'Good taste? Frankly, no. Rather like Mrs Mac-Farlane, overfussy. I can recommend one or two modistes who should suit.'

'And how do you know about them, might I

ask?' she enquired and was rewarded by the tips of Gray's ears turning pink. Or perhaps it was the wind. 'Your daughter is far too young.'

'Naturally one is au fait with the most fashionable designers in all fields,' Gray drawled. 'And, equally naturally, I have no idea how much the establishments I will recommend might charge you.' The steel-grey eyes challenged her to persist and try to make him admit he paid for his mistresses' gowns. Or that he had a mistress at all.

He must, surely? He's a virile man, and I can't believe he frequents bawdy houses, he seems far too fastidious.

But she was not going to fish for a response, that might imply that it was of some concern to her. Which, of course, it was not. Gaby shivered.

'You are cold.' Without waiting for her response Gray unfastened the neck of the heavy boat cloak he was wearing and flapped it out so that one half settled around her shoulders. 'Move up.' He put his arm around her shoulders as he tugged her gently against his body. 'There, that will keep the wind out.'

Harmless, Gaby told herself. *Mutual warmth and shelter from the wind. Perfectly acceptable.*

Only it was not just the cloak that was warming her. There was the heat of the big male body so close to hers and her own heat that had nothing to do with an absence of cold breezes and everything to do with a purely feminine desire to unbutton Gray's coat, rip open his waistcoat, push him back against the bulkhead and bite his neck. *Then rip open his shirt and lick all the way down—*

'The captain asks if we will join his table at dinner. And Miss Moseley, of course,' Gray said. 'Can you get access to any of the port—my port? I could donate a bottle or two to the occasion.'

Gaby blinked, pulled out of erotic imaginings.

Oh, yes. Make love to a man in front of an interested audience of half a dozen sailors, two shippers known to me and a pair of very respectable-looking Portuguese matrons. A man who made it quite clear he was far too prudent to indulge in any such thing, audience or not.

She took a careful half step to the side, opening up just an inch of air between them. 'The port is in the hold, except for the two dozen assorted bottles jammed into my cabin. I never know when I am going to find a new buyer so I always make certain some is to hand. I will certainly choose a few bottles for dinner.'

Gray simply looked at her, the hint of two vertical lines between his brows, and Gaby realised she could read his frowns so much more easily than his smiles. The smiles hid things—they were a mask he used quite deliberately, but the frowns were thoughtful, genuine. And not hostile either, however severe they made his face seem. This one held a hint of amusement at her presumption in bringing wine for him, a touch of admiration for her entrepreneurship and the merest suggestion of banked heat that caught the breath in her throat.

This man wanted her and she wanted him and, it seemed, neither of them was going to get what they wanted—Gray because his past held something that had soured his view of relationships, she because it would be wrong to ask for what she needed from him.

'Will this do for a few days?' Gray turned on his heel, the better to inspect the sitting room of the suite he had engaged for Gabrielle and Miss Moseley at Grillon's Hotel on Albemarle Street.

Beside him the manager voiced a mild twitter of protest at his choice of words. 'This is one of our best suites, my lord. Many ladies of rank express themselves most satisfied with its amenities.'

'It appears to be just what is needed, Mr Montjoy.' Gabrielle came out of one the bedchambers with an expression that Gray had no trouble interpreting as displeasure at the manager for addressing him, not herself. 'Have our luggage brought up directly, if you please. And a tray of tea and cakes for Miss Moseley.'

The manager bowed himself out, expressing his delight that Miss Frost found the suite suitable.

'No tea for us?' Gray queried.

'I was hoping that you would take me to call on Aunt Henrietta and she is sure to ply us with refreshments. I thought it good tactics to take her by surprise before she discovers we are in London.'

'I agree. We could call on my man of business on the way and set him to finding you a house.'

'And so present her with a fait accompli?'

'A statement of intent, certainly, if you mean to begin as you will go on. But do you not want to bring Miss Moseley?'

'She is lying down and resting and I do not need a chaperone when I have you, surely?'

Gray silently reviewed the parts of his anatomy Godmama would attack at the news that he was squiring her niece around London unchaperoned. He shrugged. He was most attached to all of them, but he could probably move faster than she could. 'On your head be it.'

Gabrielle tied the ribbons on a particularly el

egant bonnet and paused to admire the effect in the mirror. 'Well, this is what is on my head at the moment—the best the Lisbon milliners can produce.' She picked up her reticule. 'Lead on, my lord, and we will face her wrath together.'

Gaby was not certain whether she was terrified or excited at the prospect of bearding Aunt Henrietta in her den. Probably both. It certainly felt like one step she must take to clear her way to fulfilling her plans for the future. Besides anything else, if she was able to find a suitable, willing father for her child she did not want him dissuaded by rumours that she was promised to George.

Gray's stables at his town house were shut up so he had hired a carriage, complete with driver and a smartly liveried groom who jumped down from the back to knock as they arrived in Mount Street.

'They are in residence.' She had been harbouring a sneaking hope that the knocker would be off the door and the family in the country. But of course, if Aunt Henrietta had been expecting Gray to bring her back, she'd be in London, scheming.

'She is waiting for me to return with you meekly at my side,' Gray said as the door swung open and the groom presented his card. 'Expecting it. See, the butler has not even had to enquire whether his mistress is receiving.' He stood as the man returned to let down the carriage steps. 'Chin up, shoulders back. I tell myself that it can't be any worse than a dressing-down from Wellington.'

'You have never been on the receiving end of one of those, surely?' Gaby took his hand and allowed herself to be helped down in a decorous manner. Aunt was doubtless peeping from behind the curtains and it would not do to begin the encounter by leaping out of the coach like a hoyden.

'I once queried an order.'

'No! Isn't that tantamount to mutiny?'

'Fortunately what I was suggesting was rather more, shall we say, aggressive, than his original intent, so he could hardly accuse me of cowardice. I escaped with the words, *impudent*, *improvident* and *impetuous* ringing in my ears, but with no further damage.'

They were through the front door as Gray finished speaking and Gaby suspected she had been most effectively distracted from any nerves she might be feeling. Gray was relieved of his hat and gloves and they were ushered through to the front drawing room. Out of the corner of her eye she saw the curtains sway slightly. Yes, they had been observed.

'Gabrielle, dearest child!' Aunt Henrietta swept down in a cloud of elegant dark blue draperies. 'Gray, dear boy, I knew I could rely upon you to bring her home to me.' She moved too fast for him to dodge a kiss on the cheek before she whirled on Gaby and gathered her in a fond, and very uncomfortable, embrace against a substantial bosom embellished with a fine diamond brooch.

They were not alone, Gaby realised as she extricated herself. A stocky young man she vaguely recognised had risen to his feet from one of the sofas flanking the fireplace. 'Welcome home, Gabrielle.'

'Thank you for the welcome to your home, Cousin George,' she said with emphasis on *cousin*. 'But hardly mine, I think. I hope I find you both well. And my uncle Orford?'

'At a house party in Herefordshire. He will be desolated that he was not here to welcome you,' Aunt Henrietta said with the air of woman not to be contradicted. Given that Lord Orford spent as much of his time out of London and away from his wife as possible, Gaby took leave to disbelieve this. 'And this will soon be your home, just as it became mine when I left Portugal for London and marriage. Now, we have a guest to meet you.' She gave Gray a very arch look. 'Someone you will be happy to see, Gray. Caroline Henderson is staying with me for a few weeks. Caro, dear, see who is here.'

A young lady rose from the other sofa. A very young lady, Gaby saw. Pretty and blonde and as sweet and shy as a chick just hatched from the egg. And she was gazing at Gray with the air of a juvenile saint sighting a vision. *Oh, no.* Beside her she felt Gray stiffen and, in the sudden awkward silence, she realised that her aunt was matchmaking twice over. But Gray to this girl?

'Lord Leybourne.' Miss Henderson's cheeks were pink and her copybook curtsy wavered along with her voice. 'I am very pleased to meet you again.'

Something had to be done. Someone—her aunt, presumably—had given this child expectations of a match and Gray was being put in a position where, unless he was exceedingly rude, he was going to reinforce those expectations. He was a gentleman. Fortunately she, Gaby, was not.

'How nice to meet you, Miss Henderson. Are you an old friend of Gray's?' she asked warmly and slipped her hand through his arm, moving in tight to his side. 'How lovely for you, darling,' she added with a melting look up at him.

For a second she thought he would fumble the catch. His eyes widened, the pupils dark, then he smiled, that charming, concealing smile. 'I believe I had the pleasure of meeting you here on one occasion before I left for Portugal, Miss Henderson, did I not? Will you be making your come-out under my godmother's wing? That must be very exciting for you.'

He used the avuncular, faintly patronising tone of a much older man and the girl's cheeks lost their colour and her lower lip trembled for a moment. Then she said, 'Yes, I am very fortunate,' in a flat voice and sat down again.

Gaby felt a stab of guilt at hurting her, but it was best done now. She would be hopeless for Gray, and he for her, even if he had the slightest intention of going against what he had said about remarrying. Her aunt had been filling the child's head with fairy tales and now she would be able to recover from her infatuation as quickly as possible.

'Gabrielle? Gray? What is this?' Aunt Henrietta was staring at them, not her trembling protégée. George stared blankly from his mother to Gabrielle.

'You must wish us happy, Godmama,' Gray said. 'We had not intended to make such a pre-cipitate announcement of our betrothal, though. My Gabrielle is nothing if not impetuous.' He laid his free hand over hers on his arm and gave her an unseen pinch. His eyes narrowed when Gaby smiled sweetly at him. Now that expression she could read as clearly as if he had spoken. He wanted to give her a good shake.

'But…but, Gabrielle, this is so…'

'I know, Aunt. But the feeling was mutual, at first sight almost. Thank you so much for sending him to me. Now, we have come upon you unex-pectedly and you have a guest. Gray will take me back to my hotel and Miss Moseley, my compan-ion, and just as soon as I have found a house you are all invited to dinner. And George must bring a partner, because I am certain you are courting some eligible young lady, cousin.'

'Er…no, not exactly.' George sent his step-mother a look of confused appeal.

'A hotel?' Aunt Henrietta demanded. 'Your *own* house? What are you saying, Gabrielle?'

'Of course I cannot impose upon you, Aunt, es-pecially as I have business to transact in London and I know you would not wish anything hinting at trade to be carried on from this house. Darling

Gray's man is finding me somewhere suitable and a staff and, of course, I have Miss Moseley with me to add countenance.'

'We really should be going to inspect that first property, my dear,' Gray said to her. 'We will be late, but you would insist on calling on Godmama as soon as possible.' The intense look he gave her was almost enough to send Gaby off into giggles, but she kept a straight face throughout a brisk exchange of farewells.

Gray bundled her into the carriage, snapped something to the driver and climbed in beside her. He fell back against the squabs and turned his head so he could meet her gaze. 'Has my hair turned white? What the devil are you about, Gabrielle?'

'Saving you from that child, of course. Aunt has been filling her head with dreams about you. Then you turn up unexpectedly, looking precisely like any girl's dream lover, and do nothing to repel her in those first vital seconds.'

'Dream lover?'

'Titled, handsome, free. All your own teeth, remember? That girl is like a flawless peach—almost ripe, ready to be bruised for ever by the wrong handling. You'd be a disaster for each other and it would be almost as bad if she was to have her expectations and dreams reinforced by your gentlemanly reluctance to snub her. This is much kinder. She will have a little weep for a few days, then emerge unscathed except for the delightful memory of a tragic love with no reality to it to damage her.'

'And meanwhile—and you must forgive me for seeming ungallant if I do not seem ecstatic at the thought—you and I are to be leg-shackled? You have forgotten, perhaps, that I told you I had no intention of marrying again?'

'Of course I had not forgotten. Before the end of my visit you will realise that I am quite hopeless for you. I will be driven to distraction by your disapproval and attempts to curtail my business concerns and we will agree we do not suit. Aunt will not say anything to anyone until she absolutely has to because she will hope just such a thing will happen and George will follow her lead. Miss Henderson is unlikely to say anything, given her own disappointed hopes. You are quite safe, Gray. Provided you steer well clear of Miss Henderson once you are free again, that is.'

He studied her face, his own set in a thoughtful frown. 'And you had every confidence I would play along with your outrageous scheme?'

'Of course. Did you not tell me that Wellington, no less, called you *impudent and impetuous*?'

'Do not forget the *improvident*,' he growled.

The sharp vertical line between his brows was
just too tempting to resist. Gaby reached up and
smoothed it with her thumb. 'Don't scowl at me,
Gray. You look as though you want to box my
ears.'

'No. What I want to do is this,' he said as he
pulled her towards him and kissed her full on
the mouth.

Chapter Ten

Surprise warred with instant arousal. *He still wants me?*

Gray sat back, released her almost before she could complete the thought. 'Damn.'

They stared at each other, then Gaby put both hands around his neck, knocking off his hat in the process, and kissed him back, slowly, thoughtfully and with great care. 'We cannot carry on like this,' she observed when she, too, subsided back into the seat, breathing heavily. 'I believe we have established that we have no desire to marry each other.' It was quite difficult to manage a sentence of that length—and number of syllables— without panting.

'You want an affaire?' She was not the only breathless one.

'Yes.' Brazen, immodest. Honest. 'I am not a virgin, and neither of us is committed to anyone else. I am here for only a short time. What harm can there be?'

'You are certain?' Gray looked at her intently, every ounce of his formidable attention focused on her.

'Yes.' It was foolish in the extreme, of course, and not for any reason that a moralist would give her for avoiding such behaviour. How could she seek for a father for her child, her heir, if she was enmeshed in an affaire with Gray? But surely this was simply a flare of passion, an instinctive desire? Satisfying that desire would end the compulsion, it would burn itself out and his presence would no longer fill her senses and disturb her dreams and she would be able to think clearly about what—and whom—she wanted.

'Then come with me now?' She could not escape the heat in those eyes she had thought so hard, so cold. When she nodded, he knocked on the carriage roof and, when it halted, dropped the window glass, leaned out and called something up to the driver. 'My town house,' he said as he slammed the glass back up and reached for her again.

Gaby slid her hands under the lapels of his coat, felt his heat and the hard movement of his muscles under her palms, arched into his kiss as his hand slipped up her leg, over silk, over the ribbons of her garter, over bare skin towards her heat and her secrets.

The windows were unshielded, and they were trotting demurely through fashionable, crowded Mayfair and this controlled, disciplined man was giving way to his desire for her in the most un-inhibited, dangerous manner. She loved it. Her hands pushed at his coat, wanting him, wanting to touch his skin as he touched hers, burning.

Her skirts were heaped in her lap now, there was cool air on her thighs, his hand—

The coach turned a corner, slowed and they fell apart.

'I've lost my mind.' Gray closed the blind beside him with a jerk, leaned across her as Gaby fought her skirts into decency and dealt with the other, then tugged his coat back into place and pushed his hands though his hair. 'And, what's worse, I cannot seem to care.'

'No,' she agreed. She found her bonnet on the floor, put it on and pulled down the veil that, thank goodness, Jane had insisted she pin to it. 'Am I fit to be seen?'

Gray released a blind, letting some more light in as the carriage came to a halt. 'Yes, we will pass muster.'

Considering that she was trembling like an aspen leaf in a faint breeze, Gaby thought that she managed to dismount from the carriage and climb the front steps of Gray's town house with admirable composure. She had no idea where they were, the view through her veil was blurred and she was too agitated to ask.

The door was opened by a small man in a butler's formal black with a striped waistcoat. 'My lord. Madam.'

'Fredericks, this is Miss Frost, Lady Orford's niece visiting London from Portugal. I am assisting Miss Frost in finding a house for a few months, so doubtless you will be seeing a great deal of her.'

'Miss Frost, welcome to England. My lord—'

'Miss Frost and I have business to discuss. Please have refreshments sent to the study and then see that we are not disturbed.'

'My lord,' the butler said again with enough emphasis to stop Gray's march down the hall. 'Mr Pickford is in residence. He arrived last week and, as you told me before you sailed that you had offered him open house, I did not hesitate to accommodate him in the Chinese suite.'

'Gray!' A cheerful voice floated down from the landing, followed by a pair of long legs in pantaloons and Hessian boots which belonged, Gaby saw, to a younger, fairer, shorter version of Gray. 'You see, I made up my mind to take the plunge and hazard my new future and I am heartily glad of your offer to stay while I put it all in place.' He stopped in front of Gaby, who had flipped back her veil. 'Ma'am.'

'Miss Frost, my cousin Mr Pickford. Henry, Miss Frost, Lady Orford's niece from Porto. Lady Orford, you will recall, is my godmother.'

'Who can forget?' Henry Pickford thrust out his hand and shook Gaby's. 'Are you staying with the old battleaxe, Miss Frost? Or…er…perhaps she is your favourite relative, in which case I apologise most heartily for the description.'

'Please, do not apologise, Mr Pickford. I quite agree, Lady Orford can be…demanding. Lord Leybourne is assisting me to find a house in town for a few months so I can live there with my own household and companion.' She managed a smile and to put warmth into her voice and could only hope that he was a very unobservant young man. If he wasn't, then the best she could hope for was that he might think that her colour was naturally high and that she suffered from some kind of breathing complaint.

Beside her, when she glanced up, Gray was

wearing one of his most deceptive smiles. So much for an afternoon of sin amid the teacups on the desk in the study… Or perhaps there was a sofa in there. Or his bedchamber led off it.

She was not going to find out today. Perhaps she never would if the pair of them came to their senses and pretended this had not happened, that Gray had not had his hands on her bare thighs in the carriage, that she had not been trying to tear off his coat and scratch her nails down his naked chest.

Somehow she found herself in the drawing room, making polite conversation with this member of Gray's family. Or rather, she was making polite conversation—he obviously felt a pressing need to unburden himself to anyone who would listen.

'I am definitely going to America to make a fresh start there, in Boston. My father left me heavily in debt when he died last year, you see, Miss Frost.'

'I, um… I am so sorry for your loss.'

'Thank you. We were not close, far from it.' He grimaced. 'It has taken me all this time to sort matters out, everything was in the most appalling state and there was such a scandal.'

Gaby cast a frantic glance at Gray, but he merely shrugged.

'Father embezzled money from the bank, you see.'

'Oh,' she said faintly.

'But I have sold up everything and it is completely paid off and I have just enough to relocate and leave all this behind me. I hope to find employment where my name is not known. I'm not afraid of honest hard work, you see.' He smiled at her, suddenly shy. 'I'm sorry, I have embarrassed you, storming on about my ghastly family troubles, And money, which makes it all worse.'

He's young, she thought. *My age, but inexperienced and not worldly-wise.*

Suddenly she felt at ease with him. 'I do not think money makes anything worse, Mr Pickford. Clearly embezzling someone else's money does, but it sounds as though you have acted in great good faith and with energy. I produce port and I certainly do not find discussing matters of trade embarrassing.'

'Port?' He sat up even more alertly. 'I am exceedingly interested in wine.' Before she knew it she was immersed in a blizzard of questions about young growths and vintages and bottle maturation.

* * *

Gray settled back in his chair, drank tea and let them talk. He liked his mother's nephew Henry, who had been faced with a hideous situation when his father had shot himself. The only hint of a silver lining to the cloud was that Mr Pickford's wife had died many years before and Henry had no brothers or sisters, so he had only himself to extricate from the mire his parent had left behind for him.

Henry had refused offers of financial help, but had clutched gratefully at advice and moral support. Gray could wish that he had not been quite so open-handed in his invitations to come and stay at any time, for as long as Henry needed. Tea and biscuits were absolutely no help at all in combatting intense sexual frustration.

It might be for the best, of course. It had been passion and impulse that had brought them there and his own anger at his godmother's blatant attempt at matchmaking. He found himself thoroughly in sympathy with Gabrielle's resistance to Lady Orford's schemes now, when before he had felt that she was right and that Gabrielle's life needed organising in a way that reflected what society expected of a young lady.

Having the tables turned so that he was being

manoeuvred into doing what society expected of an unmarried earl, however… That was something else entirely. Gabrielle was right, Miss Henderson was an innocent little chick and utterly unsuitable for him in every way. Just as he would make her a dreadful husband.

That said, it was something of a turnaround to find himself shifting from advocating a respectable marriage for Gabrielle to taking the young lady in question as a lover. Contact with Miss Frost was beginning to turn his view of the world on its head and he was struggling to find his balance. Was he doing what he wanted because he could, or was he doing what they both wanted and it was something that would do neither of them harm, might even enrich their lives for a short while?

He did not know, all he did know was that once before when he had been faced with understanding what a woman wanted, truly needed, he had offered what had seemed right and proper without thinking it through. Then he had turned away, left for the army again, avoided the issue by simply not being there.

There was nothing he could do about Portia now, but Gabrielle was his responsibility for the moment, although he could imagine what she would have to say if he told her that was how he regarded her.

He watched now as she talked to Henry, completely immersed in the conversation, listening intently to his mixture of confidences, questions and plans. She was beautiful, desirable and yet not, he would have said a few weeks ago, his type. He had always favoured blondes, sweetness. Intelligence, yes, but not challenge.

Gabrielle's dark eyes challenged with every look. They offered debate on every topic and disagreement with his opinions, his observations, his desires. She wanted to lock horns with him because she could, because she enjoyed sparring with him. And he enjoyed being challenged, which was a surprise to him. Cavalry officers, especially those raised as heirs to earldoms, did not, as a general rule, find themselves flouted and defied very often, let alone teased.

It was refreshing as well as arousing. He ate a biscuit, then another, and applied himself to convincing his body that it was getting no satisfaction that day and probably not until Gabrielle was established in her own house. By that time she would probably have thought better of it.

He doubted he would be having second thoughts. Gabrielle was unlike any woman he had ever encountered and he feared that she was becoming increasingly addictive. Perhaps making love to her would satisfy both of them, satisfy their curiosity, remove the mystery. That would be best.

'My lord?' Fredericks had come in without Gray noticing, in itself an indication that he needed to get his brain disentangled from thoughts of smooth skin, strong limbs, the haunting scent of jasmine-scented woman and back to the present.

'Yes?'

The butler was offering a salver with one unfranked letter in the middle. 'Lady Orford's footman brought this, my lord. He is waiting for a reply.'

Gray broke the seal, read, mentally rolled his eyes and coughed. The two deep in conversation broke off and looked up. 'Miss Frost, your aunt has sent a note to say that should you wish to attend Lady Altringworth's soirée this evening, her dear friend is only too pleased to welcome you and that she and George are at your disposal as escorts.'

'I do not have anything fashionable to wear for evening yet, not by London standards.' Gabrielle bit her lip in thought. 'I could be Portuguese and eccentric, I suppose. I would certainly like to go. Will you accompany me? I can write and thank her and say I would not dream of taking them out of their way to collect me, but I will be most grateful for her chaperonage at the soirée.' She smiled mischievously at him. 'That sounds suitably dutiful, doesn't it? Then we can escape if it is too tiresome.'

'It sounds like a good compromise. I have no doubt of being acceptable as your escort at the Altringworths' house, even uninvited. They're a hospitable family. The footman is waiting and the writing desk is over there if you want to pen a note.'

He strolled over to take the seat next to Henry. 'How are the plans shaping up?'

'Well, I thank you. It really is exceedingly helpful having this house as a base in London because I have several possible contacts here and having such a good address is a great help. Meeting Miss Frost is a stroke of good fortune.' Henry sat forward, hands clasped between his knees. 'I was interested in the wine trade, but had no focus for that. Now I am wondering if I can find an opening in Boston, which was the city I most favoured trying my fortune in. Miss Frost is being most generous with advice, but there is so much I would like to ask her. She has promised me a letter of introduction to someone she corresponds with in Boston, you know.'

'Has she agents in America?'

'Apparently not. There are issues about shipping port such distances, apparently, but Miss Frost says—'

'You must tell me later. Now I must take Miss Frost back to her hotel and return here to change.'

Gabrielle eyed Gray ruefully across the width of the carriage. By unspoken consent they had taken opposite corners, sitting with the utmost decorum in almost laughable contrast to the way they had arrived, flushed and tumbled and aching to strip the clothing from each other.

'Your cousin is a very interesting gentleman.'

'He is definitely a good one, I believe. I admire his moral certainty and his energy in righting his father's wrongs. He has set himself a hard path, but I think, with luck, he will flourish in the New World.'

'Are you sorry he had taken you up on your invitation?' she asked. She had resolved not to mention it, not until they had both spent a night considering the matter.

'I could have wished the poor devil almost anywhere else in the universe,' Gray said, with an intensity at odds with the stillness of his body.

'Then why are you over there?'

'Because I am not going to tumble you in a carriage like some member of the muslin company.' His hand clenched on his thigh. 'And besides, there is a strong possibility you have thought better of it.'

'You must think me very fickle, or indecisive.' She wanted to reach out, touch that betraying fist, but that would be like cutting a cord under high tension—the recoil would send them into each other's arms and Gray was right, the first time should not be hasty and furtive in a carriage. Even so… 'I agree about not making love in a carriage—the first time.'

Gray looked at her directly at last. Even in the uncertain light of the carriage she could see the intensity of that regard and her body responded, softening, warming, aching. 'The first time?'

'It might be rather stimulating on some other occasion, don't you think?'

'I am trying very hard not to think about it at all,' he said, the growl in his voice reverberating down her spine. 'Now I doubt I will get any sleep tonight doing just that.'

Thank goodness. He still feels the same way.

She was not at all sure what she would have done if Gray had changed his mind. Dissolved into a puddle of lust on the carriage floor, probably. 'I had never thought that misbehaving in London would be quite so difficult.'

Gray laughed and the tension became less charged, less dangerous. 'It is if one party is encumbered with a chaperone and the other is attempting not to compromise her. If it were not for Miss Moseley we could lock ourselves away in your hotel room. If it were not for the risk of you being seen we could take a room for the day at any one of a number of obliging accommodation addresses.'

'You seem to have considerable experience in arranging this kind of thing.' It came out sounding sharper than she had intended. Jealous, even.

'I have not been a monk since my wife died, if that is what you are asking.' Gray kept his tone even and that deceptive smile was back. 'But, no, I have never attempted to make a rendezvous in London.'

Gaby did not make the mistake of asking if he was keeping a mistress. No, surely not. Gray was not a man to make love to one woman while keeping another. 'I beg your pardon, that was inquisitive.'

The smile disappeared, but he laughed again. She found she trusted his laughter more than his smiles. 'And I parted company amiably with the lady who had been in my keeping two months before I left for Portugal, just in case you were biting your tongue over that question.'

'I was curious,' Gaby admitted. 'Is she a beauty?'

'Oh, ravishing. A green-eyed redhead.' His hands moved, sketched curves in the air.

She suspected he was teasing her. And she more than suspected that she was becoming green-eyed herself. 'Was she too expensive for you? Or had she a fiery temper?'

'Neither. She was ambitious and had her eye set on a marquess. She lamented that he was balding and stout and that she had the poorest of expectations of his performance in the bedchamber, but what was a girl to do if she is determined on a duke one day?'

'Goodness, that was a very frank conversation to have with a lover!'

'Neither of us deceived ourselves that what we had was a meeting of hearts,' Gray said.

Did he love his wife? Has he known what it is to lie with a lover whom one loves? Gaby wondered.

She had not loved Laurent, she knew now, somehow. But her feelings had been close to love.

The loss of him had been an agony, but then the thought of not having known that attachment, that feeling of closeness, that was unbearable. And now she was becoming melancholy.

'Will I enjoy Lady Altringworth's soirée?' she asked, giving herself a mental shake. 'I have no experience of fashionable London entertainments.'

'She is a good hostess.' Gray seemed willing to accept the change of subject. 'There will be music, intelligent conversation, cards if that is what you want—and excellent food. She is very much of the *ton*—expect to see only the most fashionable in society, although London is thin of company at this time of year, of course.'

'Then I must indeed aim to be eccentric, for I have nothing that will pass muster as fashionable. Not yet. Is there a taste for that in London or will I simply succeed in embarrassing myself?'

'Eccentricity with style and wit is always acceptable. I find myself looking forward to seeing what you create.'

The carriage halted. They were at the hotel, she realised.

Gray handed her out, escorted her to her door and kissed her fingertips before he opened it for her. 'Pleasure postponed can be the greater for it,' he murmured. The pressure of his fingers on hers pulled her in towards him until his breath was warm on her cheek.

Gaby lifted the hand he held and brushed her own lips over the ungloved back of his. 'There will be two of us unable to sleep tonight.'

Beside them the door began to open. 'Is that you, Gabrielle? Ah, yes, it is.' Jane stood on the threshold, spectacles perched on the end of her nose, notebook in hand. 'Good afternoon, my lord.'

'Miss Moseley. I will collect you at nine, if that is convenient, Miss Frost?'

'Very, thank you.' And then he was gone and Gaby was inside and trying to think of how to report a most unsettling day to Jane. 'Have you been out?' she asked, playing for time while she sorted out her thoughts, got her breathing under control and tried, very hard, not to dwell on the sensation of Gray's breath on her cheek.

'British Museum, Lackington's Circulating Library, three bookshops and the British Institution,' Jane said briskly. 'And how was your aunt?'

So much for distraction. 'I have convinced her that Lord Leybourne and I have an understanding.'

'Indeed?' For once she had succeeded in surprising her companion.

'Simply a ruse, of course. But she was planning on matchmaking for him, too, so I killed two birds with one stone, as it were.'

'And what does Lord Leybourne have to say about that, pray?' Jane removed her spectacles, the better to subject Gaby to a beady inspection.

'He is suitably grateful for being rescued, of course.' She ignored Jane's snort and went through to the bedchamber. 'And Aunt has secured invitations for you and me to a soirée this evening, from which I deduce that she entertains hopes of separating me from Gray. Or did not believe a word of it in the first place.'

'I doubt that.' Jane followed her and stood in the doorway while Gaby shed bonnet and gloves.

'Really?' Surprised, she turned, one glove half-off. 'I had not thought her very perceptive.'

'She can see what is in front of her nose, I suspect.' Jane came right into the room and perched on the side of the bed. 'The pair of you clearly have a strong attachment.'

'We have?' Surely, surely, they had done nothing that might make Jane suspect? Until that day nothing had been agreed between them, they had behaved with restraint, hadn't they?

'I may be a spinster,' Jane said primly, looking

every inch the model of one. 'But I also know a great deal about the mating habits of mammals.'

'*Mammals?*'

'Humans are mammals.' The tip of her companion's nose was pink now.

'And we are not *mating.*' *Not yet, anyway.* 'Gray is a very attractive man. I may flatter myself that I am not exactly repulsive to the opposite sex. Obviously there is a mutual…awareness.' Now her own face was reddening, she could feel it.

'Yes, dear. As you say. I do not think I will accept your aunt's kind invitation. Will you require any assistance dressing for this evening?'

'Are you not going to give me a little lecture on proper behaviour?' Gaby enquired, halfway between being horrified by Jane's perception, when she had thought her companion would hardly notice if Gaby was entertaining half the men in the valley, and embarrassed that she was being obvious in her feelings about Gray.

'I hardly think that this is the time to start behaving like a conventional chaperone, is it?' Jane stood up and turned to the door. 'And especially after your Frenchman, poor young man.'

'You *knew* about Laurent? You never said anything.'

'It is none of my business. But I can interpret

the memorial stone. If he had been an English officer, I believe you would have said something about him. As it is…' She put on her spectacles again and drifted out of the door, closing it behind her with a little click.

Chapter Eleven

Gray paced slowly up and down the entrance hall of Grillon's Hotel. He had arrived at nine, sent up a footman to announce his arrival and, from previous experience of escorting ladies to balls, was expecting to spend a good half hour before Gabrielle appeared.

'You look like a caged beast in a menagerie,' Gabrielle remarked from immediately behind him.

'I was settling down to wait,' he confessed. It was ridiculous the way his pulse leapt at the sound of her voice. 'You are admirably punctual, Miss Frost.'

'I dislike being kept waiting myself.' She tipped her head to one side and studied him gravely. 'I thought you most elegant in Portugal, but clearly you had tossed some old rags into your valise for travelling, because now you look magnificent, my lord.'

'I thank you.' Her serious, lingering study was both flattering and arousing. 'It is not the custom for ladies to compliment gentlemen on their attire, I should warn you—just in case you encounter Prinny and are swept away in admiration of his appearance.'

'From what I have read of the Prince Regent, I beg leave to doubt it,' she said with a chuckle.

Gabrielle was enveloped in a long black evening cloak with a large hood which covered her hair. All Gray could see beside her face was a flash of deep crimson at the front edges of the cloak when she moved and a subdued hint of the same colour in the depths of the hood.

'You look enchanting,' he said and meant it.

'You cannot see more than my face,' Gabrielle protested as she took his arm.

'Just what I said—enchanting.'

She nipped his arm in reproof at what he supposed she thought was teasing and he glanced down to see that instead of conventional long evening gloves she was wearing black lace fingerless gloves through which her skin glowed creamily.

There were no rings on her fingers, not on either hand, he saw when she gathered up her skirts to mount the step into the carriage. Of course, she would hardly bring jewellery on a voyage to England, even if she had very much. He should have thought of that, offered to lend her some. Buying jewellery at this stage in their not-quite affaire might be a sensitive issue, but he could certainly hire something suitable on her behalf. He made a mental note to suggest it.

The Altringworths' house was not far, in a street to the west of Berkeley Square. Torchères were blazing on either side of the door, a red carpet was down from the steps to the kerb and two burly footmen were on the pavement to assist arriving guests and deter the crowd of onlookers from pressing too close.

Gray delivered Gabrielle to the ladies' cloakroom, shed his own hat, cloak and cane and joined the group of other men waiting for their partners in the front hall. He was listening his old friend Freddie Stansfield's account buying a team of matched Welsh bays for his mother's carriage when Freddie's voice trailed off and his jaw dropped as he stared over Gray's shoulder. Gray turned and felt his own mouth open. He snapped it shut and moved, fast, before any of the transfixed men beat him to Gabrielle's side.

'You look ravishing,' he murmured, too low for

anyone else to hear. 'I want to take you home, kick Henry out on to the street and make love to you all night.'

Gabrielle kept her composure, although her cheeks turned a warm, flattering pink. 'I was aiming for mildly exotic and eccentric,' she murmured back.

'Unique and elegant.' He took her hand and led her towards the foot of the staircase where a receiving line snaked down. When they were brought to a halt two steps up he turned again and studied her from head to toe.

Gabrielle was wearing a sophisticated version of her everyday working costume. Over a tightly fitted shirt of white lace with long sleeves, a slit at the neck and a stand-up collar framing her neck, was a black brocade waistcoat. A perfectly plain skirt of deep crimson silk whispered down to her toes. Her hair was caught up in an elaborate plaited coronet held in place by silver combs studded with rubies and diamonds and long ruby drops crusted with more tiny diamonds fell from her earlobes. At her throat glowed a single tear-shaped ruby surrounded by yet more glittering white stones and held on a silver chain to lie where a shadowy hint of cleavage showed at the neckline.

'Those gems—you brought them with you? How?' He wouldn't have had a moment's sleep on the ship if he'd known she was carrying a fortune with her. 'They must be part of the Frost Fire parure—I had heard of it, but I thought it was a legend.'

'How I carried them is my secret. But, yes, these are Frost Fire pieces. The rest are safely locked away at the quinta. My great-grandmother was Portuguese nobility and it is said that the stones were originally a gift from King John the Fifth, the Magnanimous, when he came to the throne in 1706. Family legend says that she was his mistress when he was the crown prince and this was his farewell gift when he became king.

'They were reset like this about seventy years ago. That's when they became known as the Frost Fire jewels, because of the contrast between the rubies and the glitter of the diamonds,' she explained, lifting her skirts a little as she climbed, revealing a hint of lacy petticoats.

They climbed a few steps and Gray became aware that they were being eyed with varying degrees of discretion by the guests around them. Gabrielle was looking stunning, but he suspected that her jewels were what were riveting the attention of most of the onlookers. The entire parure, which would include a tiara and bracelets, rings and necklaces, must be worth more than the entire quinta. No wonder his godmother wanted to secure Gabrielle for her stepson: any prudent mother would want her as a daughter-in-law.

Gray had a sinking feeling that not only was he going to have to guard her against predatory mamas, covetous jewel thieves and fortune hunters, but that Gabrielle was set on thoroughly enjoying herself with as much verve as the most dashing young matron.

'I imagine you are going to be a great success,' he said drily as they reached the top and turned to their hostess.

'I know. I could have a face like a carthorse and the disposition of a scorpion and still be a catch,' she agreed. She said it lightly, almost flippantly, but there was something in her tone that did not ring quite true.

Someone has hurt her, he thought. *Some fortune hunter. No wonder she resents her aunt so much. And no wonder that her trusted neighbours' matrimonial scheming had angered her so.*

Lady Altringworth was gracious, warm even. Her eyes had widened at the approach of a young lady in such an unconventional gown, then her smile had widened, too, at the sight of the great ruby on Gabrielle's breast.

'Welcome to London, my dear Miss Frost. You will soon find yourself quite at home, I am certain.' She favoured Gray with a coy look that managed to imply that he was a cunning dog to have attached himself to the heiress so promptly and then they were past and into the main reception room.

Gray took a deep breath and surveyed the throng. The room was already crowded and warm, the scent of expensive perfumes, hothouse flowers and hot beeswax mingling with the smell of food and wine and, far less pleasantly, hot humanity.

It was his duty as escort to present Gabrielle to the hostesses who would invite her to the most select parties and, he supposed, to anyone she might find useful for her wine business. That would have to be more discreet, avoiding any hint of trade, but he could probably rely on Gabrielle to manage the situation once he had pointed her in the right direction.

Her gown attracted attention, and some compliments, from the various matrons they met. Gabrielle was charming, poised, and, he was certain, would be a success. Lady Parslow introduced her to a small group of younger people, including her own recently married daughter and Gray decided he could leave her to her own devices for a while. Besides any other consideration he did not want to appear as anything but the escort her aunt had happened to select for her that evening.

'Abandoning the heiress, old chap? Not good tactics, not until you've got her firmly attached. Too many interested hounds sniffing around.' It was Freddie Stansfield again, this time with two mutual friends, Lord Peter de Clare and Malcolm Fitzwalter.

'I am not fortune hunting,' Gray said mildly, cursing mentally. That was precisely what he did not want to appear to be doing. 'Simply doing my godmother a favour by squiring Miss Frost about until she finds her feet.'

'She is certainly an original, and a beauty,' de Clare said and they turned to watch Gabrielle as she stood laughing at something one of the young men clustered around her was saying.

'Any single woman with gems like that is a beauty,' Fitzwalter, a man in no need of a rich wife, observed cynically. 'Didn't know you were planning on a stay in town, Leybourne. Care to join us at the theatre tomorrow night? Thought we'd dine at Brooks's and go on from there, finish up with some cards.'

'Thank you, yes,' Gray agreed, half his attention on Gabrielle.

'Watch out, the cavalry's arrived,' Freddie said, nodding towards the door where five men in scarlet dress uniforms were entering.

'That's Turner and Appleton. I haven't seen them since we left France,' Gray said. 'Excuse me.'

He made to intercept his old comrades, but the room was now crowded and he was detained several times by acquaintances he could hardly push past and ignore. By the time he located the officers they had joined the group around Gabrielle and, it was clear, she knew all of them.

'Now, let me see if I have learned everyone's names correctly,' she was saying. 'Lady Ferris, Mrs Horton, Miss Platt, Lord Knighton and Mr Horton, may I introduce Major Lord Appleton, Major Carfax, Captains Sir James Grigson, Turner and Colney.' She glanced round and saw Gray. 'And I am sure Lord Leybourne is known to all of you.'

'Colonel.' The officers came to attention, although Appleton and Turner were grinning at him, old friends he had known too well for considerations of rank off-duty, even when he was one of them.

'I'm a civilian now,' he said as he shook hands and endured some brisk backslapping. 'No need for the rank, I assure you. It is good to see you and we must catch up with our news another evening, I'll give you my card. But I see you already know Miss Frost, whose aunt, Lady Orford, is my godmother.'

'We often met Miss Frost when we were based in Pinhão,' Appleton explained and made a gallant bow in her direction 'She was the ornament of all the best dinner parties in the district. You were off on the Staff, as I recall. We got shouted at less and had the better port, I would make my guess.'

'It is good to see you are all safe and sound,' Gabrielle said. 'Once you had left to chase the French out of Spain we had no idea what had happened to anyone, and then I had no idea which of my old acquaintances fought at Waterloo. I tried to check the casualty lists, but they were so long.'

There was a moment's silence when they all were clearly thinking of just what those lists in smudged black newsprint signified. 'We've had a charmed life,' Carfax drawled with a grin, breaking the mood. Then he sobered. 'Except, of course, for poor Norwood.'

The rest of the group, the civilians, had drifted

away, taking Captain Colney with them. 'Poor Norwood?' Gray queried. 'Major Andrew Norwood, the intelligence officer?' He'd never quite taken to the man and now it sounded as though the major had not made it back.

'That's him,' Carfax agreed. 'He was pulled out of the river downstream of Pinhão just before we moved behind the lines.' He flicked a glance at Gabrielle as though wondering what to say. 'Been knifed in the ribs, very efficiently.'

It was Gabrielle's very stillness that told Gray of her distress. She had gone pale now and he recalled that Norwood had been the man who had involved her brother in the spying work that had led to his death. When she had spoken of the riding officer before she had been cool, almost hostile.

'Perhaps an angry father or husband,' she suggested, her voice unemotional. 'He had a certain reputation, I believe.'

'Er, yes. That could be it. Shouldn't have mentioned it at all, not a fit subject for a lady's ears,' Carfax apologised. 'Do you make a long stay in London, Miss Frost?'

She answered readily enough and the talk turned to theatre and the opera, but Gabrielle was still pale, her eyes dark and shadowed, and Gray had a disturbing memory of the long, thin-bladed knife in her hand that day on the terraces, and the easy competence with which she used it. Had she blamed Norwood for her brother's death and taken her revenge, a life for a life?

He reined back the tumbling thoughts. Norwood had been a tough soldier and a big man. There was no way a slight young woman, even a fit and courageous one, could have overcome him, let alone dragged him to the river and thrown him in.

But her staff would do anything for her, a little voice whispered in his ear. Anything. *Oh, hell.*

Gray thinks that I killed Norwood. He had gone very still, his eyes watchful despite the easy social smile on his lips. She had come to distrust that smile, it was his mask. She had betrayed too much when she had spoken of Thomas's death, of the way Norwood had recruited and used him. His eyes had narrowed when Carfax had spoken of the knife wound and she, so foolishly, had shown off just how good she was with a blade.

Gaby kept her chin up, her tone light and amused, and fought the urge to close her eyes as though to hide from that assessing, judging, look.

I did not kill him, she wanted to shout. *But I might as well have*, her nagging sense of guilt amended. If she could have done so in those desperate, frantic moments, she would have, she knew that. But not in cold blood. She did not think she could kill anyone, whatever they had done, whatever they were, with premeditation.

She dropped her fan, gave a pretended mutter of annoyance and dipped to pick it up, colliding with Lord Appleton and Major Turner, who both dived to rescue it. It gave her a moment's respite, broke the temptation to give in, like a mouse held by a snake's cold eyes, and confess all.

The trance broken, she found she could breathe again. Gray had turned away and was saying something to Grigson about a sergeant they both knew who had lost a leg at Waterloo and was now running a successful posting inn on the Brighton road.

Lord Appleton offered his arm. 'Shall we take a look-in at the refreshment room, Miss Frost? I hear great things of the fruit tarts and we need to get there before Grigson or there will be none left.'

Gaby laughed at the sally and at Sir James Grigson's half-hearted denials of gluttony and found herself with both men as escorts to the supper room. It was easy enough to eat, especially when she found cheese tartlets and lobster patties. Tension always made her hungry rather than the reverse and neither man seemed to find her manner strained.

'I will have a dinner party when I have my house and I have settled in,' she promised. 'If you are all still in London, you must help me with my house-warming.'

That was greeted with enthusiastic acceptances and suggestions on what they might bring as house-warming gifts.

'A basketful of kittens for catching mice might create more mayhem than the mice,' Gaby said, laughing over Sir James's fanciful ideas of what constituted a suitable present. 'I do hope you are not serious.' She felt the smile stiffen on her lips as Gray came to the table.

He made no move to sit down. 'I believe you said that you wished to return to Grillon's by midnight, Miss Frost. If you have finished your supper, perhaps you would allow me to escort you?'

She had said no such thing, she was sure of it. Gray, she supposed, had decided he must get to the bottom of Norwood's murder sooner rather than later. *Murder.* Gaby had never thought of it like that. It had been self-defence, Norwood had been the aggressor.

'Of course, how thoughtful.' She managed to

get some warmth into her tone, despite the cold finger of apprehension trailing down her spine. 'Thank you, gentlemen, I look forward to being able to invite you all to dinner.'

If I am still in the country and not fleeing back to Portugal...

Gray maintained a flow of easy conversation as they walked back through the reception room. He stopped and introduced her to several of his acquaintances and behaved as though he had nothing more on his mind than making a leisurely departure from the party. By the time she had retrieved her cloak and he had sent a footman for his carriage, Gaby was ready to scream.

He said something to the driver that she did not catch. It might have been an instruction to drive to Bow Street, it might have been an order to drive round and round in a circle until she confessed. Gaby made herself put her fan and reticule beside her on the seat rather than clutch them as an illusory safety barrier and leaned back, trying to appear merely slightly weary and ready for her bed.

'Well?' he said as the carriage moved off. 'Are you going to tell me about Norwood?' Gray had settled on the opposite seat, his back to the horses, even though there was room next to her.

All the better to interrogate me, I suppose.

'I did not kill him, if that is what you mean.'

'So who did?' Still the same even tone without either sympathy or accusation. Gaby found she had no idea whether Gray believed her or not.

Chapter Twelve

'Laurent killed Major Norwood. Must I tell you everything? It still makes me feel sick.' The moment she had spoken, she despised herself for sounding feeble, but everything about it was appalling, from the realisation that Norwood would stop at nothing, including rape, to marry her and secure the wealth that Thomas's death had left entirely in her hands, to the splash as two bodies had hit the fast-flowing river.

'I think it would be as well, don't you?' She could not see his face, but his voice was that of a doctor telling the patient that a painful procedure was entirely for their own good. There was no reassurance that it would not be agonising. Nor was she under any illusion that she could bluff her way out of this. She might find Gray deeply attractive, he might feel the same about her, but that was not going to stop him finding out the truth, whatever it took.

'Very well.' Gaby took a moment, organising her words to get it over with as quickly as possible. 'I was in the garden. I had just left Thomas's grave where I had been planting flowers and dusk was falling. It was almost time to go in to wash and change for dinner. Norwood found me there and proposed marriage.

'At first I thought it was genuine. He said all the right things, went down on one knee, even. He had always been attentive, rather more than was comfortable, but I had not thought him dangerous, merely insensitive. And of course I blamed him for encouraging Thomas to join the *guerrilheiros*. I refused him, politely, but he persisted. He got up off his knees, tried to kiss me, but I sensed this was a pretext, a display of affectionate ardour. When I moved from hinting to outright rejection to no effect it began to dawn on me that he wanted the quinta, the Frost Fire jewels he had seen at a dinner party, everything.'

Gray muttered something under his breath, a quick curse, perhaps, but she could not see his face very clearly.

'The more I refused, the angrier he became. He let something slip about Thomas and I realised that it might have been he who betrayed him, simply to leave me the sole heir. I threw that at him and he laughed. I had the soil from my brother's grave on my hands and he *laughed*. I told him he was despicable, that I would write to Wellington, and he grabbed me, started to pull at my clothing, force me to the ground. I don't know whether he was simply too angry to control himself or whether he thought that if he ravished me I would have no choice but to marry him.' Gray made another sound and she broke off. 'What did you say?'

'Nothing. I think I was grinding my teeth. Go on. You had your knife.'

'No, only a hand fork and that was blunt. I tried to stab him with it, but he twisted it out of my hand, threw it away and I screamed, even though I knew all the staff were at the back of the house, preparing for dinner. Then, suddenly, he was dragged off me. Laurent was there, dressed like one of the local farmers. Norwood drew a knife, went for him. They fought, right on the riverbank, and then they went in, both of them.'

She sometimes woke out of a nightmare with the sound of that splash in her head, scrabbling at the bedclothes as she had scrabbled at the ground, trying to get to her feet, trying to reach Laurent. After a moment she managed to continue.

'There was this huge splash, then silence, nothing but the sound of the river, and it was getting darker. I was going to run back to the house, get someone to help me launch the skiff, then Laurent came out of the bushes further down. He was cut, on his arm, his shoulder, his face, but he was alive.'

'And Norwood?'

'Laurent said they had been washed into a fallen tree only a short way downstream. He managed to keep hold of a main branch but the one Norwood grabbed was thinner and broke off. Laurent lost sight of him, but he knew he had got at least one serious blow home. That must have been the knife wound they found in his side.'

'Did no one know Norwood was at the quinta? How did he get there?'

'He rode and Laurent took his horse with him when he left. And, yes, I did check the saddle-bags before I let him take it, so do not accuse me of being careless with secrets.'

Gray merely grunted, which she supposed might have been a denial he had thought that.

'No one came and enquired after him. But then, I doubt he went around announcing that he was setting out to try and entrap an heiress into marriage by whatever means.'

'Taken at the worst you could be accused of being an accessory after a murder and of aiding and abetting a spy,' Gray said.

'Laurent was *not* a spy and I did nothing to aid the French cause unless you count perhaps improving the morale of one young officer,' she said sharply. 'And just what do you intend doing about it now you have me convicted?'

'Nothing.' Gray shifted suddenly, leaning forward and taking her hands. 'Why, Gabrielle, do you think I do not believe you?'

'You certainly sound like the counsel for the prosecution! Have you any idea how your voice drips icicles?'

'Damn it, I am trying to get the facts straight, to see if there is any weakness in your defences we may need to strengthen. It sounds as though no one suspects anything and there is nothing that could connect him with you that evening. Certainly if his movements were not known, then no one is likely to have calculated that he went into the river from your property.'

'You do believe me?' It was an effort to keep her voice steady, but not, it seemed, a very successful one.

'Gabrielle, darling. Of course I believe you.' Gray pulled her into his arms. 'Hell. Are you crying?'

'No.' She managed not to sniffle into his shirt front. 'I've never spoken of it with anyone but Laurent. I didn't expect it to affect me so…'

Breathe. You are not going to weep all over him. Breathe.

'You seem so strong, so decisive, that I did not think how my questions must have affected you,' Gray said, his voice soft. He seemed to have his cheek against her hair, which was soothing, although the thud of his heart against her chest was anything but calming. 'I was trying to be logical, methodical.'

'You sound very much the senior army officer sometimes, especially when I cannot see your face,' Gaby confessed, burrowing a little closer.

'I've been an officer virtually all my adult life. You must forgive me if it takes a little time to change, become a civilian. Gabrielle—what are you doing?'

'Smelling you,' she confessed, her response rather muffled with her nose among the folds of his neckcloth.

'I had a bath before dinner,' Gray protested.

'I know. You smell of lemons and spice and starch and warm man.'

'And you smell of jasmine and rosemary and warm woman. It is somewhat arousing.'

'I can tell.' She was sitting across his thighs, after all, and not everything she could feel was muscle.

'The sooner we find you a house, the better.' His voice was a husky growl now.

She stayed still, aware of how unfair it was to push his self-control so far. 'You think I am safe now from any questions about Norwood?'

'I am certain of it. If anyone had seen something, suspected it and had wanted to betray you, they would have done so long ago.' His arms tightened around her. 'I can see now why you are so very resistant to the thought of marriage.'

'The fear of fortune hunters?' Gaby sat up, then moved carefully to sit next to him, bracing herself against Gray's shoulder as the carriage lurched. He seemed reluctant to let her go, but one of them had to move or they would spend the night driving round and round London and, tempting though that might be, it was hardly sensible. And she supposed that being sensible was the right thing, although it was hard just now to recall why.

'No, it is not that, not the complete truth. I was not hiding anything when I told you why I do not wish to marry. It is not because of Norwood,' she assured the shadowy figure opposite her. 'Not every man who would want to marry me for what I have would be a venal as he was. But *whoever* it was, as a married woman I would lose control of everything that is mine, that I and my family have built. It would not matter whether I married a rich man or a poor man, a man who loved me or a fortune hunter, the effect would be the same.'

'Would it not be worth it if you loved him in return?' Gray asked. 'What if Laurent came back, had not been killed, after all? We are at peace now. Would you marry him?'

'I… No.' Where had that come from, that certainty?

'You loved him.'

'I had strong feelings for him, although perhaps they were not love. I would never have become his lover if I had not cared for him, but I do not think I would love him now.' The certainty was unsettling. 'I think we would have grown too far apart.' Gaby tried to work out why she was suddenly so definite. 'We were young and in the strangest of situations, a world away from normality. I was grieving and he, I am sure, was homesick and exhausted by fighting. We were right for each other then. But not now, not for ever.'

Not now when she wanted something else from a man, something…more? But Laurent had been brave and gallant and kind. What more *could* she want? Other than to make love with the man before her. The man who had interrogated her with such cool insistence and yet who promised her his silence and his understanding, promised her safety.

'I think I want to go back to the hotel now. I am so tired all of a sudden.'

'Confession tends to be exhausting, don't you find? A letting-go of a tension that has been held a long time.' Gray reached up and banged on the roof of the carriage and it slowed, turned.

'What have you to confess?' Gaby found she had the energy to tease a little.

'Youthful idiocy,' he said after a moment. 'Then poor judgement followed by misguided gallantry followed by an inability to… Never mind, that is in the past now.'

He is talking about his marriage, she realised. The temptation to press him for more details, here in the darkness when she, at least, was in confessional mood, had to be resisted. Gray was a proud man and a private one and she owed him too much to indulge in vulgar curiosity.

The silence as the carriage wound its way back through the night-time streets was curiously companionable. All either of them said when they reached her hotel room door was her thanks, his 'Goodnight.'

Gray bent his head, brushed his mouth across the lips she raised to him, then, as she opened the door he turned and walked away.

A lamp was burning low on the table in their sitting room, but when she peeped around the door of Jane's bedchamber she was fast asleep on the bed, still in her wrapper, a book fallen open on the coverlet. She pretended that she was a brisk, unsentimental woman, but even so, she stayed up at night to see Gaby safely home.

With a sudden surge of affection Gaby moved the book, found a spare blanket in her own room and draped it carefully over her companion, then took the lamp and put herself to bed.

She had told Gray that she was tired and so she was. Yet her brain would not let her sleep. *I could love that man if I am not very careful,* she thought. She wanted to be his lover, she had agreed to become so, but something suspiciously like her conscience was telling her that had been a serious mistake.

If she was not very careful she was going to forget her reason for coming to London—to find a man to father her child and heir. She could hardly be Gray's lover and, at the same time, seek out another man. Nor, she realised, could she indulge her desire for him and then promptly end the liaison. She would be using him, she saw that all too clearly.

For a moment there was the tempting thought of being both his lover and hoping she would fall pregnant by him. *Gray's child.* She could almost see the little boy. Somehow she was sure it would be a boy with dark hair, his father's eyes… Gaby shook her head resolutely as though that would stop the dull ache of longing inside. Gray would never agree to father her child and to try to trick him would be despicable.

Which meant that she must tell him she had changed her mind and as quickly as possible. It would be a lie—she wanted him, desired him, ached for him. Telling him that they should not be lovers would hurt. It was not going to be an easy conversation, Gaby thought as she pulled the covers over her head and burrowed down. Not easy at all.

* * *

If anyone had told him a month ago that he would hear about a fellow officer being killed by a Frenchman in civilian disguise, aided by a loyal Englishwoman, and that he would decide to do nothing about it, Gray would have thought them either insulting enough to challenge, or a fool.

But here he was doing just that, he thought, as his valet moved soft-footed around the dressing room disposing of garments as he shed them. Why?

Because he believed Gabrielle, he supposed. And if the positions were reversed, he would certainly do his utmost to rescue a Frenchwoman from an assault by one of her own countrymen, whether or not they were at war. Norwood was not a man he had ever warmed to or admired. There had been an essential coldness about him. Not that Gray expected to form a warm friendship with every officer he met, but he had never seen Norwood grieve for a friend lost, or put himself out for someone who needed help. And there had been whispers about women, young women, seduced and abandoned.

It was not hard to believe that the intelligence officer might want to secure a wealthy wife, not too great a stretch to visualise him forcing the issue. Had he been so ruthless as to plot the death of a patriotic young man to increase his gains? Possibly, Gray realised with a sense of shock that the idea came so easily.

'My lord?' Tompkins was standing patiently, a nightshirt folded over the back of the chair beside him, the red silk banyan draped across the seat.

Gray realised that he was down to his evening breeches and must have been standing there, his hands on the fastenings, for several minutes while he thought. 'I'm sorry, just puzzling something through.'

'Of course, my lord.' Tompkins whisked away breeches, stockings, evening pumps and shook out the nightshirt. When Gray took it and pulled it over his head he added, 'Mr Hotchkiss, the agent, left a portfolio for you. I thought perhaps it was somewhat bulky for night-time reading, but I have placed it on the table in your bedchamber. Can I do anything else for you, my lord?'

That must be the first selection of houses for Gabrielle. It might be better to stop brooding on Norwood's death and do something practical. 'Light a candelabrum for the table and bring me a pen and ink and the brandy, Tompkins. Then take yourself off to bed.'

The agent had included details of eight houses and two apartments in the portfolio. Gray tossed two of the houses aside as being insufficiently good addresses. Gabrielle, with the faint taint of trade and her anything-but-faint air of independence, needed the most fashionable and respectable of addresses to lend her consequence.

Two would be too small, one, too large. Another street he knew to be very noisy at all hours. That left four. He scribbled a note to Hotchkiss to be sent first thing in the morning and closed the lid on the inkwell. Inspecting four houses with Gabrielle might be a diverting way of spending the day. The sooner she was established in her own household the better for the sake of his ability to sleep, let alone his ability to keep his hands off her. He wanted her in his arms, against his skin. He wanted to be over her, in her, with her.

Gray picked up the details of the apartments that he had initially discarded without more than a glance. A house with Miss Moseley in residence and a complement of servants was not going to be suitable for a liaison either. But if he took one of the apartments himself, then they could use that for trysts in complete privacy. He uncapped the ink and picked up his pen again.

*I have details of four houses if you would care
to inspect them tomorrow. Also apartments,
which might prove useful.*
   Might I suggest a bonnet with a veil?
G.

Oh, yes, he was beginning to ache for Gabrielle
Frost, he thought as he addressed and sealed the
note. Gray snuffed out all the candles and took
himself off to bed, where he proceeded to toss
and turn until he sat up again with an oath, wide
awake.

What the devil was the matter with him? Tomorrow he and Gabrielle might be lovers. Certainly
the day after. With that definite he could surely
compose himself to sleep? He was not some randy
seventeen-year-old lusting after his first wench.

But for some reason he could not stop thinking about Gabrielle. Not her in bed, although that
image was always there in the back of his mind.
Not her part in Norwood's death either. Just Gabrielle. How she smiled, how she looked when she
was sad. The sudden flashes of humour, her seri-
ousness about her quinta and her love of Portugal.
The curve of her neck, the gesture of her hand…

*I am on the brink of falling in love with her.
Hell and damnation.*

He would marry her tomorrow, love or not—this was close enough for him, love was a dangerous emotion. But she would not have him, he knew that much about her now. The resistance to marriage was engrained in her, confirmed by Norwood's cynical manoeuvrings. And he was not in a position to simply walk away from England and his obligations, even if she could be persuaded to marry him and believe that he would be a sleeping partner in the business of the quinta, as she might if he was a younger son without ties to England.

Gray lay in the darkness, staring up at the ceiling mouldings made mysterious by shadows.

He had children here, estates and obligations here. A seat in the House of Lords. Responsibilities. Many people would say that one of those was to find a suitable bride who would get on with his mother, love his children, support him socially and politically.

But that was not going to happen. His record as a husband had convinced him that he should not try again and Gabrielle Frost was simply impossible. Except as a lover. Perhaps after a week or two they would have worked this mutual desire out of their systems. He could only hope so, he felt he had enough regrets about women as it was.

Chapter Thirteen

'This one,' Gaby announced, turning a slow circle in the little drawing room of the house halfway up Half Moon Street.

'Are you sure?' Gray queried. 'The property in Charles Street has been redecorated more recently and the St James's Place one is larger and we still haven't seen the one near Grosvenor Square.'

'This is close to Green Park. The street is quiet and the house has a good feel to it. There is a pleasant sitting room and bedchamber for Jane and one for me, and the dining room and this drawing room are quite adequate for any entertaining I might do. The domestic quarters are good, too, which will help in attracting suitable staff.'

'If you are sure? The rent, I have to admit, is reasonable and Hotchkiss says the landlord will be flexible about how long you take it for. Property is in demand in the area and he will have no trouble reletting it if you decide to leave at short notice. I'll send him a note now.' He took a notebook from his pocket, scribbled a few lines and folded it. 'Are you ready to look at the apartments?'

'Yes.' This was what she had been dreading, she thought as she followed him out to where his groom waited with the phaeton. Gray obviously thought that taking an apartment would be a discreet way of conducting an affaire and he was right. Only she now had to tell him that she did not want one. Or, rather, that she did, but her conscience would not allow it. He might very well ask why her inconvenient conscience had not informed her of this at the first kiss, by the second caress. A very fair question, she supposed.

The groom took the note, handed the reins over to Gray and walked briskly off down the street. He had even thought of that, she thought gloomily, finding that she did not have the courage to tell him while he was concentrating on the traffic.

They went through Berkeley Square, crossed Bond Street and drew up outside a house in a quiet backstreet. 'Veil,' Gray murmured before he gestured to a crossing sweeper, handed him sixpence to hold the horses and promised him the same when they came out.

The lad grinned, bit the coin, pocketed it and went to stand at the horses' heads, holding the reins firmly. 'Dun this afore, guv'nor, they'll be all right wiv me. Prime pair of prads.'

Gaby allowed herself to be helped down and followed Gray up to the front door. The landlady had obviously been expecting them, a key was handed over and the woman retreated back into her downstairs front parlour without any attempt to look at Gaby, for which she was truly grateful.

They climbed one flight of stairs in silence, then Gray unlocked the right-hand door on the landing and held it for her to walk through to a sitting room with a view of the street. 'Gray—'

'Not bad,' he said after a swift glance round, turned back, caught her up in his arms and gave her a rapid, hard kiss, then let her go. He opened another door. 'Ah, the bedchamber. Very pleasant, what do you think?'

'Gray.' She stayed where she was in the middle of the sitting room.

'What is wrong?' He turned back, then closed the bedchamber door. 'The landlady appears discreet, the place seems very clean and respectable.'

'I can't do this. I realised last night.' She braced herself for his reaction.

'By *this* I assume you mean have an affaire? A rather sudden change of mind. Is it something I have done? Or not done?' He was very clearly not pleased, but he was hanging on to his temper, which was a relief. She realised her knees were not quite steady and her mouth was dry.

'No. It is nothing you have said or done, or not said, not done. I want to be your lover, but I cannot, not with a clear conscience, and I realised it last night when I thought it through without a haze of desire consuming me. Gray, the reason I came to London was that I need to find a father for my child, a man who will agree to surrender it to me without making any claims. Someone I can trust to vanish and allow me to return to Portugal as a widow, raise the child respectably.

'I cannot begin an affaire with you, then just stop and coldly go looking for another man for that purpose. It would not be right, not fair to you. And I don't think I could bear it, it will be hard enough as it is.'

She had expected an explosion or a lecture or disgust. Possibly, probably, all three. Instead Gray looked at her, that steady frown on his face, and seemed simply to study her. After a moment he asked, 'You are in the market for a stud?'

'I am looking for a man I can trust not to black-mail me,' she said, her tongue stiff in her mouth. 'An intelligent man. A decent man without any ties. I realise this may be an impossible quest.'

'So you lied to me when you told me that you were coming to London to allow any tension be-tween you and your neighbours, the MacFarlanes, to cool. You intended to find a father for your child all along.' One hand rested, clenched, on the door frame of the bedchamber. He was angry, she saw clearly. Angry and hurt.

'That was a partial reason. It makes sense. If I return, apparently married and widowed, every-one who knows about the MacFarlanes' schemes will assume I acted on the rebound from that dis-covery.'

Gray lifted his fist an inch, thumped it once against the door frame, then walked away to the window. 'The tenderness of your conscience is at odds with your prowess as a schemer, it seems.'

'If my parents taught me anything, it was to listen to my conscience and be guided by it,' she said bleakly, to his back. 'I allowed my feelings for you to overcome that. It was tender enough when I considered how I must be honest with this man—if I ever find him—but, somehow, desire was not so easy to resist as it should be.'

'And that is what you feel for me? Desire?'

'And liking and, I had hoped, friendship. But that is a forlorn hope now, I can see that.' It was more than the loss of friendship that was tearing at her, making this so hard and bitter.

I could love him. Perhaps I already do and I have deceived him and wounded him and he deserved none of that.

That mention of friendship had been too much like a plea for forgiveness, a pathetic, craven hope that perhaps what she had done was not so dreadful, after all, and he would turn from his contemplation of the street with a smile, with a hand held out, with a reassurance that he understood.

Gray did turn then, his hands by his sides, his face blank of expression. 'I had best return the key.' He went to the door, held it open for her, then locked it behind them before preceding Gaby down the stairs. She remembered to lower her veil before the landlady came to the door and took the key and then they were out on the street again. Gray's hand was steady and impersonal as he helped her mount on to the seat and he remembered to toss the crossing sweeper the promised sixpenny piece as the lad released the reins.

It seemed that she was the only one with shaking hands and an inability to think straight.

'I will have Hotchkiss deal with you directly in relation to the house in Half Moon Street,' Gray said as the phaeton swept out into Old Bond Street, across into Grafton Street and down Albemarle Street. She had not realised how mercifully close they were to the hotel.

'Thank you.' Her voice sounded scratchy, but at least she was not weeping, which was a miracle because she felt as though she had lost something precious and had only herself to blame. 'I fear this will make things difficult if my aunt asks you to escort us anywhere.'

Gray managed to shrug while simultaneously guiding his team around a wagon, unloading crates outside the Royal Institution. 'I will simply refuse on the grounds of prior engagements.'

'Of course.'

When they drew up in front of Grillon's, Gray gestured to the doorman, who hurried forward to help Gaby down. 'Without my groom I fear I cannot escort you inside, Miss Frost.'

'I quite understand, Lord Leybourne. Thank you for your assistance. And understanding.'

She glanced up to catch an expression on his face that she could not read. It was gone as soon as she glimpsed it, a starkness that went beyond frustrated desire or anger at her foolishness.

'You are welcome to the assistance, Miss Frost. I fear you may have to manage without the understanding. My regards to Miss Moseley.'

She stood there watching his broad shoulders as he drove towards Piccadilly.

'Ma'am?' It was the doorman. 'Are you entering the hotel?'

'Oh. Yes, I am sorry. I was wool-gathering,' she murmured. Gray's words had been too low to have reached the man's ears, she hoped, thankful for her veil. 'Thank you.'

Somehow she gained the suite and found it empty. On the table in the sitting room was a note from Jane informing her that she had gone to investigate Earle's Circulating Library at Number Forty-Seven and might be gone for some time. As it was meticulously timed, it was clear that Jane had been gone only a few minutes. Gaby went into her room, locked the door, took off her bonnet, gloves and pelisse and repressed a sniff. Weeping was not going to help matters. On the other hand, she rather thought it was that or ring for a decanter of brandy and attempt to drown her sorrows.

Tears won. It was such a long time since she had allowed herself to weep—not since she received the locket and the news of Laurent's death—that it was hard, almost painful. Afterwards she did not feel any better. Gaby looked bleakly at her reflection in the mirror. All she had achieved was a stuffed-up nose, reddened eyes and a headache. And she was going to have to find some explanation for Jane, who might often be preoccupied, but was bound to notice something wrong, even after Gaby had bathed her face and done her best with the rice powder.

She would tell her that an argument with Gray had meant the end of his visits, but that they now had a house of their own, Gaby decided as she whisked powder over her cheeks and pinned back her hair. And then, somehow, she had to decide what she was going to do next. The idea of trying to find a father for her baby now seemed not only difficult but, emotionally, impossible, she thought as the sound of a key in the outer door warned her that Jane had returned.

Deep breath, chin up, she told herself as she opened her bedchamber door. *You did the right thing, telling him no. You did it too late, but it was right.* Somehow that was going to have to suffice.

Gray turned the phaeton into the mews without conscious thought. Somehow he had arrived home and it might have been through a riot or a snowstorm for all he had noticed. He snapped back to attention as one of the grooms ran out and, behind him, Henry. There was a post-chaise standing by the stable, unhorsed, and a pair of postilions lounging against the mounting block.

'Thank God,' Henry said as he reached the phaeton. His face was screwed up with anxiety. 'I had no idea where to find you or how long you'd be.'

'What's wrong?' Gray tossed the reins to the groom and got down.

'A message from Winfell. Little James fell from a tree and they can't get him to regain consciousness. Your mother sounds frantic.'

'When?' Gray demanded. 'Is the man still here?'

'The day before yesterday. Your mother sent the message down by the post-chaise so there would be no delay getting back with reliable changes. Forgive me for opening it, but it was so obviously a crisis.' Henry gestured towards the vehicle. 'The horses will be rested for the first stage back, they came in just after you left this morning.'

'Hitch up,' Gray shouted at the postilions. 'I will leave within the hour. You did right,' he added to Henry as they strode inside. 'Find Tomkins,' he snapped at the butler, who was in the hall.

'He is already packing, my lord. Cook is assembling a hamper so you will not need to stop to eat.'

Gray was already halfway up the stairs, Henry at his heels. He wanted to stop, to howl at his own impotence. He was almost two hundred and fifty miles away from his five-year-old son, who might already be dead, and his little daughter, who would be terrified. And his mother, still in mourning for her husband. And he could do nothing except leave as fast as possible and not stop until he got to Winfell. And then comfort and grieve? Or… He shook his head, angry at himself. Speculation and false hope were weakening. In twenty-four hours, accidents aside, he could be there.

'Hotchkiss came round, said he had a message from you.'

Gray kept going into his bedchamber. 'Tompkins!'

'Here, my lord. All packed. I have my own valise ready, as well.'

'No. Stay here.' He couldn't bear the thought of being cooped up with someone else in a chaise for that long, having to maintain his composure in front of another human being. 'Henry, tell Hotchkiss to deal direct with Miss Frost over the house in Half Moon Street. She's at Grillon's.'

'Of course.' Henry waited while he snatched up the bag from the end of the bed and followed him downstairs. 'If there is anything I can do while you're away, just write. I'll pray for you all.'

That was the last thing Gray was conscious of before he strode out of the back door and into the mews. One of the footmen was stowing a hamper in the chaise, the postilions were mounting up, two of them for the four horses. He could always rely on his mother, they'd make the best possible time. 'Shortest route to Harrogate,' he ordered as he slammed the door and the coach lurched into motion.

The next morning breakfast was an almost-silent meal. Jane kept her attention firmly on a book in German on rock formations that she had found in the circulating library and tactfully re-marked neither on the dark circles under Gaby's eyes nor asked for details of her falling-out with Gray.

Eventually she took herself off, announcing that she had a ticket to visit the British Museum and assumed Gaby would not be interested.

Gaby agreed that indeed she would not, wished

her a pleasant day and rang to have the table cleared, keeping back a cup of coffee.

She sipped it while she fought the strong inclination to book passage on the next ship back to Porto, however strange it might seem to her friends and neighbours for her to return so swiftly. She would settle on the house, take it for two months. Then she would go and call on her aunt, permit herself to be fussed over and, somehow, manage to break her false betrothal to Gray whilst not encouraging Aunt Henrietta's matchmaking schemes for George. If she had no social life, she could meet no gentlemen and if she met no one there was little hope for her plan.

If it has any hope at all, she thought, cupping her chin in one hand and stirring far too much sugar into her coffee.

There was a tap at the door. Had she ordered more coffee and forgotten about it? 'Come in!'

One of the hall porters entered. 'Gentleman at the front desk asked if he might call, Miss Frost.' He proferred a small salver with a card. 'He apologises for the early hour, but begs the favour of a brief word.'

Gaby frowned at the rectangle of pasteboard. *Henry Pickford.* How very strange that Gray's cousin should come to call at that hour. 'Please ask him to come up directly.'

The porter escorted him in a few minutes later, then left, closing the door behind him.

'Miss Frost, I do apologise for calling so early.' Henry shook hands and looked around. 'Ah. You appear to be alone. Forgive me, no doubt you would prefer to come downstairs and talk in one of the public rooms. If you can spare me a few minutes, that is?'

'There is no need, Mr Pickford, I feel quite safe with you.' He blushed, but took the seat she gestured to as she sat down. 'May I ring for some coffee for you?'

'Thank you, no. I came merely to let you know that Lord Leybourne has had to leave town for a few days. I know he has charged Mr Hotchkiss to speak to you directly about the house in Half Moon Street, but he left in such haste that he was not able to let you know about his absence and I felt you might perceive it as some unintended neglect.'

'Nothing is wrong, I hope?' Surely Gray had not fled London because of her refusal to become his lover? He was neither a man who sulked, nor one who lost control of his temper, she was certain. Henry Pickford was looking uncomfortable and she immediately apologised. 'But I am prying into family business.'

'Not at all. You are concerned, I understand that. It is a family matter of some urgency, but I do not know the details and I am not in a position to speak of it.'

'Of course not.'

'Forgive me, Miss Frost. I realise this is not something that one should say to a lady, but you seem a little pale. Might I offer you my escort for a stroll in the park, perhaps?'

'I—'

I want to go back to bed and pull the covers over my head and pretend none of this has happened. I want to be back home at the quinta with nothing to worry about but the price of barrel staves and an outbreak of mould. I want Gray. And I do not want to dissolve into a wet puddle of feebleness and throw away everything the Frosts have worked for over the decades. Everything I worked for.

'Thank you, I would appreciate your escort very much, Mr Pickford.' Gray, whose judgement she trusted, thought well of his cousin, considered him an honest and honourable man. He was a perfect, safe escort.

Chapter Fourteen

'When do you expect to move house, Miss Frost?' Henry tucked her hand under his arm as they strolled through the north-eastern gate of Green Park.

'Within a few days, I hope, Mr Pickford.' They paused on the brink of the reservoir and looked out towards Westminster Abbey in the distance. 'The air is very smoky again today.'

'It must seem unpleasant after Portugal. I imagine clear blue skies and sunshine every day,' he said as they began to walk again.

'Most days it is like that, but it can rain. It can be cloudy and grey and we have frosts, too, sometimes. You are bound for the north-east coast of America, if I recall. That has cold, snowy winters.'

'I may yearn after sunshine but I aim to find work where the commercial heart of the country is,' he explained earnestly. 'I have a living to earn.'

'When do you leave?'

'I am waiting to hear back from a number of businesses to whom I have written. Various trading concerns, you understand. Gray has been very helpful in finding recommendations and having checks carried out for me. I cannot afford to start off on the wrong foot with an unreliable company, there is too much at stake. I mean to make my life out there, not merely go for a few years.'

'Marry and start a family in a new country?' She liked his earnest enthusiasm.

'Indeed.' His voice was wistful for a moment. 'It will be years before I can afford to support a wife and children, but that is my ambition.'

He's a lonely man, Gaby thought. *But not one to grab at happiness without thought for his responsibilities.*

'If you are able to investigate the market for port in Boston and the area, then I would be very interested to hear your thoughts on the matter,' she said slowly, thinking it through as she spoke. 'If I could export, then I would need an agent. But exporting port long distances by sea has proved tricky in the past. I can make no promises, you understand.

'No, of course not.' Pickford slowed down and turned to look at her. 'If you can tell me more about the things I need to find out, you'll find me a fast learner.'

'Come to dinner tonight,' Gaby offered. 'My companion, Miss Moseley, will be there, naturally, and we can eat in the hotel dining room and talk.'

'Thank you, I should like that.'

They began to stroll again, talking of other matters, but Gaby felt herself calm a little at the prospect of something positive to do, some aim that had nothing to do with Gray. What had sent him from London at such speed? She hoped there was nothing wrong... Then she reminded herself that Lord Leybourne was none of her business any longer, that he wanted nothing more to do with her and that she should feel the same about him.

And yet she could not help but worry.

Gray forced himself to sit still as the chaise jolted northward at ten miles an hour. There was nothing else to do. He couldn't drive—that was in the hands of the pair of postilions, the new ones who had taken over at the last change at Biggleswade. He could not give in to the urge to abandon the chaise, hire a horse and gallop on because he had no way of knowing whether he could get reliable, fast remounts. Besides, there was no virtue in arriving home saddle-sore and exhausted.

He was an adult. He was responsible, so he had to be sensible and calm and think of something, anything, but the limp body of a small child. He should try to sleep so as to be rested to face whatever he found when he reached Winfell. He had to be strong for his mother and for Joanna and for himself, but when he forced the useless speculation and worry to the back of his mind all he could think about was Gabrielle and her insane plan to secure her precious quinta.

Gray knew he should value her honesty, the fact that she listened to her conscience and had been—finally—open with him. It did not help at all that he could feel nothing but hurt and resentment and a regret that he knew diminished him. Frustrated desire was one thing and, of course, no gentleman would try to persuade a reluctant woman against her will, however much he knew she yearned to give in. But the depth of his reaction warned him that this was more than simple sexual desire. He was falling for Gabrielle. Had fallen.

And she was a woman who was resolved not to wed. Ever. A woman who intended to get herself with child by some stranger, who would risk so much—her feelings, her safety, her reputation.

Gray shifted across the seat as though finding a different viewpoint through the glass in front of him could help. He could get her with child, he could keep her secrets—and… No. Not *and*. The word was *but*. *But* he could never, ever, give up a child of his to be raised a stranger, he knew that as clearly as he knew his own reflection in the mirror.

And how could he think about another child when he might have already lost one of his, his little Jamie. Bright as cut steel, active as a puppy, funny and loving and brave and, if he was conscious, wanting his father. Joanna would certainly be wanting him. He had convinced himself that at their age they needed the feminine influence of their grandmother more than they needed his daily presence. Now guilt for that ate away at him, a gnawing sensation beneath the worry. Was he a bad father? Could he add that to the thoroughly merited charge of being a poor husband?

You only married me because you thought it your duty, Portia had spat at him once, making *duty* sound like an accusation of the vilest kind of depravity. *You ruined my life and then you think it can all be made well again with a wedding ring. Well, my lord, it cannot.*

She had written to him when she had discovered that she was pregnant and the letter, much battered and soiled, had reached him in some remote Spanish village, months after she had sent it.

I hope you will be satisfied now. You have done your duty, married the Wronged Woman, planted an heir on her. The world will say what a fine fellow Colonel Graystone is. What a fine earl he will make one day.

At least I will have the raising of your son. Perhaps I can work out where your mother went wrong and rear a boy with a heart.

The chaise began to slow. Eaton Socon, Gray saw as he looked through the window and recognised the familiar shabby exterior of the White Horse. He resisted the temptation to pull out his pocket watch even though the passage of time felt as though he was walking through mud with blistered heels.

Portia never had the opportunity to raise her son. Gray was not at all certain that she had even been aware that she had borne him, or his twin sister. When a man returns from the wars eighteen months after his wife dies in childbed, no one is very eager to describe the harrowing details to him.

The watch was in his hand, although he had no recollection of taking it from the fob pocket. He watched the hand tick round for five minutes, then the chaise lurched into motion again and he tried to make his mind a blank. Strangely the blankness produced the image of a pair of expressive brown eyes, not scornful or imperious or even heavy with sensuality, but warm with sympathy and concern and understanding.

Gabrielle.

Gaby had confessed her scheme to bear a child to Gray and that had been a disaster. She would have said—been prepared to swear to it—that she would die rather than admit it to anyone else. It was a shock to find herself, only three days after he had left so mysteriously for the north, curled up on the sofa in her new drawing room and telling Henry, as Mr Pickford had rapidly become, all about it.

Quite how it had happened she was not certain. She was heartsick over Gray and he was, clearly, anxious about his cousin and they could not talk of him—he for reasons of discretion, she because it was all still too raw. Yet, they seemed to need each other's company and Henry threw himself into helping her move into the new little house.

They talked of the wine trade and travel, of Henry's family problems a little and rather more of his ambitions for the future. Jane had dismissed Henry early on as harmless and took no pains to chaperone them on either walks or long conversations, or when Henry spent an afternoon walking backwards and forward, shifting the hired furniture about in the receptions rooms until Gaby was satisfied.

And now with everything to her liking and an excellent dinner behind them she kicked off her satin slippers, curled her feet up under her, leaned her chin on her hand and smiled at Henry. She felt slightly sleepy and very comfortable.

'There must be someone in Portugal waiting impatiently for your return,' Henry said, as he settled back in an armchair with a glass of port in his hand.

'My staff, I suppose. But my manager writes regularly—I had a letter only today. All is well.'

'No.' He smiled and shook his head at her. 'That's not what I meant. Some man. A special man.'

Gaby shook her own head in return. 'No one.

How can I marry? If I do, Frost's becomes his, and I lose all control.'

He frowned over that. 'It would be the normal thing, would it not? You could deed the business to some relative if it is important to keep it in the family name.'

'I have no relatives, none I would want to have control of the quinta, at least. No, you do not understand.' Perhaps she had drunk too many glasses of wine at dinner, she thought as she began to explain both her idea and her problem to the man sitting opposite her, nodding sympathetically in the candlelight.

'Impossible, I know,' Gaby finished. 'How to find the right man? And how to ensure his silence? And then how to produce a plausible proof of the wedding and cause of death? I should not even think of it.'

'Hmm.' Henry neither laughed, nor exclaimed in horror. 'Tricky, of course, but the marriage itself is no problem. Nor is making you a widow.'

'What?' She stared at him, realised her mouth was unbecomingly open and closed it with a snap.

'Murder, of course,' Henry said. Then he did laugh. 'I am teasing you. No, but the marriage part is easy. When you find the man he needs to procure a special licence. A special, not an ordinary one, mind. That enables you to be married without *banns* being called and anywhere you choose.'

'Yes, but then I will be *married*. And the entire point is that—'

'And he gives a false name for himself. You can marry him where and when you like—but it will not be a valid marriage because the licence is based on a false declaration. Mind you, the man had best leave the country, because if it did come out, then he lays himself open to all kinds of trouble with both civil and church law. So, he goes on a voyage and is shipwrecked. There you are holding a licence and a genuine entry of marriage in the register—and with a sadly drowned husband. What does it matter that you will have to wait seven years, or whatever it is, to have him declared dead? You do not want to marry in reality, after all.'

'Henry, that is *brilliant*.'

'It is, rather,' he said with a grin, then sobered abruptly. 'I do hope I have not developed a talent for deceit as good as my late, unlamented father's.'

'I cannot see any flaw with that.' Absently Gaby reached for the decanter and poured herself another glass of port, then leaned across to pass the decanter to Henry. 'All that would remain is to find a suitable gentleman and that, I fear, is going to be even harder.'

Henry filled his glass almost to the brim and then had to spend a few moments lowering the contents to a safe level. 'I…er…may have another idea, one that would solve that difficulty.'

'Tell me.' Gaby sat up straighter. 'You are a miracle worker.'

'Not here.' He glanced up at the ceiling as a floorboard creaked overhead, reminding her that Jane's room was just over where they sat. 'Look, I know this is a shocking thing to suggest, but we do need complete secrecy about this matter. All your servants are newly hired and you cannot trust their discretion if they were to catch even a hint of it. We really should not have been discussing it so freely just now. Miss Moseley said something about dining with acquaintances after a lecture tomorrow, I think? You were not intending to accompany her?'

'No, I was not.' Gaby shook her head with some emphasis. 'The conversation around a dinner table full of geologists is not something I can even follow, let alone participate in.'

'Then dine with me, at Gray's house. We will

have all the time of the lecture, and her dinner party, to ourselves. Gray's servants are discreet and if I suggest to the butler that I wish to dine alone with a lady I believe we can be confident of being left in peace.' He grimaced. 'But saying that would suggest to them a liaison and would damage your reputation. I should have thought of that. Perhaps we should confine ourselves to talking in the middle of Green Park.'

He looked so hangdog that Gaby couldn't help but laugh. The sound startled her. Perhaps it was the first time she had felt like laughing since she and Gray had parted. 'There is no need for such scheming. Tell them that it is a business meeting. Unbend to the butler and confide that I am asking you to investigate the markets in Boston. They all know that Gray has been assisting me, they will think nothing of it. We will plunge into tedious detail before dinner—with the door wide open—and by the time we sit down to the meal they will think nothing of it when you vaguely wave them out of the room and say we will serve ourselves.'

'You, Miss Frost, are an intelligent and cunning female.'

'I know,' she admitted, making no effort not to sound smug about it. She still couldn't help but feel that she was going to return to Portugal heartsick and childless. Henry was enthusiastic and optimistic and his idea about the false details on the marriage licence was inspired. But she was rapidly losing all faith in the idea of finding, and then losing, a father for her child in a way that she could feel was both safe and morally right.

Still, Henry was a good friend, she enjoyed his company and an evening spent talking about things that interested them both was something to look forward to.

Finally. The chaise turned between the tall stone gateposts, rattled round the first curve of the driveway and there, at the end of the avenue of battered old oaks, was Winfell. *Home.* Gray fought the instinct to stop the carriage, get out and run. He wouldn't get there faster, he knew that. Slowly the house came into sight, as grey as the gateposts, as battered as the oaks, as old as the hills.

He strained his eyes but he couldn't see if the curtains were drawn across the windows in the front, couldn't see if there was any black crepe on the knocker.

The chaise made the last turn, pulled up as he almost fell out of the door and began to run at last.

The front door opened and there was his mother on the top step, Joanna in her arms. They were both weeping.

Chapter Fifteen

'Mr Pickford suggested the Small Chinese Drawing Room upstairs, Miss Frost.' Fredericks, Gray's butler, took her evening cloak. 'It is used by the family for intimate dinner parties, rather than the Red Dining Room, which, I venture to say, is somewhat cavernous for fewer than twenty.'

'Thank you, Fredericks. I certainly would not enjoy an echoing dinner,' Gaby said, as she followed him across the hall to the sweep of stairs.

'Quite, Miss Frost. Along here, if you please. I regret it is quite a way, tucked along here at the end past the various suites, but the present earl's grandmother had it created because it was the only room of the right size to use a fine shipment of Chinese wallpaper.' He opened the door. 'Miss Frost, Mr Pickford.'

Henry jumped up from his chair and dropped

a book on the side table. 'Good evening, Miss Frost. May I pour you a glass of sherry? Or do you despise the products of Spain?'

'Absolutely not. Thank you, Mr Pickford.' Gaby sank on to the sofa facing the window and looked around. The room had a bay window around which several chairs and the sofa had been arranged and at the back of the room there was a large alcove with a dining table and six chairs. The whole room was papered with a delightful hand-painted design of Chinese scenes.

Henry returned with the wine and they sipped and made conversation about the wallpaper, which was one mass of intricate detail, while footmen arranged a wine cooler and then took up their position against the walls.

It was easy enough to move the conversation on to the port wine trade and what knowledge Henry had managed to glean of commercial conditions in Boston. By the time Fredericks had come back to announce that dinner was served Henry appeared engrossed and Gaby suspected that the footmen were becoming cross-eyed with boredom.

'We'll serve ourselves,' Henry said vaguely. 'I will ring if we need anything.'

'Sir.' The butler bowed himself out and began to pull closed the door.

'Leave the door, if you please,' Henry called.

'Of course, sir.'

With the door open they could see from the table clear down the corridor to the first turning point. 'This is much better than having it closed. No one can approach,' Henry said, ladling soup. 'And we have given the impression of being concerned about appearances.'

Even so, they spoke of innocuous matters while they ate. Henry used the bell at his right hand at the end of every course and the footmen glided in, cleared and re-laid place settings with practised efficiency.

Gaby found she was becoming decidedly restless, waiting to hear what Henry's idea might be to solve the problem of the father of her child. She eyed the array of desserts set out and helped herself to a cream and pureed chestnut confection that would probably be ruinous to the digestion, but which looked too good to resist.

'Thank you, that will be all. You may clear later,' Henry said and they watched the last footman vanish along the passageway. 'That should have established our innocent intentions for the evening,' he added as they disappeared. He made rather a business of peeling himself an apple.

'Henry, if you do not tell me your bright idea soon I am going to sit here and empty this entire bowl out of sheer frustration and then I will be very ill indeed.' Gaby bit the end off a wafer and pointed the sharp remnant at him. 'You have been keeping me in suspense all evening.'

'I have been trying to find my nerve,' he admitted ruefully. He put down his knife, pushed back his chair and frowned at Gaby.

'Henry—' she threatened.

'Very well. I am single, unattached, committed to your interest in this and in good health.' He pressed on doggedly as she stared at him. 'I am about to leave the country on a journey which might plausibly end in shipwreck. I have no intention of returning to Europe. What about me?'

'You?' It came out as a squeak. Henry's face fell. 'No, I am sorry. I did not mean you are impossible for any negative reason. But, Henry, we are friends—'

'I find you extremely attractive,' he confessed, blushing rather charmingly.

Gaby blinked. *He has just asked me if I want him to make love to me, to father my child. He has made it real, a possibility.*

Henry's blush deepened as she stared at him. 'I foresee no problem with… That is, should you decide…'

'I hadn't thought…' *Pull yourself together. We cannot spend the entire evening stammering at each other.* 'It is very—' *Kind?* '—thoughtful of you, Henry. I had not considered… Not that I do not like you. But, we have been friends and now you propose something so different and I am having trouble thinking straight about it.'

'I am not suggesting that our emotions might be engaged in any way beyond friendship.' Henry seemed to have both his composure and his voice under control again, although his colour was high. 'Perhaps, if we were to kiss? You might be able to judge whether this is something you could take a little further? I realise that as a…er…lady without experience, it might seem daunting.'

'I am not a virgin,' Gaby said. 'An old love affair, he is dead.'

'I am so sorry.' Henry got up, walked to the sitting area, his back to her, presumably out of tact.

'It was years ago and not relevant to this discussion except that you need not have concerns on that score.' She got up, too, pushed the door closed and went to him. 'You are right. Let us kiss and see.'

There was nothing alarming about kissing Henry. He was gentle and respectful but not hesitant. *He has obviously done this before*, Gaby thought, reaching for humour to calm her nerves. He gathered her in against his body and she was aware of solidity and strength and a pleasant scent of cologne and warm man.

She closed her eyes, tipped up her face and his lips covered hers confidently. She tasted wine and the sweetness of the pudding he had just eaten and… *He is really quite good at this.* She tried to relax, to kiss back. It was not so very difficult. There was comfort in being held in his arms, and some pleasure, although no surge of excitement or desire.

Henry's tongue slid along her lips and she opened to him, responded. *I can do this and he seems to be enjoying it.*

Then Henry gathered her in closer and she realised that he was, indeed, finding pleasure in the embrace and that when he had said he could foresee no problem, then, as far as his responses were concerned, that was the truth. The thought, the pressure of his arousal against her, carried her deeper than she had intended going. This had been only a kiss. Just a kiss. A tiny, harmless experiment.

She felt his hand lift from her waist, come to rest on her right breast, his fingertips stroking gently at the swell of bare flesh exposed by the low lacy neckline of her evening gown. He gave a soft growl, deep in his throat.

With the sound she was suddenly sure. This was wrong. She could not do this, not with this man. And she knew why. He was not Gray and she was in love with Gray. She couldn't have him, she knew that, but she loved him and to make love with any other man would be a betrayal she would never recover from.

Gaby jerked back, shocked by the realisation, shocked at herself for enjoying, however mildly, Henry's kiss. She twisted sharply away from his embrace and he released her instantly but his fingers caught in the lace as she turned. There was a ripping sound, a sudden coolness on her skin and she looked down to see the bodice torn away on one side, exposing her breast above the tight edge of her corset.

'Hell, I'm sorry, Gabrielle.'

'Accident,' Gaby stammered. 'It wasn't your fault, Henry. I'm sorry, I can't. It isn't you, honestly.' She was backing towards the door, not frightened of him as he stood there, making no attempt to touch her again, but of her own feelings.

'I know it isn't,' he said, his expression rueful. 'It's him. It is Gray. I should have thought.'

He knows. It is that obvious?

'Don't be sorry. You were trying to help. This is my fault. I must go.' Her back touched the panels and she reached for the handle.

'Gabrielle, your gown—'

'I will fix it, I've pins in my reticule.' The handle kept slipping as she tugged at it.

He did move then, to pick up her reticule, hand it to her, open the door. 'There are spare bedchambers along there. Go and pin it, recover a little, then I will ring for the carriage for you.'

'No. I'll go down myself and tell the butler that I have suddenly remembered something. I'll be all right, Henry, honestly. Please, just leave me to myself.'

He must have recognised the desperation in her voice, the need to be alone, because she saw on his face the struggle to overcome his instincts and step back. 'Very well. Call me if you need me.'

She fled. There was no other word for it, she realised. Not flight from Henry, dear, harmless, gentlemanly Henry, but from her thoughts and desires, as though she did not carry them in her head, in her heart. Inescapable.

The turn in the passageway was in front of her

and Gaby tried to slow to a walk. There were bed-chamber doors just beyond, she recalled. If she could just go into one for a few moments, pin up her bodice, straighten her hair and compose her-self, everything would be perfectly all right. Any appearance of distress in her demeanour could be explained by her being flustered over forget-ting that she had to meet Jane. She would dither and twitter to Fredericks about it and he would dismiss her as an empty-headed peahen, but that did not matter.

She was still half running when she rounded the blind corner and her speed sent her thudding into a large, firm, male body. For a second she thought it must be a footman. *I must pretend the collision tore my gown...* Then arms came around her in a supporting embrace and every sense told her that this was Gray.

'Gabrielle? What on earth are you doing here? What is wrong?' He held her away from him to look at her.

Gray had just turned from opening one of the bedchamber doors, she realised as she glimpsed the mahogany gleam of a half-tester bed, rich dark green hangings and the glow of lamplight. He looked tired and travel worn. There were shadows under this eyes, his neckcloth was crumpled and he had not shaved recently.

'Gray?' She found that her hand was cupped against his cheek, the prickles of a day-old beard on her palm, but it dropped as his gaze slid from her face to her bosom and back to her lips. She touched them and found them sensitive, swollen from Henry's kisses.

His expression changed from puzzled to something horribly like a sneer. 'Foolish of me to ask. I left the field very clear for you. Henry makes an ideal candidate for your stud, of course. And he needs money. How much are you paying him to get you with child?'

'Nothing! And we haven't.' Gaby stopped, took a deep breath and tried to speak calmly, not like a hysterical woman fleeing from her lover's embrace. 'We are not lovers. We talked about it. Discussed the possibility, the practicalities.'

'I can see that, although the talking does not appear to have involved words and the practicalities appear to have included practice.' Gray reached out and ran the pad of his thumb slowly along her lower lip, then dropped his hand to flip at the torn bodice. 'What stopped you? Did you hear my arrival? Really, my dear, you should have simply stayed in Henry's bedchamber. Who am I

to chaperone you?' he asked, his fingers still toy-
ing with the ripped lace.

Oh, yes, that is a sneer.

'I did not know you had returned. I realised I
could not make love with Henry.'

'Why ever not? He's a pleasant, handsome, up-
standing young man about to leave the country
for good. He sounds perfect to me. What did your
sensitive conscience find to object to this time?'

'Because he is not you!' she flared, batting
away his hand, turning to run. If she reached
the hallway he would not, could not, follow. Not
without making a compromising scene in front
of his staff.

It took one stride for him to catch her, spin her
round again. Gray held her, his hands cupped
around each shoulder.

*He isn't holding tight. I could twist away, free
myself.*

Then Gaby looked properly into his face, into
his eyes. The hands that curved around her shook
slightly.

'Gray? What is wrong? You look—'

'I have been down into hell,' he said flatly, as
though he was reporting visiting Richmond. 'Into
hell.' His eyes were dark with remembered pain,
the purple smudges under his eyes were more

than tiredness. He had been gone only a few days and yet she could swear he had lost weight.

'Tell me.' Gaby moved forward, lifted her hands to his face, her fingertips on the thin skin of his temples, where the blood beat in the vein, blue under the skin.

'My son. He had a fall, knocked his head. He wouldn't wake. We thought—'

'*No,*' she whispered.

'No,' he agreed. 'He recovered consciousness the day after I reached home. He doesn't remember the accident, but he is all right.' His arms closed round her and she realised his entire body was shaking, a fine tremor, almost imperceptible. Nerves and endurance stretched almost to breaking point. 'Perfectly all right. Talking and walking and wanting to play.'

'But you are here.' Her voice was muffled against his neckcloth.

'I want a London doctor to examine him, just to be perfectly certain. He is travelling down by slow stages with my mother and his sister and a small battalion of nursemaids and grooms. I will have their rooms made ready and discover the best doctor for head injuries tomorrow. There is no concussion—I know enough about blows to the head to check for that and for fractures. Our local doctor agrees. I am talking too much,' he added, sounding surprised.

'Relief. Exhaustion. How much sleep have you had since you left London?'

'I have no idea. None going up. When I tried to think about something else, all I could do was think about you. Not very restful. I slept in the carriage coming back, I think.'

'You should be in bed now.' She was so tight against his body that she felt the change come over him, felt the energy flowing through him, just like the startling electric current she had experienced when she had attended a demonstration at the Institute in Porto.

'Gabrielle.' It was a question and she answered it, tipping back her face to look up at him.

'Gray, you know what I need. You cannot give it. I cannot ask it.'

'Forget that tonight. Forget all of it. Make love with me, Gabrielle. Just us, tonight. We will worry about everything else tomorrow. Who knows what will happen? Life is a chance suspended by a thread and I have just found out how fragile that is.' When she hesitated, he stepped back into the bedchamber, leaving her cold and alone on the threshold. 'I am sorry. I am not thinking straight. You want to go and I should let you.'

'I want to stay,' she said, suddenly certain. She loved him, wanted him. He wanted her and needed her. Tomorrow, rested and with his family to worry about, he would know this had no future, but that was tomorrow. Now was all there was. This minute. This man.

Gaby stepped into the room, closed the door behind her, felt for the key and turned it in the lock.

The sharp click seemed to break a spell. Gray swept her into his arms, kissing her on the way to the bed, falling on to the wide green covers with her, still lip-locked, his hands pulling her back into a close embrace. Fully clothed, they strained together, their bodies frustrated by layers of cloth, their legs tangling. She knew his taste now, his scent, the feel of his mouth over hers, and yet it was all new. And not enough, not nearly enough.

She pulled and tugged at their clothes, her fingers clashing with his until finally they calmed enough to work together, unbuttoning, shifting, tugging. Her torn gown fell to the floor, her petticoats and stays after it. Gray knelt back on the bed like a half-naked god in a sea of green and looked down at her. 'You are so beautiful, I do not have the words.'

Gaby opened her mouth, then closed it again as he bent over her garters. *Beautiful?* She would take that from Gray, treasure it. She watched as he untied the ribbons, rolled down her stockings, kissed the crease of her knee, making her laugh. She was naked now, bare to only the second man she had ever lain with and it was a long time since Laurent. She should be nervous, perhaps, but she was not.

'You still have far too many clothes on, Gray.' His shirt was half out of his breeches so she found the hem, pulled it over his head and then stopped. They were on their knees facing each other and she let her gaze wander down his torso. There was the scar on his shoulder, the wound that had brought him back to England. It was a white dent now, surrounded by a network of spidery lines. The triangle of dark hair on his chest, brown nipples, tight and puckered now with arousal, that tantalising trail of hair down towards his navel… Gaby ran one finger down it, pressing against the hard muscles of his stomach, then gripped the waistband of his breeches, pulling so that they swayed together.

Gray came up on his knees and she saw just how aroused he was. Still she could feel nothing but excitement, anticipation. Need. *Love, but I must not say it. Let him believe it is all desire.*

'You are wearing too much,' she said, meaning to tease, her voice breaking, husky with longing.

'Only fair. You've already seen me in the river.' There was laughter in his eyes now, but hunger, too. 'Mind you, the water was very cold, I was hardly at my best.'

'It whetted my appetite.' Finally she managed to find the fastening, released his falls and reached for him. He filled her grip, hot and proud and eager, magnificently male.

Gray kicked away his breeches and tumbled her back into the silken covers. 'I want to spend hours making love to you, slowly, inch by inch, exploring every private corner, every dimple, every freckle.' His mouth trailed down her neck, detoured so he could nibble at her ears, nuzzle behind into the soft, vulnerable skin there. 'And if I do that I will go out of my mind. Gabrielle, I'm beyond finesse. I need you now. Forgive me.'

'*I* need you now.' She wriggled beneath him, loving his weight, his hardness over her softness. He pressed between her thighs and she lifted to meet him, gasped as he touched her intimately, one finger penetrating, his thumb playing fire and sweetness between her folds. She was already wet for him, but she was beyond modesty, pushing against his hand, demanding more.

He shifted, nudged against her and she opened to him, lifting again, gasping at the pressure as he filled her. It had been a long time, but her body wanted him as much as she did. Gray rocked gently, inexorably into her: advance, retreat, slide and press. He filled her, caressed her, claimed her.

Gaby met every thrust, sighed at every withdrawal, tightened her legs around him until all at once he was totally within her.

They both stopped moving. 'Are you all right, Gabrielle? Have I hurt you?'

'No,' she said, confused at the concern in his voice. Then she realised her cheeks were wet, her lashes clogged with moisture. 'I am crying because I am happy.'

He smiled then, the rare true smile that she trusted as much as his frown. 'I haven't done anything to make you happy yet.'

'Liar.' She tightened her muscles and he closed his eyes and began to move again, each thrust and withdrawal so slow and sure that she could have believed that he was far less shaken by this than she was, until she felt the tension in his shoulders where her fingers held him, felt the thudding of his heart over hers.

Then her own driving pulse took possession of her and thought and reason took wing, leaving only sensation. Gaby was not certain where her body ended and Gray's began, only that nothing else existed but this man and the heat of his body, the scent of him, the slide of his skin over hers, the depth of his possession of her.

'*Gabrielle.*'

What was he asking? Or perhaps it was just a statement, she thought hazily as the pleasure built and twisted so tightly it was almost pain. She felt his rhythm become uneven, his breath ragged and let herself go, let the pleasure soar. Gray pulled away and, even as she gasped a protest at the loss of him, she felt the hot spill of his passion against her belly. *He is taking care*, she thought hazily. Then she welcomed his weight as they collapsed together, his head heavy on her shoulder.

Chapter Sixteen

Gray came to himself slowly. Still half-awake, eyes still closed, he felt beneath him softness, sweet-smelling bare skin. Someone was breathing close by his ear. *Gabrielle.* He knew who it was although his exhaustion-drugged brain could not quite recall *where* he was or how he had come to be there. He had made love to Gabrielle and the aftershocks of pleasure were still running through him.

'Gabrielle.'

'Gray,' she murmured, her breath tickling his ear. She moved under him, the soft curve of her belly against his rapidly growing arousal.

He shifted and she moved with him, opening to him, welcoming his body back into hers with the sensual generosity that he realised was typical of her. He plunged into the tight, moist, hot velvet of her and she rose to meet him, clenched around him, murmuring, then gasping, encouragement. He should make this slow, something told him, although he could not quite recall why, and his body did not want to go slowly. It wanted to possess, to give and take pleasure, to lose itself in her.

The pleasure built as her legs twined around him, her heels hard on his buttocks, her thighs gripping him. The sensation in the base of his spine twisted, intensified to the point of pain as his climax built and suddenly he remembered where he was, what he was doing. It was almost too late, he was past the point of no return and her legs, her grip as she cried out in the throes of her own passion, was strong. Somehow, knowing he might have hurt her, he wrenched back, gasping as much with relief than with release as he spilled on to her thigh.

'Gabrielle? Did I hurt you?'

She blinked up at him. 'No. We forgot ourselves, both of us. It is all right, you remembered in time.' She reached for him, pulling him close again.

'I fell asleep on top of you.' He nuzzled into her neck for a self-indulgent moment, then rolled to one side and sat up, scrubbing his hands over his face, over the stubble that must have fretted her skin. 'You must wonder what sort of selfish lout you've taken to your bed.'

'An exhausted one.' Gabrielle propped herself up on her elbows and studied his face. 'I have no complaints at all, but you should rest. When did you last have a full night's sleep?'

'I have no idea.' He wanted to stay there all night, just looking at her as she lay there, relaxed and pleasured and quite unselfconscious. Warm, olive-toned skin, just now flushed pink over her breasts. Long, sleek muscles in those elegant limbs, high, small breasts he wanted to take the time to worship thoroughly. A nest of dark curls hiding delights he could spend hours exploring. 'I do not feel like sleeping now.'

'But you should. And I should go home.' Gabrielle sat up abruptly as the clock on the mantelshelf struck one. 'Jane will be back by now and wondering where I am. I must not worry her.'

She scrambled from the bed. 'Will there be water in the dressing room?'

'It will be cold,' he warned as he got up and searched for his breeches. He needed to escort her out as though they had spent the past hour in innocuous conversation. 'But I can hardly ring for more. I must see you to the door.'

Gabrielle was already splashing in his dressing room. 'It will do,' she called. 'Can you see my stockings?'

Gray tucked in his shirt and scooped up her clothes. 'Here, let me be your lady's maid.' His fingers, usually so sure, fumbled over the laces of her stays, the fastenings at the back of her gown, but somehow between them they managed to get her dressed tidily, her hair smoothed into submission, the rent in her gown pinned up invisibly.

'Gray, your hair is on end and where is your neckcloth? Oh, there, under the bed.'

'I will come and see you tomorrow,' he said as he cracked open the door, checked up and down the passageway. Perhaps when he had slept for nine or ten hours he might know what he was going to say to her. In a way it was a mercy that there was no time to talk now.

'In the afternoon,' she agreed, walking demurely beside him to the head of the stairs, just as though she had not bitten his shoulder just minutes before. 'Don't forget that we're at Half Moon Street now. And, please, do not be angry with Henry. He was trying to help me.'

Henry? He had forgotten his cousin. That was going to be an uncomfortable encounter. Unless— 'Do you want me to pretend I know nothing of your meeting with him?'

'That would be best, don't you think?' she murmured as they reached the hall. 'Oh, Fredericks, thank you.' His butler appeared, carrying her cloak and gloves. 'Look at the hour! I was just about to leave when Lord Leybourne came in and we quite lost track of time, hearing the good news.'

'Good news indeed, Miss Frost. I will send round to the mews for your carriage, it will be here directly.'

Gray knew he should make polite conversation while they waited. Easy, confident meaningless chit-chat, instead of standing there, wanting to take her in his arms and carry her back upstairs to that all too empty bed that would hold her scent, perhaps her warmth. Gray racked his tired brain for something innocuous. 'The house in Half Moon Street is proving comfortable, I trust?'

'It is delightful.' Gabrielle sounded perfectly awake and sensible, thank heavens. 'I do appreciate your help finding it.' She chatted on, holding up a one-sided conversation while he stood and looked at her and prayed silently that her tender, thoroughly inconvenient conscience was not going to give her—and him—hell tomorrow. Because he wanted her again. And again. He wanted—

'Your carriage, Miss Frost.' Fredericks was already at the door.

Gray pulled himself together, said all the right things to speed a guest on their way in the presence of the butler, then turned and made himself put one foot in front of the other towards the stairs.

'I will send up your man and hot water for a bath, my lord.'

'No. No, thank you. I can undress myself and I would only fall asleep in a bath. Tell Tompkins I don't want to be disturbed until at least ten tomorrow. Go to bed, Fredericks. I am sorry to keep you up so late.'

He would make himself wake early to check for any trace of Gabrielle. When he reached it the room was scented by Gabrielle's light perfume, by the musk of their loving. He threw open the window, shook out the bedcover thoroughly, then jammed it to the foot of the bed as though his restless sleep had trodden creases into it. A quick survey on, under and beside the bed revealed not so much as a hairpin. Even so, he must wake by nine to check in daylight.

Everything had changed and Gray had no idea how to feel about it, other than that his tired body had no trouble in luxuriating in the memory of their lovemaking, of the feel of Gabrielle filling every sense. Gray pulled off his clothes, tossed them on to a chair and fell into bed. He was vaguely aware that he had forgotten to snuff the candles, but he did not have the will to stir again. *Let them gutter out.*

'I expect Lord Leybourne to call this afternoon,' Gaby said casually, affecting an interest in the choice between marmalade and cherry jam for her breakfast toast.

Jane looked up sharply, then folded the learned journal she had been reading and set it down by her plate. Clearly Gaby was not as successful in feigning unconcern as she thought. 'And why might that be? I thought that you and he had fallen out.'

'Not exactly fallen out. And he has been away in Yorkshire. This cherry jam is very good.'

'Gabrielle.'

'Very well,' She put down the toast. When Jane chose to be perceptive there was no point in trying to evade her. 'I believe he may come to propose.'

'Marriage?'

'Yes.'

'I understood that the appearance of attachment

you were making was to quash your aunt's match-making schemes for the pair of you and that it was simply a pretence.' Now Jane was studying her over the wire rims of her pince-nez.

'There is a degree of mutual attraction,' Gaby admitted warily.

'Is there a reason why Lord Leybourne *should* be making you an offer?'

She was blushing, she knew she was. 'Yes,' Gaby admitted.

'I cannot say that I blame you,' Jane remarked. 'Really, my dear, the wind will change and fix you in position with your mouth open like that. I may be a spinster bluestocking, but there is absolutely nothing wrong with my eyesight. He is a very superior specimen, physically and mentally, and he has an admirable war record. If you did not succumb to him, I would be wondering about your state of health.'

'Jane.'

'I had always understood that my role was to give you the appearance of respectability, not to lecture you on your conduct,' Jane said crisply. 'However, as we are discussing the matter, I had believed that you did not intend to marry because of the loss of control of the business that such a state would entail. I confess I find myself puzzled that you are now contemplating matrimony.'

'I am not. But Gray might well be.' She was not going to contemplate what being married to Gray might be like because if she did she would probably put her head down amidst the toast crumbs and the butter, and have a good weep. And tears, she had finally fallen asleep telling herself at three in the morning, would be counterproductive. She was an impossible wife for an earl with vast responsibilities in England. He, or any man, was impossible as a husband. Impossibilities were not worth crying over.

'He is a gentleman with a code of honour. He is not going to be pleased to be refused.'

'He might not ask. We had agreed to be lovers, he knows my feelings on the subject of marriage, and yet, somehow, last night I felt something had changed.' It had for her. She was in love with the man and it was no good pretending that she was not. 'He made a point of saying he would call, but as he was almost asleep on his feet and the butler was showing me out he could hardly elaborate.'

Jane made a sound that in any other woman would be a giggle. 'Asleep on his feet? My dear Gabrielle—what *had* you done to him?'

'I suppose I had better explain. I had dinner at

Gray's town house with his cousin Henry. If you recall, I told you that Gray had left suddenly for his Yorkshire estate? As I was leaving I met him coming in. Just outside his bedchamber door.' She explained about little James and Gray's long journeys and lack of sleep. 'I think his mother will arrive with the children tomorrow.'

'So now you will have Lord Leybourne, your aunt *and* his mama all expecting the match.'

'I am sure he will not have said anything about me to his mother and she can hardly approve of a bride for him who is in trade. That might help.'

'You are no more in trade than he is, selling the agricultural produce of his estates. You are hardly operating smoke-belching factories or coal mines. Your lineage is impeccable, your upbringing that of a lady,' Jane said in a tone that brooked no argument.

'I am going to have to return to Portugal. That is the only way out of it.'

'Run away?'

'A strategic retreat,' Gaby countered. *Yes, run away.*

'And what about all the things you—*we*—planned to do while we were in London? Do you want to sacrifice the theatre, the opera, the exhibitions and the shopping just because you cannot say *no* firmly enough to a suitor? And how will it appear if you arrive back home within weeks of leaving?'

'You are quite right,' Gaby said with a sigh. *I must be fair to Jane even if I don't care what the neighbours will think.* 'I will speak frankly to Gray this afternoon if he proposes. Refuse him without any ambiguity.' *Break my heart.*

Gray was at the front door at three o'clock, quite the correct time for a morning call should anyone have observed him. He was turned out in the most elegant outfit of dark grey pantaloons, glossy black Hessians with silver tassels, a swallowtail coat of darkest blue superfine and every appropriate accessory in restrained good taste.

If it were not for the dark circles under his eyes and the lines of strain between his nostrils and the corners of his mouth no one would think anything was wrong. Anyone seeing him, and the tasteful bouquet of roses and ferns he carried, would have deduced that this was a gentleman setting out to court a lady, Gaby thought.

She made herself smile and greet him as though the night before had not happened. When Gray presented her with the flowers she exclaimed with pleasure, rang for the footman to take them and place them in water and bring them back directly. He shook hands with Jane, made polite conversation, accepted a cup of tea.

The flowers were brought in arranged in a silver vase and Jane admired them. Gaby continued to smile and wondered if she was going to scream. She felt like it.

And, finally, he turned to her. 'Miss Frost. Gabrielle. I wonder if I might beg a word alone with you?'

'Of course, Lord Leybourne. If you will excuse us, Jane?' She rose, he rose, Jane sipped her tea without comment. 'If you would like to come through to the—'

'Lady Orford, Miss Frost.'

'Gabrielle, my dear. And Gray.' Her aunt looked rather less pleased to see him. 'Good afternoon, Miss Moseley.' She sat down, took a cup of tea with a vague word of thanks and plunged straight in. 'Now, my dear, it is a positive age since I saw you and I know you have not attended a single one of the events for which I obtained invitations on your behalf after the first one, so what have you been about?' She took a sharp bite out of a biscuit and fixed Gaby with a reproving stare.

Gaby, with a despairing look at Jane, sat back

down again. Gray was left with no option but to sit in the only free chair next to his godmother.

'You are not shy of society, surely? Or has Leybourne been taking up all your time? It is too bad of you, dear boy, if that is the case.' She leaned across and tapped Gray on the forearm with one beringed finger.

Gaby was conscious of her gaze flicking between them and smiled with more determination, avoiding Gray's eye.

'Now, you must have advanced your plans, the two of you. You are very wicked to keep me in the dark, Gabrielle. You know I would dote on the chance to arrange a wedding, especially as I have no daughter. Sons are not the same.'

'We hope to make some decisions soon,' Gray said. 'At the moment we are at that stage which my friends tell me is almost inevitable—we cannot agree on anything from the venue to the date, let alone the guest list or the organ music.'

'Or even which country,' Gaby added.

Gray sighed, the very picture of the put-upon betrothed man, she thought as she suppressed an entirely inappropriate giggle. It was probably hysteria. 'Portugal would mean a saving on the wine bill, I agree,' he added and she had to bite the inside of her cheek.

She must stop enjoying this mutual teasing of Aunt Henrietta. It made him seem like an ally, a friend. She must not find more things to like or her defences against him were going to crumble like a pile of sand in front of the incoming tide.

'How is Cousin George?' she asked before Gray could add any more embellishments.

'He is not your cousin, dear.' The firming of Aunt Henrietta's lips were clear proof that she had not given up on her plans for Gaby. 'He is very well and has taken to squiring Miss Henderson about. Such a charming unspoilt girl and her uncle is Viscount Worthington, of course.'

Miss Henderson? Ah, yes, that pretty child Aunt was trying to pair up with Gray. Is she trying to make me jealous? Surely not, no one would think I would rather have George than Gray, even his besotted stepmother. Or perhaps she is dangling the girl in front of Gray in the hope of detaching him from me.

'Very sensible of George,' Gray said heartily. 'Good for him. She's an absolute infant, of course, but I expect she will grow up eventually and George has some maturing to do himself. They'll suit.'

Aunt Henrietta looked a trifle daunted at that. *Surely,* Gaby thought, *she will give up now.* Her aunt did indeed draw a deep breath and the smile she had fixed on her face seemed a trifle artificial now, but she showed no sign of departing.

Gray rose. 'Look at the time! Miss Moseley, good afternoon. Thank you for tea. Gabrielle, I will send a note to tell you how I fare with those theatre tickets. Godmama.' The door closed behind him, leaving the three ladies gazing at the tea tray. The front door banged as the footman came in with fresh hot water. Aunt Henrietta refused a second cup of tea, informed them that their new cook needed to put more ground almonds into the orange biscuits and took herself off.

'Surely she cannot want you to marry George now that he has attached Miss Henderson,' Jane observed.

'I believe she is trying to make us both jealous that the others are not pining for us. She really does not like to be thwarted and I am sure I will bring more money with me than Miss Henderson will.'

'That is certainly a consideration,' remarked Gray, right behind them. 'At least, Godmama would think so. I wonder how she intends to separate us.'

Both of them jumped. 'I thought you had gone.'

Gaby righted her sliding teacup and tried to tell herself that her speeding pulse rate was a result of shock.

'As far as the dining room. Your new footman is admiring the shiny guinea he has just earned. We were about to talk, Gabrielle.'

'Yes. No, don't disturb yourself, Jane. We will go to the dining room.'

'I suppose I should warn you to leave the door open.' Jane reached for her journal. 'However, it is probably a case of shutting stable doors, not dining room ones.'

Gaby knew she was blushing, but she left the room with as much composure as she could muster.

'Miss Moseley is aware of what happened last night?' Gray closed the dining room door.

'Yes. In, er, outline.'

Gray looked at her, then walked around the long table and hitched one hip on it. 'Gabrielle, I realise that you have a rooted objection to marriage with anyone.' He held up a hand when she opened her mouth to speak. 'And I understand your reasons and can sympathise with them. But we *should* marry, you know we should.'

'I know that when we spoke of becoming lovers

before, there was no question of marriage. What has changed?'

'I thought—if I thought clearly at all—that with a lover in your past and a refusal to marry you were like a widow, someone who could live an independent life provided you were discreet. I should have known better.'

'Why? Nothing has changed and you have described my position exactly.'

'We have become lovers and now I am thinking clearly. I have feelings for you, Gabrielle. Feelings that go far beyond the desire to lie with you and certainly beyond friendship.'

Something inside her seemed to stutter, as though her heart had jumped at his words. 'Are you saying that you are in love with me, Gray?'

'I do not know. How does one know?' He twisted round and looked her full in the face across the expanse of gleaming mahogany. 'I have never been in love before.'

'Your wife—'

'I cannot discuss Portia. I made a mull of that marriage.'

'No?' Gaby realised that she was angry. Where had that come from? 'You want me to marry you because you *might* be in love with me. Possibly. Because you have *feelings*. It has been clear from what you have let slip before that you did not have a happy marriage. Now you refuse to talk about it, yet you expect me to become your second wife without any idea what went wrong before? Do you expect to make a mull of it this time?'

'Gabrielle, the story does not just involve me.'

'You were unfaithful to her?'

'No.' Gray got to his feet, abruptly, without any of his usual grace. The question had obviously struck a raw nerve.

'She was unfaithful to you?'

'No.'

'It does not matter.' Gaby threw up her hands in exasperation. 'Why are we even discussing it? Nothing has changed. You have vast responsibilities and ties here. I will not surrender my control of Frost's. It is hardly as though you seduced a virgin—I knew exactly what I was doing.'

She understood why he had put the width of the table between them. If she touched him, if he touched her, her resolution would go up like smoke. But she could not talk to him like this. She came round the table until she was just out of reach and tried to make her tone more reasonable, less fraught with tension. 'My idea of finding a father for a child is impossible—you were quite right about that. I intend staying in London for perhaps another month, six weeks. Jane has commitments, interests. I will shop and visit the theatre and galleries. Then I will return home and research my family connections. Perhaps somewhere I can find a suitable successor with Frost blood in their veins.'

'And if this is not simply desire and liking? What if I am in love with you?' he asked, a proud man driven to laying his feelings, his heart perhaps, at her mercy.

As I am with you? He felt desire and liking, yes. Emotions a lover and a friend would feel. But it was not enough. Hearts did not break, it seemed. Not with a crack and a splintering noise, at least. They just ached with a bruise that would never heal. 'Then I am sorry. I never tried to set lures or to attach you. I never intended for you to have feelings for me.'

'I know. If there is fault in this, it is mine,' Gray said with a rueful twist of his lips that Gaby did not mistake for humour.

'It is no one's fault. We played with fire and it seems we are both a trifle scorched.'

'I should, in all honour, marry you.'

Yes, that would prick his conscience as a gentleman. 'You haven't ruined me, I was not a virgin, some innocent you seduced. If I had been, then, yes, I agree, you are honour-bound to offer marriage. But I was not.' He had nothing to say to that, it seemed. 'We can manage some pretext to end our betrothal a week before I leave. I do not trust Aunt Henrietta not to promptly matchmake again, whatever she says about George's attachment to Miss Henderson.'

'Gabrielle—' He broke off, reached for her hand and lifted it to her lips. 'I cannot—we cannot—continue as lovers.'

'I know.' She intended to sound firm and definite. It was not as though she disagreed with him. 'It would be too difficult to separate emotions and desire, would it not?'

'Your emotions are engaged?' Gray held on to her hand and pulled her closer. 'Gabrielle?' His hand was warm and when her fingers instinctively closed around his she could feel his pulse beating strongly. Last night, his heart had beaten over hers as they made love.

'I desire you. I like you.' *You are breaking my heart.* 'I want to be your lover still and I know I should not. I would be an impossible wife for you and marriage is not for me. I cannot afford to allow my emotions free rein, to wonder *What if?*'

Chapter Seventeen

He might as well be battering his head against the wall for all the good this was doing, Gray thought. Whatever it was that Gabrielle felt for him, and perhaps it was only self-delusion that he thought she felt more than she was admitting, it was clearly insufficient to compensate for the legal penalties of marriage.

Gray released her hand. Their fingers seemed to cling of their own accord for a second, then she was moving away from him, tension in every lovely line of her back, in the way she held her head. Yes, Gabrielle felt more than just desire and she was hurting, perhaps as much as he was.

What did he want? Surely he could not *wish* to love when he could not have her? No more than he could not wish her to love him, because it would hurt her.

What could he do? He could not change the

law for her and even if she trusted him enough to believe that he would leave all the power over Frost's in her hands, that still left the little matter of geography. He could not move his estates or hers closer together or drain the Bay of Biscay. If he had been a younger son he would not be tied to estates and responsibilities, to the House of Lords and thousands of acres, hundreds of lives. But he was not a younger son.

'I cannot blame you,' he said, as she reached the door. She stopped. She did not turn, but at least she was listening to him. 'I wish I could. I wish I could call you unwomanly and foolishly independent and make this all your fault. But I cannot. I admire what you do, what you have. I understand why you cannot surrender it into a husband's hands any more than I could hand unconditional control of my estates to a wife.'

'Thank you,' Gabrielle said. Her head was bent, baring the vulnerable pale nape of her neck. He wanted to touch it, to kiss it, somehow soothe himself with the taste of her. 'I believe you.' She reached for the door handle and he thought that was her last word. Then, as she went through, she said, 'That makes it worse.'

Gray stared at the closing door. How could his understanding make it worse for her? Unless…

unless she felt more than just the desire and liking she admitted to and sensing that she could trust him only made refusing him harder. He gave her a few minutes, then went out to the hall, retrieved his hat and gloves from the expressionless footman he had tipped to hide him, and left.

The choice in front of him was stark, he thought, as he walked up the slight slope towards Curzon Street. He could try and suppress his feelings, not examine them, not try and puzzle out if this was love. Then he could meet Gabrielle in social settings, act sufficiently well to keep his godmother at bay until it was time for them to stage their falling-out. Gabrielle would return to Portugal and he would do his best to forget her.

And unicorns will dance in Grosvenor Square.

Or he could admit that this was more than lust, more than liking, discover if he could love.

And then I can drive myself to distraction trying to find a solution to an insoluble conundrum and end up with a broken heart.

A broken heart? he sneered at himself, turning right into Curzon Street. Broken hearts were for romantic girls and long-haired poets, not adult male aristocrats. A high brick wall loomed on his right and he realised he was at Berkeley Square. Where was he going? What he felt like doing was beating the hell out of someone or something, and the civilised outlet for that desire was to continue along to Old Bond Street and Gentleman Jackson's establishment. He could find someone to spar with or, if he was in luck, the Gentleman himself might take him on.

On the other hand, Dover Street and Manton's, the gunsmith, were closer. He could go to their shooting gallery, relieve his feelings with some target practice and possibly look at their latest guns.

Which is probably the equivalent of a lady deciding to buy a new bonnet when she's upset, he thought grimly. *I should be at home harassing the staff about making up the rooms for Mama and the children or interviewing doctors.*

These feelings were the very devil, distracting him from what was reality, what he could—and should—be doing.

He turned on his heel and found himself confronting a solid six-foot male obstructing the pavement. With a muttered apology he sidestepped and the man put out a hand to stop him. *Giles.*

'Hey, it's me, Gray. What the devil's the matter with you? You look like a man who's lost a sovereign and found a groat.' The man in front of him frowned. 'Oh, hell—they said when I called just now that Jamie was going to be all right. They aren't just putting a brave face on it, are they?'

'No, he's fine. I was thinking about something else.' He found he could smile. This was, after all, Giles, Marquess of Revesby, his oldest friend. 'Good to see you. When did you get to town and how is Laurel?' Laurel was Giles's wife, another childhood friend, despite a residual tension between them ever since the events which had led to him marrying Portia.

'She is flourishing, although she really ought to be back home in the country with her feet up, if you follow me.'

'You are anticipating a happy event? Congratulations.' Gray shook Giles's hand with genuine feeling. 'I'd say come down to the club and we'll drink to it, but I've got to track down a doctor I've had recommended to check Jamie over.'

'Couldn't anyway, tempted though I am.' Revesby cast a harried look at his pocket watch. 'I'm supposed to be collecting Laurel from the dressmaker's in five minutes. But come to dinner tonight if you're free. Relax before the family descends upon you, which your Cousin Henry tells me is likely tomorrow.'

'I'll do that, with pleasure.' They shook hands,

restrained by the location from anything more demonstrative, and Giles strode off northward while Gray took a moment to give himself a mental shake. This was not the time to be bloodying his knuckles or wasting ammunition on harmless targets. He should be calling on Dr Templeton and arranging for him to call and examine Jamie, then he should be reviewing the arrangements the staff had made for his mother and the children. Giles mentioning Henry had given him a telling insight into one of the reasons he was feeling so unsettled: he had a strong desire to hit his cousin, knock out a few teeth.

Henry had acted in good faith in offering to help Gabrielle, he knew that with the rational, sensible part of his brain. His suggestions would have helped keep her safe from discovery, would have kept her from encountering men far less honest than Henry. And his cousin could have had no idea that Gray's feelings for her were any more genuine than the pretence they were making for her aunt's benefit. None of which reasonableness stopped the desire to pulverise the man. Henry had kissed her, he had put his hands on her, even if her torn gown was not his fault, as she insisted.

Mine, something primitive and fierce snarled

inside Gray as he changed direction yet again and made his way towards Brook Street and the doctor's residence. He could have sent a note, but a personal call would give him time to get his thoughts into some sort of order. *Mine*. It was no comfort to realise that Gabrielle was never likely to be anyone's, now or in the future. He didn't want her lonely and celibate, even if that meant there was no one to be jealous of. He wanted the impossible.

It must be love, he concluded grimly as he let the knocker drop on the imposing front door. *So cope with it. Bite your lip and keep it to yourself. Learn to live with it and without her, and focus on what you can control, like finding the best man for Jamie.*

If Templeton could afford this house his practice was profitable and fashionable. It remained to be seen how effective he was, although the replies he had received from his hasty notes to fellow officers who had suffered head injuries in combat and who were now recovered and home in London had produced two direct recommendations and a mention of this man's name.

He handed his card to the butler who answered the door. 'I have no appointment, but I would be grateful if Dr Templeton could spare me a few minutes.'

'My lord.' The man bowed him inside. It seemed a title gave immediate access here. That did not particularly impress Gray. He didn't care whether Jamie was examined by the king's doctor or a slum physician, provided the man knew his business, he thought as he took a seat in an elegant waiting room. The local doctor had been reassuring, had almost convinced him that nothing was wrong, but he would not be satisfied without a second opinion.

'You look charming, Gabrielle.' Aunt Henrietta gave an approving nod towards the new evening gown revealed as Gaby handed her cloak to an attendant. 'And Gray is not here to see you. I do not understand the man.' She sounded a touch smug. 'How long is it since you last saw him?'

'Oh...three days, I think.' *Three days, six hours, twenty minutes...* 'He is sure to be anxious about his son and I doubt he wants to leave his mother just two days after she has made that long journey,' Gaby said, following her aunt towards the receiving line for Lady Carsington's reception.

'You are *sure* and you *doubt*? Are you not talking to him?' Aunt Henrietta gave her a searching look. 'Do I detect a little rift between the pair of you, dear?'

'Not at all, Aunt.' Gaby produced a smile. 'We try not to live in each other's pockets. So unfashionable, don't you think? And besides, we are not ready to make our understanding known—too obvious a degree of attention would betray it.'

'And why are you not ready?' her aunt demanded.

'Because, as Gray said, we cannot agree on the venue, or our wedding trip or any of the practical details and until we do there is no point in advertising the matter. I suppose we are both strong-willed people who have been used to having our own way. I am sure we will manage to compromise in time.' Gaby saw with relief that they had arrived at the end of the receiving line. That, at least, was sufficient to silence her aunt for a few minutes and once they were inside the reception she could surely escape her.

'Henrietta! Cooee, Henrietta!'

Even better, one of her aunt's bosom friends, rushing across the room, all flying ribbons and bobbing plumes, to pass on the latest titbit of gossip. Gaby ducked neatly to one side behind a large gentleman and his larger wife and emerged on the other side of two potted palms.

'Oh, excuse me.' A lady came from her right-hand side suddenly and almost knocked into Gaby. 'Did I tread on your toe? I do beg your pardon, but I was trying to avoid catching the eye of Mr Parsons, who is convinced I want to hear him recite his latest poetry. I made the mistake of admiring some out of sheer politeness last week and now he haunts me.'

'No good deed goes unpunished,' Gaby said and the other woman laughed. Her hair was dark and glossy, her eyes a deep brown, both like Gaby's, but her skin was the roses and cream that English ladies seemed to specialise in.

'I am Laurel, Lady Revesby. My husband is that improbably handsome blond creature over there looking politely interested while having his head talked off by Lady Jersey. I haven't met you before, have I? Are you new in London?'

'I live in Portugal.'

Lady Revesby dropped her fan, fumbled a catch and stared. 'Portugal?'

'Yes, the Douro Valley. I am Gabrielle Frost.'

'Frost's port?'

'You have heard of us? Ladies so rarely have—their menfolk guard the wine buying, and certainly the port drinking, so jealously.'

'I have heard of *you*.' Gaby could not interpret Lady Revesby's tone. 'Lord Leybourne was a neighbour when I was growing up. So was my husband. My godfather's daughter was Gray's first wife.'

'So you are aware that I know Lord Leybourne?' She knew and she sounded distinctly wary about the fact, Gaby realised. 'I presume you also know that he is my aunt's godson and was kind enough to escort me from Lisbon.'

'Yes. He had dinner with us the other night.' Lady Revesby looked directly at Gaby, her gaze frankly curious. 'Something is wrong with Gray.'

'His son had an accident, I am sure he told you.'

'He did and apparently the London doctor has given him a most satisfactory report and little Jamie is not suffering as much as a headache now.' The other woman was still studying her with those candid brown eyes. 'Will you come and talk with me? I am supposed to be sitting down or my husband will fuss. I tell him that I am three months pregnant, not sickening from some dire disease, but he takes no notice.' She stood on tiptoe and scanned the room. 'Look, that alcove near the string quartet is empty. There is only the one sofa and we can spread out and not be interrupted and the music will mean we can talk in confidence.'

'We need to talk in confidence?' Gaby enquired rather tartly, but she followed Lady Revesby none the less. 'And if you are worried about Lord Leybourne, then I suggest you speak to him about it,' she added as they sat down. Lady Revesby shifted uncomfortably on the sofa, her eyes on her reticule. 'That was not an accident just now when you bumped into me, was it? You knew who I was and you intended to speak to me.'

'Oh, very well, I admit it. Gray said you were intelligent—which is one of the few pieces of actual information we managed to get out of him. That and the fact that he obviously likes you. Even Giles couldn't get to the bottom of it and he and Gray always used to tell each other *everything*.'

The bottom of what, exactly? 'Then perhaps Gray does not want even his friends to interfere with his life.'

'Ouch!' Lady Revesby turned a reproachful face to Gaby. 'It is not interference out of simply curiosity. I owe him something to make up for the fact that I misjudged him for years.'

'Really? What could Gray possibly have done to earn such enmity? I thought he was generally considered above reproach.' She knew she sounded sarcastic and brittle, but she could not seem to help herself.

'Oh, don't be angry and sharp about it.'

Gaby started to rise and the other woman caught her hand. 'Please, don't go. Call me Laurel.' After that sudden burst of confidence Lady Revesby went back to examining her reticule with painful intensity.

'You can call me Gabrielle, Laurel. Listen, whatever it is in the past that worries you so, I have no desire to hurt Gray. If you confide in me I most certainly will not break your confidence and I have to admit to being curious about his wife, if that is what this concerns.'

'I thought you might be interested. He is so silent on the subject that it is enough to arouse the curiosity of a stone! Well, as I said, we all grew up together. I did not know it then, but my father and Giles's father always intended for us to marry. All I knew was that Giles was my friend—I was too young to have any other kind of feelings for him.

'Then one summer, when I was just beginning to be aware of men as something…different, and particularly aware of Giles, I overheard him and Gray talking in the hayloft. I know now they were fantasising as young men will. But they were talking about Portia, my godfather's daughter. She wasn't much older than I was, but far more mature and very, very lovely. I did not realise that what I was overhearing was wishful thinking—I thought the two of them had been... That they had seduced Portia. I was so upset I ran back to the house looking for somewhere to hide and overheard our fathers—mine and Giles's and Portia's—discussing Giles and me becoming betrothed.'

'Goodness...' Gaby breathed. 'You must have been confused and upset to put it mildly.'

Laurel grimaced. 'I stormed in, all righteous indignation about the pair of them and poor Portia. But she had been eavesdropping, too, I discovered when she promptly rushed into the room and had hysterics. It was dreadful. I refused to have anything to do with Giles. Godpapa was insisting that either Giles or Gray marry Portia. They were furious and humiliated and said they would do no such thing because they had done nothing to deserve it. That set Portia off again. Then the two of them took off to London—Giles joined his cousin who was off to Lisbon on a diplomatic mission and Gray joined the army.'

'Good Lord. They must have been very young.'

'Only just eighteen. Gray's father supported

him and bought him a commission, although Giles's father was livid that his plans for the pair of us were thwarted. They were estranged for some time, although it is all right now. But Gray felt guilty about Portia because she almost refused to have her Season and was ice-cold to all her suitors when she did come out. So eventually he proposed and she accepted him which was a grave mistake by both of them because they really were *not* happy together.'

'So he married her out of a sense of responsibility, even though he had done nothing beside indulge in some loose talk with his friend in private?'

'She was lovely enough to turn a man's brain to porridge,' Laurel said ruefully. 'Anyway, she died giving birth to the twins and, ridiculous as it might sound, I think he felt guilty because he did not love her.'

'I can understand that, I think. All the time they were married he was probably wishing he had never proposed and that he wasn't married and then, when she died, he would have felt awful because he somehow wished it on her. Poor woman.'

Poor Gray, trapped by his own sense of honour.

'Poor both of them. Giles and I were lucky. We found each other again, years later.'

They sat in silence for a while as the string quartet worked its way through its repertoire of light music.

'Is Gray unhappy now because of you?' Laurel asked abruptly. 'Have you turned him down?'

'I— Oh, no, look. Gray is here.'

Chapter Eighteen

Gray emerged through the crowd by the doors looking starkly handsome, all in black and white except for a flash of ruby from his cravat pin and the gold of his watch chain across his admirably flat stomach. She knew how those muscles felt under her fingertips. She knew where the skin was unexpectedly soft, where the dark hair revealed and concealed, how Gray had twitched when her finger circled his navel and how he had laughed when she teased him for being ticklish.

He was not laughing now. His face was the bland mask he adopted for social occasions. There was a deceptive half-smile on his lips and that tiny frown line between his brows as he surveyed the room. Then he saw them and it deepened into a furrow as his eyes narrowed.

'Oh, blast,' Laurel murmured. 'He's seen us. He looks furious.'

'And he's coming over.' Gaby felt a strong urge to flee, although quite where to, she had no idea. Hiding behind the sofa was clearly impossible and they had trapped themselves in their alcove.

'Lady Revesby. Miss Frost.'

'Don't be stuffy, Gray,' Laurel said with a laugh that had an edge of nervousness.

'And don't play the airhead with me, Laurel. I've known you since you were six and I can tell when you are up to something at forty paces.'

'Very well, Gray, if you must have it, we are talking about you, of course.'

Gaby almost bit her tongue.

'That is hardly a surprise,' he said, the treacherous false smile curving his lips. 'You don't know each other and I must be the only thing you have in common. Besides you, Laurel, have never been able to resist interfering.'

'Then you admit there is something to interfere in?'

'Hasn't Miss Frost told you all her secrets? I would beware, Miss Frost, Laurel carries the equivalent of thumbscrews with her. You'll be pouring your most intimate confidences into her ear before you know where you are.'

'No, I have told her no secrets and no confidences, Lord Leybourne. I have been hearing all about Lady Revesby's own romantic marriage.'

'And what led up to it, no doubt.' There was no hint of a smile, false or genuine, now.

'That, too.'

He was angry, she realised suddenly, with a stab of alarm. She had seen Gray in many moods, but never furious. It was cold anger, controlled anger, that showed in his eyes, in the way he held himself, not in his voice.

'You will do me the favour of walking with me for a while, Miss Frost.' That was not a request.

What could he do if she refused? Drag her to her feet and haul her around the room? Throw her over his shoulder and march outside to the terrace? She searched for the least provocative way to refuse, but beside her Gaby could feel Laurel's tension, and across the room she could see Aunt Henrietta watching them. The last thing she could afford at the moment was a display of antagonism towards Gray, or George would be on her doorstep, primed for courtship by his mother.

'I must say that a breath of fresh air would be welcome, it is becoming very stuffy in here. If you will excuse me, Lady Revesby? It was a pleasure to meet you and I do hope you will call.' She took one of the cards that had just arrived from the stationer and handed it to Laurel, ignoring the sensation that she was standing next to a man about to hiss with impatience like a boiling kettle.

Not that it showed on Gray's face, Gaby thought as she placed her fingertips on his proffered arm and allowed herself to be led towards the terrace doors. It was a fine night, unseasonably warm for almost the end of October, and several couples and one small but noisy group were already out on the sheltered flagstoned area amidst lanterns and a scattering of small tables.

Gray selected a table in the far corner, pulled out the chair with its back to the house for her and sat facing outwards beside her. 'I gather Laurel sought you out.'

'She is concerned about you.'

He made a sound that might almost have been a snarl. 'It seems to be my fate to be surrounded by women of exquisite sensibility.'

'Tosh,' Gaby said, startling a fleeting smile out of him. 'I have a conscience that I pay attention to. That requires no great sensibility. Laurel is a friend of yours, so she is concerned about you and sensitive to your moods. That leaves the late Lady Leybourne. Was she the woman of exquisite sensibility who made you desperately uncomfortable with female emotion?'

'My wife was a very beautiful woman who cultivated sensitivity to a fine art. I presume Laurel has told you all about that summer afternoon in the hayloft?'

'And two young men exchanging fantasies? Yes. But why on earth did you feel you had to offer for her? Surely the fathers involved knew all too well how the youthful male brain functions and weren't loading shotguns and sending for the parson?'

'Portia was hysterical, Laurel was furious and neither of us could get a word in edgeways, even if we hadn't been incoherent with embarrassment and humiliation. We took off for London before things calmed down and Portia's father realised that she had not been ravished by a pair of youthful libertines. But Portia, it seemed, did not get over it. I heard from my mother that she was unwed and was refusing to treat her numerous would-be suitors with anything but cold disdain.'

'I see. She had concluded that "all men are beasts," as my maiden aunt Clara used to pronounce, and you felt guilty.'

'Exactly. And then my mother and Portia's mother put their heads together. Her mama decided that marrying her was the least I could do and my mother was, not surprisingly, impressed by the size of her dowry. It was put to me that I had a duty to her and she was persuaded that marriage to a serving officer who was out of the country for months, if not years, at a time was better than dwindling into a spinster aunt.'

'And she was very lovely,' Gaby said drily.

'Blonde, willowy, big blue eyes, curves…' Gray shrugged. 'I should have made an effort—instead I countered her imitation of an early Christian virgin martyr with cold politeness. I should have known better, tried harder to make her happy. I didn't.'

'And so should she. There were any number of people who she could have talked to, I would have thought.' Gaby tried to feel sympathy, but it was difficult. If Portia had been assaulted, or threatened, then it would be all too easy to sympathise. Gaby thought with an inward shudder of Andrew Norwood's determined attack. Of his mouth, hot and wet on hers, of his hands on her breasts, fumbling with her skirts. Of his strength, too much for hers.

But Portia had suffered shock and embarrassment after a second-hand report of some reprehensible, and entirely predictable, adolescent behaviour. Laurel, her shock fuelled by a jealousy she was probably unaware of, had stirred up an almighty row, the fathers had overreacted, Portia had responded with hysteria and the young men themselves had made matters infinitely worse by fleeing the scene, giving the entire episode an importance it did not merit.

She remembered how her own father had dealt with her brother when he had been caught sniggering over a group of village girls he had come across bathing in their shifts in the river: a tanned backside and a lecture on the conduct befitting a gentleman. The ladies of the household were not supposed to know, of course, although no one could miss the ginger way Thomas sat down for a day or two, or the way he blushed whenever a female came within speaking range.

'No doubt you should have tried harder, but I imagine that coming home on leave and having to attempt to build bridges afresh every time can't have been easy. Every time she saw you, you must have seemed harder and tougher and more difficult to reach. Anyway, it doesn't mean you would be a bad husband to a different wife, if that is what is stopping you remarrying.'

'What is stopping me remarrying now is the refusal of the lady in question to accept me.'

* * *

'You know why I refuse.' There was more than a hint of gritted teeth about Gabrielle's response, but there was something else. *Surely not a shimmer of tears as the torchlight made stars that glimmered in the brown depths of her eyes?*

'Yes. I know and I understand.' He put certainty into his voice. Conviction. 'And yet I cannot help but feel we can do better than this. Find a compromise.'

'Compromise?' Gabrielle said indignantly. 'Who would be compromising? Me. I was reading Mary Wollstonecraft the other night. *"A wife is as much a man's property as his horse or his ass; she has nothing she can call her own."* Marrying a decent man, one she…respects, makes no difference.'

A footman came out with a loaded tray while Gray wrestled with that. 'I need a drink. I am usually good at riddles, but this one has me at a stand.'

He had to walk away from her, catch his breath, which appeared to be tied in a knot in his chest.

I love her and I think she loves me, or so very nearly. But she cannot trust me and so I have to let her go.

And he had to stop saying things that would

make it more difficult for Gabrielle, even if the difficulty was simply making her feel sorry for him and guilty as a result. He understood enough about guilt to know now that it didn't have to be logical to hurt, to be an ulcer on the soul. Her lack of trust in him hurt, though, he realised, illogical though it was. Why should she trust him when the experience of the women around her, the law, the attitude of every man she met reinforced her fears?

The footman proved to be carrying champagne glasses and another followed behind him with a tray of canapés. Gray directed them both to the table and sat down again to face Gabrielle across four glasses and an array of lobster patties and assorted savoury oddments.

'Are we expecting anyone else?' The sparkle that might, or might not, have been tears had vanished and her smile was back, even if it was a teasing one.

'I thought we both needed the sustenance.' Gray lifted his glass. 'To the ghost of Alexander the Great and inspiration on how to untangle our own Gordian knot, because I think this is the same sort of unsolvable puzzle.'

'Alexander cut it with his sword because he said the prophesy did not state *how* it was to be untied,' Gabrielle said. 'It seemed the oracle was satisfied with his solution because he *did* become King of the Phrygians. We have no kingdom to conquer and I doubt that the Greek gods are keeping a watchful eye on us.' She sounded almost as though this was not personal any longer, he realised. Gabrielle was a practical woman, a strong one. Perhaps she was already putting whatever feeling she had for him aside, facing up to the fact that they would part, preparing to regret it for a while.

'True.' Gray drained his glass and reached for another. He was not prepared to give up. Not on her, not on himself. Not yet. Something was nagging at the back of his mind, but all it resolved itself into was one of his tutors—Mr Turner, was it? Or the one before him with bad breath?—prosing on about Plutarch. In the original Greek. He ate a lobster patty, but it provided no inspiration.

Gabrielle put down her glass and the tiny noise brought his attention back to the present. All four glasses were empty. That, at least, was something he could deal with. Gray raised one hand to summon the waiter and saw Gabrielle shiver. 'You are cold. We will go in.'

'It isn't that.' She had gone pale, he saw in the flickering torchlight. 'Lord Appleton has just come out on to the terrace. I had not realised he was here. He looked at me in such…such a strange way.'

'It is just the light.' Gray glanced over at the major, who stood out like a red punctuation mark against the dark-clad men around him by the doors. He did appear to be looking in their direction, that was true. Gabrielle still seemed uncomfortable and he realised that he had almost forgotten Norwood's death, the dark secret that haunted her.

'Let me take you inside and then I will distract him if he makes you uneasy.'

'Thank you.' Her chin was up, her smile was bright as she rose and went with him, and Gray wondered at her courage. She was safe, he was sure, having heard her story, but even so the trauma must have left deep scars. Gabrielle greeted Appleton pleasantly, then glanced behind him. 'I see my aunt waving to me, she must have wondered where I had vanished to. If you will excuse me, gentlemen.' Then she was gone. When Gray watched her and saw that Lord George Welford was standing beside his stepmother he realised that Gabrielle's desire to escape the proximity of Appleton must be pressing.

'You are still in town, then,' he remarked, too uneasy to think of anything more intelligent to say.

'Yes, sir. But not on leave, I'm working at Horse Guards for a few months. Helping catch up on the filing,' he added with a smile that struck Gray as false. And he'd addressed him as *sir*, which he no longer should now that Gray was not a senior officer any more. They were equal in rank now. Clearly the major's thoughts were firmly on military matters. Matters from the past?

'The filing?' Horse Guards was the army's headquarters, not a bad place for an ambitious officer to be in time of peace, but an officer with Appleton's field experience was not going to be used as a lowly clerk.

The other man grimaced. 'Clearing up intelligence material from the Peninsula, sir.'

'The French are no threat now, surely, whatever their intelligence officers might have got up to during the war.'

'It isn't the French we're worried about.' The major glanced around. 'I'd welcome your advice, frankly. But we can't talk here. Are you committed to stay longer or would you be able to join me for a nightcap? I've a bolthole in Albany.'

'I will, with pleasure, if I can help. But I'm a

civilian now. Call me Gray, all my friends do. If you aren't going against orders talking about this?'

'Not to a senior officer with your record, sir—Gray. I'd welcome your advice because you know about the situation in the Douro Valley.'

Gray did not miss the movement of his eyes towards the reception room, where Gabrielle was still talking to Lord Welford, fanning herself with abrupt, nervy flicks of her wrist.

'I was there for a while and reminded myself of the topography recently,' he allowed.

'Charming lady, Miss Frost. Always thought so when we were stationed in the area.'

'Yes. Most attractive and intelligent, too,' Gray said, doing his best to sound objective. 'I'm doing my godmother a favour by squiring her around a little. Still, she looks settled enough now, I think I can come off-duty.'

'I thought you might have…an interest,' Appleton said as they made their way towards their hostess to thank her and make their excuses.

'Not me,' Gray said, putting amusement into his voice. 'I'm steering well clear of the parson's mousetrap for the present, however tempting the cheese might be.'

I used to be good at acting, to hiding my thoughts and feelings. Now...

Once it was necessary to show the face that his men needed to see—stern or dashing, confident or cautious. He'd needed to cultivate the art of hiding his feelings from senior officers, too.

I think you're an idiot, General. No, I'm not sure I'll come out of this alive, but I'll give it a damn good go...

It seemed the feelings he had for Gabrielle were too close to the surface to allow for easy subterfuge about anything.

They were close enough to the back entrance to Albany to walk, making small talk as they went about old comrades, a good bootmaker Appleton had found, the latest opera singer taking the town by storm.

A batman appeared as Appleton unlocked the door, but he dismissed his military servant with a nod. 'We'll look after ourselves, Hodges. You take yourself off to bed.'

'Sir. The decanters are in the sitting room.'

They settled in front of the banked-up fire, brandy glasses in hand. Gray sat back, summoned up the old, hard-learned focus of army days and ignored the unpleasant sensation under his breastbone. Apprehension. A good officer did not admit to fear, however much he might feel it. But this was not fear for himself.

'I'm tidying up some loose threads around Major Norwood's last few months,' Appleton began abruptly. 'His servant told us he was spending a lot of time focused on the area around Quinta do Falcão.'

'Miss Frost's estate.'

'Yes. Then there were rumours about a lone French officer being seen in the area in uniform once or twice—and some sightings that may have been him dressed as a local man.'

'Someone Norwood had turned as an informer, do you think?'

'No. He kept notes of those in code and we've broken that. There were a couple of Frenchmen, but we know about them.'

'And what conclusions do you draw? Good brandy, this.'

Appleton swirled the liquid in his glass. 'It is. The last of my father's smuggled cask before peace broke out.' He shifted to put the glass down and Gray read unease in the movement. 'Miss Frost had a younger brother.'

'I believe so. With the *guerrilheiros*, I believe. Brave lad and tragically young when he died.'

'Yes.' Appleton cleared his throat. 'The thing is, there was definitely a source leaking information about our troop movements in the area and that stopped after young Frost was killed. Then it began again, more or less at the time this mysterious Frenchman starts being seen around the quinta.'

'Are you saying that Frost was a traitor?' Gray swallowed the furious rebuttal. 'And then what? Miss Frost takes over where he left off?'

'Good God, no! *He* might have been, of course, but I doubt it. He was hardly more than a lad. No, I was thinking one of the people on her estate, the winery manager, for example. They travel all over the area, those people. No one takes any notice of them and they could be up to anything.'

'Such a man would be loyal to the family,' Gray said. 'All those workers have been with the Frosts for generations, apparently. If Frost had been turned, the man might have carried on out of loyalty, or conviction—or just for the money— but I cannot for a moment believe that a patriotic youngster, as Thomas Frost seems to have been, would have turned traitor. He was killed by the French, for heaven's sake. Besides, even if he was and one of his men kept up the business, why would you be pursuing the matter now? He is dead and surely there are better things for an experienced officer to be doing than chasing down Portuguese peasants?'

'Because the man might have killed Norwood.' He shifted uncomfortably again, picked up his glass and drained the remaining brandy. 'And I have an unpleasant suspicion that Miss Frost knows something about this.'

'You just said—'

'I don't mean that she was a spy. She's a lady, after all.'

You should see her with a knife...

'But if she saw something of the confrontation that had Norwood killed she might be keeping silent out of loyalty to her workers. Or—and this is what really does concern us—one of the neighbouring families might have been involved. She is very close to the MacFarlanes, is she not?'

'This sounds like a complete farrago of nonsense,' Gray said crisply. 'It isn't even making bricks without straw. You haven't got the clay or the water either. All you have is a brave young man being killed fighting for his country, a grieving sister, reports of a mysterious Frenchman in the area and a dead riding officer who might have been killed at any point upstream from where he was found. And, frankly, from what I've heard of his activities, it was more likely a furious father or vengeful husband than an agent for the French. The local port producers of English and

Scottish extraction have—and had—everything to gain from an Allied victory and nothing at all to gain from a French one.'

'How so? The French had a substantial war chest for bribery.'

'Do you think the French, victorious, would encourage the production of port? Britain is the biggest market and always has been, Portugal is England's oldest ally. The French would ruin the industry.'

'A good point. And I had heard rumours about Norwood's womanising,' Appleton admitted.

'More than womanising. He was not above using force to get what he wanted.' That was true as far as Gabrielle was concerned, so even if Norwood had never forced another unwilling woman Gray was quite happy to give the impression that he was.

The other man's expression showed his distaste. 'Disgraceful. How did you know?' He narrowed his eyes as the obvious thought stuck him. Gray could have kicked himself for elaborating. 'Not Miss Frost, surely?'

'Certainly not. Local young women,' Gray said. 'Don't ask me how I know, I was told in confidence.'

'Then this could have nothing to do with the Frosts.' It was not quite a question.

'Upon my honour.' Gray spoke without having to think about it, then braced himself for the self-loathing. He had just pledged his honour in a lie to a gentleman, to a fellow officer. But there was not a twinge. His conscience, his precious honour, were both silent.

Because I love her and I trust her and that was the right thing to do.

'I think you are chasing a wild goose with this,' he added.

'I suspect you are correct,' Appleton said with a sigh. 'It felt as though I had a glimpse of something—the tail feathers of the proverbial goose vanishing around the corner, more like! Now I know about Norwood's activities I have to agree. That is a much more likely explanation of his murder than a spy among the British port producers. They are all too ready with their knives in Portugal—just like the Spanish. And if the murder is unconnected with the French, then the rest is just too vague to trouble further with. Let's open another bottle and drink to new beginnings.'

Chapter Nineteen

Two hours later, taking care how he placed his feet, Gray made his somewhat unsteady way home. Occasionally he prodded his conscience, much as he might a sore tooth, to see if it had woken up and was preparing to give him hell for lying on his honour. Not a twinge.

'It is all about trust,' he informed an unresponsive lamp post. 'I trust her. I just need her to trust me. And why should she? She's an intelligent woman with no reason to believe that once I'd got a ring on her finger I'd behave any differently from any other man.'

The lamp post offered no counterargument to this depressing statement, so Gray wandered on through the dark streets, in and out of the pools of light cast by the lanterns outside the smart town houses he passed. He was aware that he was a trifle bosky, but not so far gone that he did not keep a firm grip on his cane and an eye on the shadows, alert for trouble. The wealthier the district the richer the spoils for any footpad brave enough to try for a victim there.

'It's *empistosýni*… That's what it is,' he informed the startled footman who opened the door to him.

'My lord?'

'Trustfulness. That's what we need.' So what was he doing thinking in Greek? That damned Alexander the Great again. Definitely drunk. Most definitely time to go to bed and dream of knots.

'The Terringtons' ball is always an *event*,' Aunt Henrietta said, ten days later. 'You cannot miss it.'

'A ball before the Season starts?' Gaby asked. 'Surely no one is holding balls in early November.'

'Augusta Terrington noticed how many people are up in town at this time of year and decided that a ball held now would stand out far more than one held when absolutely everyone was doing the same thing. And now people come early just to be in London in the hope of an invitation.'

'So what is so special about it, other than being so early?'

'Augusta transforms the ballroom with a different theme every year and guests are asked to dress accordingly. There are never any half measures—last year the theme was The Frozen North and even the footmen were wearing white from head to toe, their hair powdered with silver dust.'

'So what is the theme this year, Stepmama?' Lord Welford roused himself from the pose of languid boredom that he appeared to think made him appear a sophisticated man about town. 'One needs time to find the perfect costume.'

'It is still a secret,' Aunt Henrietta said, leaning forward and lowering her voice as though they were in the middle of Almack's and not in her own drawing room with only the three of them present. 'But my abigail heard from Lady Fortune's woman, who is walking out with one of the Terrington footmen that it is something to do with the Ottoman Empire because the staff are all being fitted with baggy trousers in silk and the footmen are going to be wearing embroidered waistcoats over *bare chests*!'

Gaby suppressed a snort of unladylike amusement as George puffed out his own not-very-impressive chest. 'I do not think that gentlemen should reveal so much flesh, do you, Aunt?'

'Certainly not. You may appear the most magnificent pasha while remaining decently clad, George.' He subsided sulkily. 'Naturally I have procured an invitation for you, Gabrielle. You can partner George. I will co-ordinate the costumes.'

'It is most thoughtful of you, Aunt, but if Gray is attending then I would not want to appear to be the partner of another gentleman.'

'If he is there. I have scarcely seen him and he hardly seems very attentive, given that the pair of you maintain you have an attachment.'

'We *do* have an attachment, as you put it, Aunt. And surely George will attend with Miss Henderson?'

'Blasted poet,' George muttered. 'Long-haired prancing ninny.'

'Language, George. The ungrateful chit has got herself betrothed to Lucian Fairweather. You must have seen him—blond curls worn too long, a languishing manner, a perfect profile—of which he is well aware—and far too much money for his own good.'

'Which he spends on calfskin editions of his blo—confounded poems,' George snapped. 'He certainly does not need her dowry.'

'I am so sorry, George,' Gaby said, biting the inside of her cheek to keep her expression suitably serious. 'I do hope your affections were not deeply engaged.'

'She was never the right bride for him,' her aunt said when George glowered sulkily. 'If only you were not involved with Gray, my dear.'

Well, that is frank speaking at last!

'I thought you were fond of your godson?'

'I am, of course I am. But—' Aunt Henrietta fixed an expression of deep concern on her face. 'There is no getting around the fact that he would be a most unsatisfactory husband, fond as I am of him. His poor wife.' She sighed.

'I know all about Portia.'

'You do? But he never speaks of her.'

'I *am* his betrothed,' Gaby pointed out.

'Oh. And he has been single again for so long— he is a terrible rake, you know.'

'I have seen nothing of such behaviour.'

Except that a man does not learn to kiss, to make love, like that from having one unsympathetic wife and a lot of book study. Not that I have to worry about his habits for much longer...

'Naturally a maiden lady would not know about it and he is intelligent enough to pull the wool over your eyes.'

Gaby ran a range of retorts over in her mind. *Poppycock* seemed the most restrained. 'I am not

a virgin and I have been his lover' was the frank-
est and most likely to send Aunt into strong hysterics. It had best be *poppycock*.

'Lord Leybourne, my lady,' the butler announced before she could say anything.

'Good afternoon, Godmama. George. Gabrielle,
my love. I thought you might be here.'

My love. She smiled up as him as he bent over
and dropped a kiss on her cheek. She only had
to move her head a trifle and his lips would meet
hers. Gabrielle stayed quite still and breathed in
the heady scent of lemon verbena, starched linen
and warm Gray.

'Love you,' he murmured.

'No,' she whispered back. 'Stop play-acting.'
He had moved so that his back was to the others,
giving them a moment of precarious privacy.

*Don't do this to me, not when I have to face
people.*

Gray straightened, his eyes still intent on hers
with a message she could not read. Dared not
read. Warning to maintain the pretence or a plea
for belief?

'No, you do not,' she said again.

*Please don't love me. Please don't make this
any harder.*

Did he think that a declaration of love was all

it would take to change her mind, make her sur-render?

'I wish you could trust me,' Gray said, his smile quite gone. Then he turned. 'Thank you, no, God-mama, I am not in need of a cup of tea. I have been looking for Gabrielle to see if she has a card for Lady Terrington's ball.'

'Aunt has kindly procured one for me. Will you be attending also, Gray?'

'Of course. My valet is assembling my costume even as we speak, which is why I have hastened round to ensure that we are in harmony, Gabri-elle.'

'How do you know the theme?' Aunt Henrietta demanded indignantly.

'As soon as Tompkins discovered that it was the prestige event for this time of year he set about identifying sources in the Terrington household. A good valet is about more than well-polished boots.'

'What are you going as?' Gaby asked before George, who was scowling at his own Hessians, could speak.

'One of the sultan's Varangian guards. I thought perhaps you could be a lady from the harem.'

'The harem? Most unsuitable,' Aunt protested.

'The harem is the women's quarters within a

household,' Gray said with more patience than Gaby was feeling. 'It implies no impropriety, rather the opposite, in fact, Godmama.' He ignored her disbelieving snort and turned back to Gaby. 'A friend of mine was in the diplomatic mission to Constantinople a few years ago and brought back a number of garments and trinkets for his wife and daughters. I called on him earlier and they are very happy to lend you the makings of an outfit, Gabrielle, if you go round to see them.'

'How kind. When would it be convenient to call, do you think?' *Say now.*

'Now,' Gray said obligingly. 'If that would suit.'

'But I was going to dress you, Gabrielle,' her aunt interjected. 'I want to make certain that your costume is perfectly proper.'

'It is very kind of you, Aunt. But if these ladies have the genuine costumes it would save you both time and cost and I would not want to put you to any inconvenience or expense for the world.'

They escaped eventually, out into a faint drizzle that dampened the air and made the pavement shine with wetness. 'The fine weather has gone. Autumn is well and truly here,' Gray said as he helped her into the vehicle waiting at the kerb. 'It is a good thing that Godmama has not realised it is raining or she'd never let you go off in something so scandalous as a closed carriage.'

'She was trying to convince me that you are a hopeless rake. George's little romance, the one with the promising dowry attached, has evaporated. Miss Henderson has fixed her heart on a wealthy poet.' Gaby tried to breathe evenly as Gray settled beside her and reached up to rap on the roof. She could not, must not, let him affect her so. It was over, however much he might call her *his love.*

'I take it you are not tempted by George's few charms?'

'No. My affections are fixed on an utterly impossible rakehell earl,' Gaby said as lightly as she could. Let him think she was teasing, she thought in the split second before she was in his arms and being comprehensively, deliciously, kissed.

'We must not, you know we must not.' She gasped the moment he set her free. They were both breathing hard, she realised, both of them leaning back against the squabs side by side. Only their fingers touched. It felt like their entire bodies.

'I am not made of stone,' Gray said. 'Nor, I'll have you know, am I a rakehell.'

'I know you are not. I'm not made of stone either.'

His hand opened and curled around hers, strong

and sure—and as powerless as she was in the face of circumstance. 'Wishing it was otherwise will not help and I am not Alexander the Great, or any other hero of antiquity, to solve this conundrum.'

'Not all puzzles have a solution,' Gaby said. 'And this is not one you can slash through with an axe, not without causing endless damage.'

'This ball will be magical, a fantasy out of time, out of place. We will dance every dance, cause a scandal, have a memory to hold. You can be so alarmed at the scandal in the cold light of day that you can use it as an excuse for Godmama when you break off the engagement and go back to Portugal.'

'Oh, yes.'

'Yes to the alarm or yes to the dances?'

'To the dances, of course. But perhaps not every one—you have to live in London after I have gone, after all. Just the waltzes, don't you think? That would be shocking enough. But how is your little boy? I would have asked at once, but I did not think you would want to hear Aunt's opinions on childrearing in general, the treatment of head injuries or all the things you are undoubtedly doing wrong because of not taking her advice earlier.'

'He is doing even better than he was when I

wrote to thank you for your note and the toys you sent for the children. Jamie is flourishing, the doctors are all in agreement that he is perfectly well, although he may never recall the hours leading up to the accident. Joanna is happy now her twin is no longer sick and Mama is completely ignoring my pleas for her to rest and is cutting a swathe through every fashionable establishment in London, every art exhibition and all the intellectual salons to which her contacts can give her the entrée. She says she feels ten years younger and I live in dread of some silver-haired charmer marrying her out of hand.'

'I am so glad.' She dared do no more than squeeze his hand. 'You must have been frantic with worry.'

'When he opened his eyes and said, "Papa, what are you doing here?" I thought I would never ask for anything else, ever again, the relief was so great. I'm an ungrateful devil still to yearn after something I cannot have.'

'Gray, I—'

'Gabrielle, you do not have to apologise. Never that. It is exactly the same as it would be for me if someone told me that on marriage I lost total control of Winfell, of all the estates, of my seat in the House of Lords, that everything would become the possession of my wife. It would not matter how much I loved her, I would be losing total control of something that was at the core of who I was, *why* I was. There are very few women, other than monarchs, who face what you face in terms of what they surrender on marriage.'

'You are too understanding,' she said, piqued. 'Could you not rant and rave a little?'

He became very still and suddenly she was aware of how big he was, how powerful. 'You think me understanding? You think that simply because I have enough intelligence to see what the problem is for you and sufficient empathy to sympathise, that I feel civilised about this? Resigned, perhaps?'

She had propped her umbrella against the seat between them. Gray picked it up in both hands and bent it—metal struts, strong malacca handle—until it snapped. 'I want to break things, hit things,' he said through clenched teeth and hurled the limp, ruined thing on to the seat in front of them to lie like a broken bird.

Gaby gasped and he turned on the seat to face her. *No, he is not feeling civilised. Not resigned.*

'I could smash this carriage,' Gray said in that dangerous voice. 'I could swear and I could rant and, my God, I could rave. I could have you sobbing, terrified, distressed.' He leaned forward sharply so his face was too close to hers for Gaby to focus. 'Is that what you want? Is that what it would take for you to believe that I care? Is that what it would take for you to trust what I say?'

Gaby shook her head. *'No.'*

'No, she says. What about this?' Gray's hands closed on her shoulders.

The kiss was hard and dangerous. There was anger that made her tremble, even as she kissed him back as fiercely. She should have been afraid, but there was despair there, tenderness there, an emotion that made his hands shake with something that was not rage.

He let her go at last and she fell back, hating herself for stripping that control from him.

'Anger breaks things,' he said after a while, into silence that had grown thick with unspoken words, feelings. 'It does not bend them to our will.'

'Only this will not bend, only break, whatever we do,' she said sadly.

'We have arrived. I will take you in and introduce you to the Gibsons and send the carriage round to the mews to take you home when you have finished. I will buy you a new umbrella.'

And a new heart?

The carriage halted. Gaby straightened her hat, ordered her breathing into submission and found a social smile.

Gray, it seemed, had been doing much the same. 'I look forward to meeting my exotic lady of the harem,' he said lightly as he helped her out.

'And I my valiant guard,' she returned in the same tone. It was that or burst into tears.

Gray lifted her hand to his lips. 'Who would die for you, my lady.' He was not smiling.

'I am not at all certain that is decent.' Aunt Henrietta, who was draped in enough silk brocade to upholster an entire suite of furniture in the Prince Regent's Carlton House, studied Gaby's costume with apparent alarm.

'Nothing is actually transparent, Aunt.' She had shed her evening cloak into the hands of a maid in the ladies' retiring room and Lady Orford was seeing the ensemble for the first time.

It had taken over a week, and the work of Gaby's favourite modiste to convert the diaphanous silks and gauzes Mrs Gibson and her daughters had pressed on her into something that looked authentic without being utterly scandalous and without damaging the original garments.

'Yes, but it looks as though it ought to be. And it clings.'

Gaby was rather enjoying having a bosom that merited the name rather than the modest curves that the fashions of the day revealed. The tight little bodice lifted and compressed and presented every inch to maximum advantage and contrasted with the filmy layers of silken skirts that flirted around her ankles—her bare ankles above frivolous little sandals with bells on them.

'I do have a veil,' she offered.

'Ha! That little scrap? All it does is dangle across the lower part of your face from ear to ear and blow about in the breeze, just like that apology for a head covering does.'

'All the ladies will be similarly dressed, Aunt. And besides, everyone is staring at the footmen and their chests.'

Her aunt gave a muted shriek, but Gaby was not surprised that she stopped protesting and led the way out. The footmen's costumes—fortunately for the poor men's blushes—were not as racy as they had sounded. The edges of the waistcoats were caught together in the front so that no—*whisper it*—nipples were on show, much as giggling young ladies might crane their necks. However, a fine array of muscular arms and broad shoulders were revealed and the baggy trousers tucked into soft kid boots were undoubtedly dashing.

But not as dashing as the apparition who appeared in front of her. 'My lady, I am sent to protect you.'

Oh, yes. It was Gray, his hair allowed to go its own way, only restrained by a narrow leather band around his brow. He had apparently not shaved the day before and dark stubble shadowed his cheeks and chin. A leather jerkin with short sleeves covered his torso and upper arms—more or less—and he wore leather breeches with high boots. There was a curved sword in his belt and a predatory smile that turned her knees to jelly.

Who is going to protect me from you? she wondered, ignoring Aunt Henrietta's gasp of outrage.

'Thank you, Sir Knight.' She left, her hand on his arm, without a glance behind. This was an evening for magic, an evening of fantasy that would have to stand for all the reality she could not have and could only dream of when duty and responsibility and the satisfaction of creating liquid enchantment from grapes failed to keep the regrets at bay.

They missed the first dance by walking around admiring some costumes, laughing discreetly at others—the number of fat pashas was incredible, only matched by the number of ladies who should never have attempted filmy silk veiling.

'It was no exaggeration to say that Lady Terrington creates a fairyland,' Gaby said. Her half veil might be a total failure at concealing her identity, but it gave her the courage to ignore the curious and speculative looks they were attracting. Exquisite shades of pierced metal covered the lights throwing patterns of stars and crescents across the walls and ceiling. The colours were rich and strong, the draperies concealing and revealing alcoves and little set pieces of a fountain, or a statue half-covered in green climbers, a couch with bowls of fruit set around it, a pool with golden fish flickering in the limpid depths.

'The first set is over, the next is waltzes,' Gray said. 'Mine, I believe.'

'As you are frightening away any man who approaches me to ask for a dance, I have no choice,' Gaby said, mock severely.

Gray frowned at her, an impressive sight with his dark shadow of beard and his primitive clothing. 'No, you have no choice.' His voice was a growl and she surrendered easily as he led her out on to the floor.

They had never danced together before and beginning with a waltz was disturbingly like being in Gray's arms and making love. There was only flimsy silk between her and the bare skin of his forearms and nothing between her lips and the notch at the base of his throat, exposed by the slashed neckline of his leather shirt. If she leaned forward just a little, she could kiss him there. He smelled of male, her male. *Mine.*

Nor were the rhythms of the dance any help in maintaining her composure. She knew the basics and had a good musical sense, so she could manage the steps even though the waltz was not much danced in the company she kept in Portugal. But Gray was obviously an experienced dancer and her head whirled as he spun her round, the rise and swooping fall of the dance creating a dizzying sensuality that swept through her until it was all she could do to stop herself moving closer, pressing her lips to that tempting area of skin.

Chapter Twenty

When the music stopped and the dancers all finally swept to a halt Gaby had to hold on to Gray's forearms to steady herself. 'I need to sit down.'

'Dizzy?' Gray took her from the floor and into an alcove where they could watch the guests making ready for the next dance in the set.

'We have never danced before and it was rather overwhelming. I wanted to kiss your throat,' she whispered. 'That is a very provoking costume.'

'Now you see what we men have to put up with, ladies revealing expanses of flesh we are forbidden to touch.' Gray looked at her more closely. 'Are you sure it is not just the dance? You seem very pale.'

'It must be, I feel quite well.' But she didn't, Gaby realised. She felt a little faint and somehow…strange. 'It must be the strain of everything, that's all.' He had said nothing about love.

He must have realised he had been mistaken. Perhaps that burst of anger had cleared his thoughts, shown him his true emotions. She should be happy about that.

'Would you like something to eat? The supper room is not open yet, but I can ask one of the footmen for some biscuits? Or a glass of wine?'

'No, nothing, truly. I will sit quietly until the next dance in the set.'

'And we will do the most sedate waltz ever seen, I promise you.'

Gaby felt better by that dance and she almost laughed out loud as her dangerous Barbarian waltzed sedately, as promised. She found an appetite for supper, but oddly her favourite lobster patties did not appeal in the slightest and instead she wanted to try all the sweets, much to Gray's amusement.

'I think sugar is good for me,' she confided as they swept into the next set of waltzes. 'I feel so much better.' *And I still want to kiss you. All of you...*

Her gaze met her aunt's as she circled in the arms of a grey-haired gentleman of military bearing. Aunt Henrietta's raised eyebrows signalled more than a question. 'We are scandalising Aunt.'

'Excellent, it will do her no end of good. Where

is she? Oh, yes, I see. Is she disguised as a sofa, by any chance?'

'Er…no. I think she just kept draping herself in the hope of looking both exotic and entirely decent.'

They retreated to their alcove while the next set of country dances formed up, but Gaby was not entirely surprised when her aunt arrived.

'Godmama.' Gray stood and promptly had his chair occupied. 'Er…do make yourself comfort-able. I'll find another seat.'

By the time he returned with a spindly gilt chair, Aunt Henrietta was in full flow. 'One waltz after another and all with Gray! Have you no dis-cretion? There are Patronesses of Almack's pres-ent—all of them, I believe. You will find your vouchers have been withdrawn.'

'I have no intention of attending,' Gaby said. 'It really doesn't matter. I only want to dance with Gray.'

'But *waltzes* are so *fast.*'

'I danced a very slow one for the second,' Gray pointed out.

'And with you dressed like that, too—as if it isn't bad enough to have all these indecent footmen without you exposing your chest and your fore-arms. And you need a shave, for goodness' sake.'

'I'm one of the Varangian bodyguard. A Bar-barian.'

'Which means *bearded*,' Gaby explained.

'Latin *barba*.'

'I despair of the pair of you. And do not go sounding like a bluestocking, Gabrielle. It is not appropriate for a young lady.'

'No, Aunt.'

'Where has George got to? You should dance with him, at least.'

'I have promised only to dance with Gray. I'm sorry.'

Over her aunt's shoulder she saw Gray roll his eyes at her fib.

'Well, all I can say is that when the scandal sheets and the gossip columns pick this up and you both become notorious, do not blame me.' Lady Orford got to her feet and swept off.

'Have a glass of champagne and drink to rout-ing the enemy.' Gray raised a hand to summon a footman with a tray of glasses. 'Good God, there's Henry. How the devil did he get an invi-tation?'

Gaby hadn't seen Henry since the evening she had fled from his embrace and his offer to father her child. She knew it was cowardly, but she'd been glad of it—what on earth was the etiquette under such circumstances? She ought to speak to him, reassure him that he had done nothing to offend her. She should have written the next day, she thought guiltily.

'Gabrielle? What is wrong?' Gray was looking between her and Henry who was making his way towards them.

'Nothing,' she said so hastily it sounded guilty, although what on earth there was to feel guilty about, other than neglecting poor Henry, she couldn't think.

'You won't want to speak to him after what passed between you last time,' Gray said. He was on his feet and ready, she saw, to intercept his cousin who was attempting to get past two over-weight pashas. Henry himself was in a similar kind of costume, although looking slim and really rather dashing.

'Yes, I do,' Gaby said. 'What is the matter? You didn't say anything to him that time when we—'

'I kicked him out,' Gray said, apparently from between gritted teeth.

'You *what*? When you knew he was only trying to help me? No wonder he hasn't been to see me.'

'Good, because I warned him not to.'

'Gray, I am not your possession and Henry did

nothing—*nothing*—that I did not want him to do. Or do you think I lied about that?'

Carrying on a furious quarrel in hissed whispers on the edge of a crowded ballroom was not easy. In fact, they were beginning to attract attention.

'Henry, have you come to ask me to dance?' Gaby stepped away from Gray and put her hand on Henry's arm. He came to a halt, smiling at her, but with a wary eye on Gray.

'If you have one free, I would be honoured. I only wanted to ask how you were.'

'Oh, look, the next set is starting.' She was on the floor in the midst of the dancers, Henry looking confused but pleased, before Gray could do anything.

'I am so sorry Gray has been disagreeable,' she said the moment the figure brought them together. 'I thought he believed me that nothing had happened. I had to tell him because otherwise I don't know what conclusions he might have jumped to.'

'I think he did believe you.' The progress of the dance meant Henry had to join hands across the circle and ended up on the far side.

Gaby kept a bright smile on her face until her own turn left her once more beside him.

'Or, rather, his head tells him to trust me, but

his heart—that's another matter,' Henry said, as though there had been no break in the conversation.

'He's an idiot,' Gaby said fiercely, then retrieved her slipping smile. 'Where are you living now? Forgive me asking, but I know your resources are limited. It isn't eating into your passage money to get to America is it?'

'No, don't worry,' Henry said, as the gentleman opposite stepped forward and she had to join hands and be whirled down the set.

'Where are you living, then?' They both arrived breathless at the end of the set, marking time while everyone else had their turn at promenading down.

'Drab but decent rooms off Fleet Street.'

'Give me your address, please. I do not want you disappearing again.'

The music came to a resounding conclusion. Gaby curtsied, Henry bowed and led her off the floor. They were on the far side from Gray, who was making his way round to them.

'Oh, bother the man, he is determined to be possessive. Quick, scribble it down for me.'

'May I borrow your pencil?' Henry dug a card out of his breast pocket, turned it over and scribbled on the back with the little pencil Gaby should have been using to note partners on the ribs of her fan.

'How did you get an invitation?' Gaby asked, taking the pencil and slipping it into her reticule.

'Your aunt, Lady Orford. I bumped into her in the Strand outside Ackermann's the day before yesterday. She asked if I was still staying with Gray and I told her not. I suspect she realised something was amiss—I pokered up a bit, I'm afraid. Anyway, she said I simply must enjoy a great ball before I vanished to the other side of the world and promised me I would be admitted.'

'Did she indeed?' Gaby said. So, her wretched aunt suspected that Henry and Gray had fallen out and was now using poor Henry to drive a wedge between Gaby and Gray. 'Oh, dear, here comes Gray and he looks thunderous. You'd best slip away.'

'I don't like to—'

'And I don't like to have the pair of you brawling over me in public. Shoo!' She gave him a little push and, thankfully, he had the sense to do as she asked.

'What the devil is going on?' Gray demanded as he reached her side. She cast a harassed look behind her, but Henry's turban was lost in a sea of exotic headgear.

'I was apologising to your unfortunate cousin for him being tossed out of your house because you are jealous and unreasonable.'

'Me? Unreasonable? He's a guest in my house and he offers to bed my—'

'Will you be quiet?' Gaby saw a door standing a ajar, took Gray's arm and towed him through it. 'If anyone overheard you, what would they think?'

'No one would hear, not in that racket.' Gray's voice sounded loud in the deserted service corridor as the door swung closed on the ballroom.

'I am not your *anything*, Gray. Henry made his offer when I was even less to you and you know it. I told you nothing happened and I do not appreciate you failing to take my word for it.'

'I apologise.' He did not look apologetic, not with the frown on his face and the darkness in his eyes and his mouth—*oh, that mouth*—set in a severe line. 'I was not at my best the next morning and he guessed what had happened and he was…judgemental and far too protective of you for my liking.'

'You believe us now?' Gaby realised that she was feeling too hot, even though the corridor was cool. The lamps set along the wall seemed to flicker strangely. For a ghastly moment she thought she might be about to faint.

'Yes. Of course.' Then Gray's tone changed. 'Gabrielle? Are you all right, you've gone quite pale.'

'I don't think I am. Gray, could you take me home? I feel rather strange again.'

'Of course.' He stood and held out his hand. 'I have upset you. I'm sorry.' He pulled her gently to him and looked closely into her face. 'Or are you ill?'

'Just rather tired. Who would have thought that waltzing was so exhausting?'

'I'm not so sure. And it was a little upsetting, arguing about Henry and then the dance with him was rather energetic.' Gray tugged off his glove and laid his long fingers against her forehead. 'I hope you haven't caught anything—a cold, perhaps. You are not used to English weather and we sat outside for a long time the other evening. Here, let me just check no one is watching.' He opened the door, steered her out into the noise and heat of the crowded room, sheltered her with his body as they made their way out.

It was good to be cared for like this, Gaby thought as she let herself be handed over to a solicitous maid in the ladies' retiring room and wrapped in her cloak and seated in a comfortable chair while Gray called the carriage. It was weakening, of course, because she was not used to it and she would have to go back to looking after herself before very long. But the way he protected her was almost as pleasurable as his kisses. Perhaps more so.

He loves me and he is letting me go. Or perhaps he does not guess how very close I am to surrendering, to marrying him, to risking everything on trust.

'I worry about you,' he murmured as they settled into the carriage, a rug across her knees. 'I should have kept my temper with Henry and I should not have spoiled your evening with my suspicions.'

'I know you worry. And there is no need. Kiss me goodnight, Gray.'

It wasn't fair to ask him to kiss her and leave her, but Gaby knew, with sudden clarity, that this would be a final kiss. None of this was fair and she was the one who had to make the break. Gray thought she was strong, thought, perhaps, that she was ruthless.

How wrong he is.

It was a sweet kiss, a gentle, quite unsexual kiss. A caring kiss from a man who wanted to love her and cherish her and she broke it as soon as the carriage came to a halt.

'Goodnight, Gray. Don't call tomorrow. I think I will rest.' It was wrong to lie in the last words she'd speak to him. It was wrong that a letter would have to serve as both goodbye and apology. But perhaps it was best. Safest. It would take so little to push her into surrender, into doing what her heart pleaded for her to do, not what her head told her was right. Sensible. Wise.

Jane was in bed when Gaby arrived back in Half Moon Street, but light showed under her bedchamber door. Gaby blew her nose and dabbed under her eyes before she tapped on the panels.

'Are you awake? May I come in?'

'Yes, of course.' Jane put down her book and peered at Gaby over her spectacles. 'I did not expect you home so soon. Was the ball a disappointment?'

'It was lovely, but I felt rather tired and a little faint. Jane, I know I said we would stay longer, but I need to go home, I cannot manage with seeing Gray any longer. There is no need for you to come and break your own commitments—I will hire a respectable maid for the journey and you can keep this house and the staff on for as long as I have committed myself.'

'Nonsense. I will come, too. I have seen and talked quite enough, I promise you.'

'Thank you, I do appreciate it more than I can say.' Gaby's eyes were beginning to water again and she dabbed at them. What was the matter with her? She was turning into a positive watering pot.

Oh, to the devil with being wise, to hell with being prudent, I just want this to stop hurting.

'What does your aunt say about this sudden departure? And Lord Leybourne?'

'I haven't told either of them. I will write just before we leave. There is a ship for Lisbon in six days' time, I saw it advertised in the *Morning Post* yesterday.' She only had to hold out for less than a week and then she would be beyond the temptation to yield and spend the rest of her life regretting her decision, making Gray regret his, betraying her inheritance and her family. For love.

'I will tell the staff that I am not at home to callers—that I have a severe head cold. We can make the booking, do our final shopping—even if I have to do it veiled in case anyone recognises me.'

She would have to write to Gray and her aunt, organise the balance of payments on the house and make sure the servants received references with an explanation for their short period of service. But it could be done in the time available. She would be busy, but that would help. And if it didn't... No one died of a broken heart, did they?

Chapter Twenty-One

'I regret that the first post has been delayed, my lord.' Fredericks delivered the news in much the same tone as he might have used to announce the downfall of civilisation as he knew it.

Gray told himself that it was ridiculous to be anxious over a late delivery. The ladies at Half Moon Street were confined to their beds with heavy colds, apparently. The footman who had answered the door had regretted that he had no information other than that Miss Frost and Miss Moseley felt unable to receive visitors, but that their affliction was nothing to cause their friends concern.

He had sent flowers and fruit, of course, and an offer to assist in any manner required, but had received nothing in return but brief notes of thanks, and not even that yesterday. Surely by today a cold, even a heavy one, should be yielding to bed rest? It would be just like Gabrielle to make light of a more serious illness, he thought, if it would stop people making a fuss over her.

'What is the problem with the delivery?' he asked.

'I sent James to ascertain, my lord. A carriage accident on Piccadilly has jammed the streets around. It is quite outrageous that it should cause the postman, who is on foot, to be delayed. Doubtless he has been gawping at the scene which James tells me is one of significant disorder. That does not excuse the delaying of your lordship's correspondence. I shall make a complaint—'

'Yes, thank you, Fredericks. I am sure it will arrive sooner or later.' *And I must develop some patience.* Muffled sounds penetrated from the hall. 'Someone is at the door now. That is probably the post now.'

'Mr Pickford, my lord.' James, the footman, opened the door on Henry, who strode in, face grim.

Hell. On top of everything else he had been unfair to Henry, Gray knew that. He should have written and apologised after the ball, but it had slipped his mind in his general anxiety about Gabrielle. His cousin had presumably had enough and wanted to have it out and he couldn't blame him. *Only not just now.*

'You damned idiot! What have you done to drive her out of the country?' He brandished a crumpled sheet of paper under Gray's nose.

'My lord,' Fredericks said urgently. 'Perhaps Mr Pickford—'

'It is all right, Fredericks. You and James may leave us.' Whatever Henry was ranting about he did not want it spreading round the entire household. 'What are you talking about?' As the door closed behind the butler Gray took the letter and smoothed it out.

Dearest Henry,
I cannot thank you enough for what you have given me, for your understanding. This is goodbye. I have to go back to Portugal, I cannot stay—the situation with Gray is impossible. I sail on the twenty-third on the dawn tide.
With much affection,
Gabrielle

He stared at it, trying to tell himself what it said was impossible. *Dearest Henry...what you have given me...the dawn tide.*

Today. She had gone. She had not been sick with a cold, she had been avoiding him for a week. She had not been well at the Terringtons' ball, she had exchanged a note with Henry, he had seen the surreptitious manner something had passed between them. Henry had got her with child, she had been sure that evening of the ball—and now she was gone, back to the quinta.

Gray was not aware of getting to his feet, of clenching his fists, of lashing out. But Henry staggered back, his hand to his face, blood between his fingers.

His cousin recovered himself fast. Gray ducked out of the way of a wild left hook, then Henry was boring in, fists flying, some science returning to his blows as he got his temper under control. Gray took a punch to the solar plexus, went down, taking a chair with him, painfully.

He surged to his feet, seeing red, knowing only that the man in front of him had put his hands on Gabrielle, *his* Gabrielle, had got her with child. He swung with his right fist and Henry went flying on to the hearthrug in a clatter of fire irons. Gray took one stride towards him and was hit in the back of the head with cold liquid.

'What the hell?' He turned, fists up, ready to take on whoever dared to intervene and found himself face-to-face with his godmother, milk jug in hand. Behind her Fredericks, normally more than capable of repelling any unwanted visitor, stood helpless.

'Lady Orford, my lord. I explained that you were not receiving, but—'

'Not receiving?' His godmother's gaze swept up and down his body, then moved to Henry who was clambering out of the hearth in a clanking of poker and tongs. *'Not receiving?* Is this how you spend your mornings, Gray? Brawling with your cousin? No wonder Gabrielle has left, poor child.'

Tomkins appeared, presumably summoned by Fredericks, with comb and clothes brush and trailed by a footman with a basin of water. 'My lord?'

Either he'd suffered a blow to the head at some point this morning and this was all some kind of hallucination or he was dead drunk or, and it seemed the least likely, he and Henry were fighting over Gabrielle and his aunt was standing in the midst of the melee as an improbable referee.

'Fredericks, please show Lady Orford to the small drawing room and bring her refreshments.'

She bridled at him, then swept out. 'I will be back in fifteen minutes, Gray.'

Henry was dabbing at his nose with a cloth

while Tomkins straightened his clothing. 'What was that for?' he demanded.

'Later,' Gray promised grimly, towelling milk out of his hair. 'When I have got rid of my god-mother. For now, try to pretend we have had a minor falling-out over some bet or another. The last thing we need is for her to be spreading this far and wide among her circle of gossips.'

Henry bared his teeth in what might pass for a smile. 'I will do my best.'

Lady Orford was readmitted to a scene which, if she chose to ignore Henry's swelling nose and Gray's split lip and reddening eye, appeared to be a normal bachelor breakfast.

'I apologise, Godmama. A minor dispute over a wager got rather heated. Will you join us for breakfast?'

'Breakfast? Certainly not. How can you eat so calmly when my niece has jilted you and fled the country?' Even so, she flung herself into a chair and added, 'More coffee,' to Fredericks.

'The post has arrived, my lord.' James proffered a laden salver. On top was a slim letter addressed in a hand he recognised.

'If I might have a moment to read my own let-ter from Miss Frost.' Gray felt sick, but he kept his face expressionless as he broke the seal.

I cannot bear to hurt you. This has become so complicated.

Several words had been heavily scored out.

I cannot deal with my own feelings for you either. Not when we are so close and I can see you, touch you. Kiss you. I wish I could tell you.

Again something had been crossed through.

I must make the break and do it at once. I see that. I must go home and be practical now. Devote myself to managing Frost's for the future...

I am sorry to leave you to cope with Aunt Henrietta...

The future. Henry had given her the future that she had dreamed of—a child and her independence to raise it. So Gabrielle had found the strength to break away, end this thing between them. Perhaps it had only been an illusion if she had been able to go to another man, lie with him like that.

She had found the strength that he did not have because somewhere, nagging at him, there was a solution to her dilemma. One she no longer needed.

Gray closed his eyes for a moment, shut out Henry's distressed expression, his godmother's indignant fluster.

Deal with Godmama first.

He opened his eyes, took a breath. 'We found we could not agree on many things, and because of that marriage was impossible. Gabrielle clearly feels that a clean break is best.'

'And because of you, my poor George lost the opportunity to woo her. It would have been a perfect match.' His godmother was shedding angry tears into her table napkin.

'Gabrielle would never have married George. She was quite clear about that.'

'You cannot be certain.' She threw down the napkin. 'Go after her, make her come back. I am past caring whom she marries—it is impossible that she is out there alone, running a *business*.'

'No,' Gray said flatly. 'I will not.'

'I don't know what the matter is with me.' Gaby clutched the side of the bunk with one hand and the basin Jane had just passed her with the other. 'I have never felt seasick before.'

'Possibly because you are not seasick.' Jane pressed a damp cloth to her brow.

'I'm not? But I am not feverish, I can't believe this is some infection or food poisoning. It is probably a judgement on me for all those lies about how we were laid up with a cold,' she added miserably.

'When did you last have your courses?' Jane whisked away cloth and basin.

'Er...' Gaby sat up and waited until the cabin stopped spinning. 'Let me see. About a week before Gray arrived at the quinta. But that's... That means I have missed two.'

'Exactly.'

'You think I am pregnant? But I can't be. I'm irregular because of the travelling and the change, that is all it is.' But she had never been irregular before, not by more than a day or two.

'You are not irregular. You are *late*. Two months late. Are you saying it is impossible that you are with child? You are queasy, you are dizzy and you are tired. You tell me you can't eat fish suddenly and you want sweet things. Can you think of any other explanation?'

'No. But I only... It was only twice and he—'

'Withdrew?' Jane said crisply. 'It is not an infallible method.'

Thank goodness for a natural philosopher, Gaby thought rather wildly.

It was true, of course. Nothing else explained this.

At least one of us is not embarrassed. And thank goodness I have discovered it here and not in London. I cannot tell Gray. He would insist on marriage. But a baby. My child. I will be such a good mother, she vowed. *But what will I tell everyone?*

Her thoughts were spinning out of control and she pulled herself up sharply. There was no way she could create a convincing marriage and widowhood now. She would just have to brazen it out and do everything in her power to keep her child happy and accepted. She was Gabrielle Frost of Quinta do Falcão, she had power and she would use it, call in every favour, to protect this baby.

They sailed into Lisbon on December first under a cold blue sky. Gaby leaned on the rail, thankful for the calming waters as the ship reached the estuary and slid between the shelter of the towering hills that contained the city.

A night to recover from her shock had done no good at all. Gaby felt unwell, thrilled, terrified— and conscience-stricken. This was Gray's child as well as hers and she had no right to keep it from him. And she knew what he would say when he found out—that they must marry.

Was she hard enough, strong enough, to go against her conscience in order to do her duty to her inheritance? The answer was *no*, even though it meant losing the company, meant that this child would not inherit one day but that James, the little boy she had never seen, would be master of Frost's—if Gray did not sell it first.

But I love him. Surely I can trust him not to sell?

She had not been able to give him that trust up to now, she acknowledged. It would be a leap of faith and the fact that she wanted to be with him, wanted to be his wife, only made it harder to decide. Was she doing what she wanted or what she ought to do?

But first she must be certain that she really was carrying a child. She knew the name of the best doctor in Porto, the one that all the ladies summoned to their childbeds. Because he specialised as an accoucheur she had never met him, so a false name would protect her privacy a little longer.

The next day Gaby managed to secure an appointment with Dr Riberro. She went to his consulting rooms veiled and returned dizzy with the knowledge that she was, indeed, with child, that she appeared to be perfectly healthy and that she now had the most important decision of her life to make.

'If I love him, then I must trust him,' Gaby said to Jane as they sipped, grimacing, the camomile tea the doctor had recommended. 'I wish I had realised that before, had not been so stubborn.'

'But you feel the responsibility to the family firm very deeply.'

'It took so long to build the quality, the reputation. All those years of work by my parents, my grandparents and their forefathers. It should have been Thomas's. Our workers have been with us for generations.'

'There is no reason to suppose Lord Leybourne would damage such an inheritance.' Jane experimented with a spoonful of honey in her tea and pushed the jar across the table to Gaby. 'Try that. It improves the taste.'

'It is trade, a business, and he is an aristocrat. And it is hundreds of miles from England. It would be a smudge on the family name and a great deal of work for what he probably thinks is foolish sentiment, although he is too kind to say so.'

Gaby looked around the tea room of the hotel. She could not go home yet, not with this decision hanging over her. If she did, she feared she would act out of sentiment alone, shut herself into the quinta and ride out the scandal, learn, somehow, to live with her conscience over deceiving the man she loved.

They were at the hotel they normally used in Porto. It was quiet, respectable and comfortable, but not one that her neighbours and friends patronised. She knew what she looked like from her mirror—pale, tense and with dark shadows under her eyes. It would be best not to be seen and her health commented upon before she knew what she was going to do.

'I love him,' she said out loud. 'And I have to do the right thing and believe that he will, too.' But the right thing as Gray saw it might well not be the same as her vision. 'I will go down to the docks tomorrow, book a passage back to England. I cannot do this by letter.'

'You must. Summon him here,' Jane said firmly. 'It cannot be good for you in your condition to go back and forth on that wretched journey. The Bay of Biscay is bad enough when one is feeling in perfect health and it is December now.'

'I have to and, besides, I am never seasick, so

the rough weather is neither here nor there.' The morning sickness would be as bad on the ship or the land. 'It will doubtless be several days or so before I find a berth and can sail again.' She leaned across the table and took the other woman's hand. 'I have to see his face when I tell him, Jane. I have to know what is in his heart.'

In hers there was joy about the baby and there would be, even if there was nothing at stake, no inheritance, she realised. Before, she had been thinking like a dynast, not a mother, not a woman. This child would be loved by her whether they grew up wanting to run Frost's or not, she realised. It felt strange to have that worry gone. It had obsessed her ever since she had begun to accept the finality of Thomas's death and now... Now other things were more important.

Chapter Twenty-Two

It was three days later that the shipping factor
sent a message to come down to the docks. There
had been a storm in Biscay, ships had been delayed and when she had enquired he had no way
of knowing what bookings were already taken.
Now ships were arriving, the note said. There
should be plenty of choice.

The wet weather, the tail of the storms, blew in
from the sea in a fine drizzle that soaked everything, made the stone-flagged quayside gleam
with damp and cast a miserable chill over the city
and the estuary. Gaby refused to be depressed by
it. There was too much else to think about and
worry over.

They were unloading a large vessel beyond the
factor's office, one of those delayed by the storm,
she guessed. Passengers, some lurching slightly
as they recovered their land legs, were making

their way towards her in the wake of porters with laden barrows. One tall figure stood out in the murk and her breath caught as she narrowed her eyes against the damp. No, obviously it could not be Gray.

'Gabrielle!' He broke into a run as she stood staring, the crowd splitting around her as though she was a rock in the river. Then he was in front of her, his hands reaching for her.

'Your face,' she said, staring. Gray was sporting a greenish-purple left eye and a healing lower lip.

'Nothing. It is nothing. Gabrielle, what are you doing here? I thought you would be back at the quinta by now.'

'But what happened? Who have you been fighting?' she demanded, a sinking apprehension in her stomach.

'Henry. A misunderstanding. He is all right and this is nothing. Gabrielle, I had to come and tell you—'

'No, me first.' Whatever he had come all these miles through the teeth of a storm to tell her must wait until he heard about the child. 'You have to hear what I need to say.'

'In here. You are getting soaked.' He pulled her towards one of the low brick buildings that lined the quay, a cake and coffee shop catering to the passengers waiting to embark or to do business. Gray pushed open the door to steam and the enticing aromas of baking and hot chocolate. 'A jug of chocolate for two,' he ordered in English, apparently too distracted to recall his Portuguese, but the woman behind the counter obviously understood.

'This booth, Gabrielle. Give me your cloak.' There was only one other couple in the shop, huddled together in conversation at the far end. Gray shook out her cloak and his greatcoat and hung them over empty chairs, then took her hands in his large warm ones. 'You are chilled through and you do not look well.' He pulled off his gloves and traced the circles under her eyes with one cold finger.

'Just what every woman wants to hear,' she said with an attempt at lightness as the chocolate and two cups were put in front of them.

The woman smiled at her. Perhaps, Gaby thought, she is being sentimental over reunited lovers. *Is that what we are?*

'Thank you.' She took the cup Gray had filled for her, sipped the rich liquid for courage and to ease her cold lips. There was no way to soften this news. She put down her cup and looked him in the eyes. 'Gray, I am expecting a baby.'

Gaby had not known what to expect when she told him. Pleasure, joy, surprise... Not blank shock.

'You are?' Gray asked when she had, finally, to let go of the breath she was holding. 'Henry's?'

'No! No, of course not. How could you—'

'It is not mine,' he said flatly. 'Damn it, I thought I'd been mistaken in him. I apologised for hitting him, for believing, even for a moment that he and you, after all, had followed that lunatic scheme.'

'What? You thought that I left England because I was pregnant?' She got to her feet, the chair legs screeching on the tiled floor. 'You thought I could...with someone else...after you and I had...'

Gray was on his feet, too, the bruises stark on his face where the blood had drained away. 'I was careful when I lay with you!'

'You are an idiot!' she flung back. 'A hateful, suspicious idiot. I told myself I could trust you, now I find this poor child has to endure you for a father.'

Gray stood looking after her as the shop door slammed, sending the bell clanking. Across the room the other couple looked up, startled. The woman bustled out from behind the counter, picked up Gabrielle's cloak and thrust it into his hands.

'*Estúpido! Burro! Imbecil!*'

'I— Oh, hell. Oh, my love.' He ran, the door banging in the wind and rain, the cloak tangling around his legs. Gabrielle was easy to catch on the slippery stones. She wasn't well, she was distressed and she could hardly see in front of her face because she was blinded by tears, he realised as he caught her. When he swirled the cloak around her shoulders she batted at it, her face worryingly white.

'Gabrielle. I'm sorry.' He scooped her up in his arms, kicking and struggling, spitting anger and misery at him. 'I'm stupid, an ass, an imbecile. I can't count. I'm jealous and fearful. I love you.' He shouldered open the shop door and the woman gestured through to another room beyond, shaking her head at him.

The wood-panelled chamber was empty and there was a fire. The woman came in with more chocolate and cups, a plate laden with *pastéis de nata*, the traditional custard tarts fragrant with cinnamon and lemon. She patted Gabrielle on the shoulder, shook her finger at Gray and bustled out, taking Gabrielle's cloak with her.

'I love you,' he said again, urgently as though

his words could bandage a bleeding wound. 'I love you. I'm sorry. When you left so hurriedly and Henry was so… I saw the letter you wrote to him and then yours to me sounded ambiguous. I feared the worst. I thought you had…'

'So you hit him.'

Was he forgiven? Gray couldn't tell, couldn't recognise this thin, tense woman.

'He hit me back. I deserved it. I was being an ass. When we finally got rid of your aunt, who managed to arrive in the middle of it, we talked. He explained what you two had been so secretive about at the Terringtons' ball, explained that what you were thanking him for when you wrote was being a sounding board to talk everything through, someone to confide in.'

Gabrielle reached out and touched the bruised skin under his eye. 'This must have hurt.'

'Not as much as I deserved.'

'And yet just now you still could not trust me?'

Gray knew he had to be honest even if it meant stripping away all his pride, laying himself utterly open to her. 'I am not used to being unsure, Gabrielle. I am not used to feeling insecure. Damn it, I have never been in love before, never felt jealousy like this. I thought I had been careful. Too careful to have got you with child. And I was not and that I could have been careless, could have risked you like that—it is hard to admit.'

'I thought it impossible, too. You were not careless, we were both too ready to believe it would be safe.' Her smile was a little shaky, but it was there and, suddenly, he felt hope. 'That is why I didn't realise until we were at sea and Jane made me work it out. It was the second time we made love. I am certain. You had been exhausted. You probably still were. You had woken from a deep, deep sleep and I think left it just a fraction of a second too long. I was rather clingy, I suspect, which cannot have helped. I saw a very good doctor the other day. He said it really is a very unreliable method.'

She is being generous, far more generous than I deserve, and now she looks so fragile.

He tried to imagine how a single woman, a gentlewoman with a reputation to preserve, must feel, realising that she was with child and alone. 'Are you well? You've lost weight, you are pale and cold and I have upset you.' He poured chocolate and put a tart on a plate. 'Eat, drink, get warm.'

'I've not been feeling much like eating, that is all it is.' But Gabrielle took the cup and sipped. 'The doctor says I am very well.' After a while she put down the cup, reached for his hand, looking down at their joined fingers, not up at his face. 'Why did you come?'

'To tell you I have solved it. I have unravelled our Gordian knot. I can marry you and Frost's will be safe.'

'And I was here to book a passage back to England. I was coming to tell you that I loved you and that I trusted you—if you still want to marry me, I would like that, too. If you love me.' She looked up then.

He did not know what she saw in his face, clearly not the startled joy that he felt, because Gabrielle stumbled on, looking back at their hands. She began to stroke her thumb over his. 'I wanted to tell you that, although I am so happy about the baby, that isn't why I want to marry you. I realised that I cannot put fear before love and I cannot love you without trusting you. Some things are more important than tradition or business or inheritance.' She looked up and met his gaze and he knew it would be all right, that his love had come to meet him halfway. More than halfway. 'Tell me how you solved the puzzle.'

'I remembered my tutor talking about Alexander the Great cutting the knot, which is what every schoolboy remembers. But there was something else. He was a real old pedant. Plutarch said that Alexander pulled out the linchpin and then he could see the working of the knot and he simply unravelled it. He did not cut it. The moral of the story is that he saw the essence of the problem, not a violent solution to it that would damage everything.'

He took a bite of the tart in front of him, realised he was starving hungry and demolished the rest. 'That's good. Yes—the problem is that, whatever we do or want, when you marry me all that is yours becomes mine. But if you do not own Frost's before the wedding, then it isn't mine.'

'Yes, but—'

'We have been fixated with the indisputable fact that everything that is yours on marriage becomes mine. So you set up a trust *before* the wedding. You put the entire business into it and you set out the terms. You, or whoever you nominate, will always have total control. There will be trustees, but you always have the casting vote. The profits all go back into the trust to be spent on the business. And you will nominate your successor or successors.

'I have never heard of a woman doing that, but I think we can organise it so that you can dissolve the trust and settle the business on a child, or children, of yours when they are ready. The lawyers I spoke to in London thought it should be possible, but there is the question of Portuguese law. But we can make it safe, keep it as you want it, even if it stays in trust for ever.'

Her face lit up as she worked it out. 'It would be difficult managing from England, but we can do it,' Gabrielle said. 'Oh, Gray, it is *perfect*.'

'I was thinking about the distances, too. There are times you would want to be in Portugal and times I need to be in Yorkshire, or in London. But I spent a lot of time talking to Henry, once we'd picked each other up off the carpet and started seeing sense. He knows enough to convince me that, if we don't mind travelling, we can divide our time between both countries.'

'You would be willing to do that?'

Gray nodded. For Gabrielle he would travel across the Atlantic and back regularly, let alone the Bay of Biscay. 'With peace in Europe, travel will become easier every year. There will be steam ships making the journey soon, I wouldn't be surprised.'

'But that is brilliant. Of course it would work— why did we never think of it before?' Gabrielle jumped to her feet, leaned across the table, kissed him full on the mouth.

'Because we were fixed on the fact that a woman's property transfers to her husband on marriage. We couldn't see past it to arranging matters so that you put the company safely aside before then.'

They sat and smiled at each other for a while as the scent of chocolate wove through the air between them.

We must look like besotted fools, he thought.

'When did you decide you could trust me?' he asked eventually when his heart rate had slowed to something almost normal and the urge to grin had subsided.

'I think I always knew, it was just that, when Thomas died, protecting Frost's became the most important thing, all that I had to hold on to of him, of my parents. Of my life. To protect it I needed a child to leave it to. And then, when I realised that the child was a reality, I saw that a business, a legacy, meant nothing. Only the baby and you mattered.

'I love you or I would never have lain with you. I love you, so it became intolerable that I could not bring myself to let go and trust you to do the right thing. I needed a good shaking, I suspect— and suffering from morning sickness in the Bay of Biscay with one very astringent female companion was certainly that.'

She was smiling, he saw with relief. Smiling even though the tears swam in those lovely brown eyes that had ensnared him almost at first sight.

'Where shall we be married?' Gray asked.

'There is an English church in Porto. We could be married there and then have a big party at the quinta.' Gabrielle seemed to come out of a happy haze. 'I suppose the sooner the better, before I cause a scandal with my flowing skirts to conceal my condition.'

'I'll send for my mother and the twins. The sooner they get to know you, and love you, the better. The children can all grow up in both countries. They will flourish on it.'

'Shall we go and find the chaplain of the English church?' Gabrielle looked ready to jump up and begin wedding planning that moment.

'Later. Now, you will eat another pastry and drink your chocolate and get warm and I will find a cab. Once we've seen the chaplain I will take you back to your hotel and we will do soothing, restful things like making lists.'

Gabrielle laughed. 'If you think that excited women making wedding plans is going to be soothing, you, my love, are in for a surprise.' But she ate another tart and drained her chocolate and put her hand into his to prove that she was warm enough.

The baker took Gray's money with a twinkle in her eye and a look of approval that had been missing before.

A romantic, Gray thought. *And I am turning into a romantic, too.*

'If we go to the agent's office I will write a letter to my mother and make sure it goes on the next ship back.'

'Invite Henry, as well,' Gabrielle said. 'He can see something of port production first hand and he can take ship to America equally well from here.'

'And I will signal that my suspicions were entirely unfounded?'

She looked up, an expression of total innocence on her face. 'Oh, yes, that *is* a good thought.'

'Scheming hussy,' Gray said. *My scheming hussy.* He smiled to himself as he pressed her hand tighter to his side. 'They should arrive just before Christmas.'

'So, we go back to the quinta now, once we have seen the clergyman and then we return to Porto to meet them and get married,' Gabrielle said as they entered the agent's office. 'The twins will love a traditional Portuguese Christmas. Would you mind them attending a Catholic midnight Mass? Only the baby Jesus arrives and is put in the crib and there will be real donkeys in church and the children love it. Papa and Mama always took me. When I was little I would sleep through the traditional meal—I don't imagine they would enjoy salt cod and greens any more than I did— and then I was awake enough for the service and for opening presents. We put out shoes in Portugal.'

'I can see Joanna borrowing my boots to put out so she has extra room for presents.' Now the smile he was trying to control escaped as a grin of pure happiness.

Letter written, and the agent lavishly paid to ensure it went with the next reliable captain to London, they emerged into pale, watery sunshine.

'You see,' Gabrielle said, 'even the sun has come out to welcome you.'

'Let us hope your Anglican clergyman is prepared to shine on us, too, and promise to marry us on the twenty-sixth.' He hailed one of the boatmen who waited at the end of the quayside and helped Gabrielle into the little ferry, even though she climbed nimbly down, quite at home on the river. She was expecting a child, his child, and it was difficult to restrain his instinct to carry her everywhere, to wrap her in wool.

'We must go home by carriage,' she said as the men tugged at the oars. 'The river is too dangerous to travel by at this time of year, unless one has no choice. And getting upstream takes an age anyway.'

On the other side they took one of the waiting carriages for hire and, when she had given the driver the address, he almost pushed Gabrielle inside and jerked the blinds closed.

'I love you. I am going to marry you and we are having a baby. And I haven't kissed you for eighteen days and twelve hours.' Gray reached for her, but Gabrielle was already in his arms, chilly woman in a damp cloak with cold hands cupping his face, hot mouth on his, hot tears that made the kiss salty, heat spearing through him with desire, with love, with relief.

'I do not know where you get the idea that *we* are having a baby,' she teased him when they finally broke apart. 'It is me who will be doing all the work. Oh, my goodness, what have you done to my bonnet? And my hair? And look at your neckcloth. The chaplain will think we have been misbehaving in a cab.'

'We have.' Gray tugged at his cravat and willed

his body to behave itself. 'And if you think I am not going to be with you for every moment of the birth, think again. If the doctor and the midwife try to shut me out, I'll break the door down.' He still had nightmares about Portia. It made no difference that no one, from the doctor to her mother, would have let him anywhere near the bedchamber: he should have been there.

'Of course. I'm sorry, I shouldn't have teased you about it. It will be the height of the summer, so you will be kept nicely occupied fanning me while I roundly abuse you for your part in the affair—I understand from married friends that it is obligatory to threaten one's husband with castration at some point during the birth.'

Gray could feel the blood leaving his cheeks. 'Ah, but they did not have their husbands there telling them how much they adored them.'

'We have arrived,' she said as they reached a high, forbidding wall. 'It is the plainest church you have ever seen because the authorities will not allow a spire or a cross or a bell. Are you ready to face the chaplain?'

'To marry you I would face the devil himself. A mere chaplain holds no terrors. And you are still too pale.'

Much to the interest of two Portuguese matrons

passing by on the other side of the road, a peasant with a cartload of hay, three small boys and two mongrel dogs, Gray took Gabrielle in his arms and kissed her thoroughly until her cheeks were pink, her eyes were sparkling and she was giggling helplessly.

'Come along and do try not to look as though you regularly seduce helpless males on the street,' he commanded, tucking her hand under his arm and settling his hat more securely on his head. 'The sooner I make a respectable woman of you the better.'

Chapter Twenty-Three

'Gray is here and we are going to be married!'

Jane looked up from the letter she was writing, carefully replaced the pen on the inkwell and smiled one of her rare, beaming smiles. 'How very satisfactory.' She blotted the page and stood up, held out her arms. 'Dearest Gabrielle.'

Gaby emerged from the unexpected embrace feeling positively tearful. 'Oh, goodness, I do not know why I am such a watering pot. I am so happy I want to run about the streets shouting the news, put up placards, order a special edition of the newspaper.'

'That would, indeed, cause some excitement,' Jane said, straight-faced. 'Where is he now?'

'Downstairs booking a room.' Was Jane going to be difficult about this?

'On this floor, I trust. He cannot expect you to

be flitting about the staircases as well as the corridors,' she said drily.

'Shh! That's Gray's voice.'

She could just hear through the door—he must have stopped right outside. 'Room six? Yes, that looks suitable.' His voice faded as he walked away.

'Next door but one,' Gaby said. 'I told him our room number.'

'Put what you need for the night in the valise,' Jane said. 'Are we leaving tomorrow? Yes? Then I will pack the rest of your things.' She cracked open the door. 'The coast is clear.'

Gaby snatched up her robe, hairbrush and toothbrush, and paused to kiss Jane's cheek at the doorway. 'Bless you. You are an angel.' Then she walked down the corridor, tapped on number six and slipped inside to find Gray and a positive heap of luggage stacked neatly against the wall. 'Where did all that come from?'

'Naturally, when running away to get married I brought my valet,' he drawled. 'Tompkins was following me along the quayside, but I had told him about this hotel, so he simply kept going when he saw us meet. He has unpacked the essentials and gone off, so he tells me, to explore Porto. What have you got there?'

'I didn't have to run away quite so far.' She put

her robe on a chair, suddenly shy. 'Jane is packing and we can be away tomorrow morning. If you want me to stay, that is.'

'No.' Gray shook his head. 'No, I do not want you to stay.' Then, before the sudden pang in her stomach could turn into anything worse he held out his hand. 'I *need* you to stay, Gabrielle. I need you to stay for the rest of time and beyond.' She reached out and took his hand in hers, let him draw her in until she could rest her head on his chest, listen to his heart beating, strong and sure. 'If I was a proper gentleman I would do no more than press a respectful kiss on your lips until the wedding night. Unfortunately I do not appear to have a gentlemanly bone in my body because what I want to do is to make love to you from now until the wedding, pausing only for sleep and food.'

Gaby listened to the rumble of his words in his chest, felt the brush of his lips in her hair and released the great shuddering breath she seemed to have been holding since the moment she discovered she was pregnant. Perhaps from the moment when she realised she loved him and could not have him.

'That sounds like an admirable programme to me,' she managed, before he was kissing her, lifting her until her whole body was plastered to his, her hands on his shoulders, dizzy with the feeling of weightlessness, with the magic of his lips against hers, the taste of him.

Gray let her slide gently down his body, his strength supporting the lingering descent until she was standing on the floor again. 'I had a very good night's sleep last night,' he remarked with apparent inconsequentiality.

'So you don't think you might fall asleep after you make love to me?' Gaby found that if she stood on tiptoe she could nibble her way around his right earlobe and trace the sharp, elegant whorls of his ear with the tip of her tongue. It had the intriguing effect of making him growl, deep in his throat.

'Shall we see?'

Her gown sagged suddenly. He had been unfastening it blind, she realised. A modest woman would make a grab for the bodice as it slid. Gaby wriggled and the entire gown slipped down, over her hips, to the floor. Gray bent his head to nuzzle at her breasts, exposed as they swelled above the edge of her corset. Then that was released and Gray pulled it up, over her head and tossed it aside.

'I am not going to ask how you learned to do

that.' It came out as a gasp as his lips fastened on to her left nipple, the sensations striking down, straight to her belly, lower, until she was shifting restlessly, her thighs tight together as though she could contain the vibrations that seemed to be shaking her.

Gray switched to the other breast, his tongue sweeping lavish, wet, delicious strokes over and over while his hands continued undressing her. She did not realise her shift and petticoats had gone until she felt the cooler air on her back, then the slide of the coverlet under her as Gray lifted her again and laid her down on the bed.

'I am wearing too many clothes.' He stripped with an urgent efficiency that was arousing in itself.

Gaby kicked off her shoes and reached for her garters.

'Leave them.' Gray knelt on the end of the bed at her feet and looked at her.

Blushing just a little, Gaby leaned back on her elbows and studied him in her turn. The winter evening was drawing in and he had lit the lamps in the room, bathing his skin in a flickering golden glow that slid over the breadth of his shoulders, the moulding of musclc in his arms and torso. She looked lower to where he was erect and felt her eyes widen as he seemed to thicken under the touch of her gaze.

'You are the most beautiful thing I have ever seen,' Gray said, his voice low. 'I thought you lovely before, but I could not have looked hard enough, long enough. I will *never* be able to look long enough.'

His palms stroked over the arch of her feet, up her ankles, the fine silk of her stockings snagging slightly against his skin. He untied her garters, one by one, his fingers steady, slow on the ribbons, his big hands gentle as he rolled each stocking down her legs and tossed them aside.

Gaby gasped as he leaned forward, pressed her knees apart, but she opened for him, bathed in the heat of his gaze. Her arms gave way as he edged up the bed between her legs and she fell back with a little cry as Gray bent his head and she felt his tongue lick up the inside of first one thigh, then the other. He teased the crease between body and leg for a while, then stilled. When she lifted her head to look at him he was kneeling between her knees, his hands curled lightly over her belly.

'There is nothing to see yet.' His fingers stroked, tender, possessive.

'No. It seems hard to believe and yet I know.'

She put one hand on top of his. 'Boy or girl, I wonder? Do you have a preference?'

'I want a child of yours. Any child of yours.' Gray leaned over, kissed her stomach, his tongue tip playing for a moment in her navel until she fell back, laughing at the tickle. Then he slid down, his shoulders wide between her thighs, and began to kiss and lick into the core of her.

Lightning shafts of delight, teasing, aching strokes of his tongue, his lips, his teeth, sucking and nibbling, dragging every exquisite, tortuous shred of pleasure out of her. She heard herself moan aloud, bit her knuckles, then flung her arms wide, her hands fisting in the sheets as he slid one, two fingers into the heat that was tight with longing for him.

'Gray.'

He answered her with the thrust of his fingers, the intensity of his kiss and she convulsed against his hand, gasping her love for him as he came up her body and took her mouth. She arched against him and he entered her in one hard stroke and then froze.

'Gabrielle,' he said against her throat, like a prayer. 'Gabrielle.' And now it was a demand, a challenge as he moved again, strong, slow, the rhythm as old as time, as fresh and new and miraculous as the moment.

'Yes.' She curled her legs around his narrow hips, dug her heels into the small of his back, clung to him and answered every thrust, every demand, gasping out her love and her pleasure as it built, tangling tighter and tighter. She felt him begin to lose his rhythm, heard his breath coming harder, harder against her face and then Gray went rigid above her as the knot of her pleasure unravelled into bliss. There was heat as he spilled inside her, the awareness that the only reality was the two of them, now one, and then she was lost in him.

'Papa, why isn't Thomas a lord? *I'm* a lord.' James, Lord Travers, peered down at the face of his new day-old brother, just visible in the swathing shawl. 'Is it because he's very small?'

Gaby watched as Gray bent over his sons, checking that Jamie, seated cross-legged on the end of her bed, was supporting the baby's head properly.

'It is rather unfair, I agree,' Gray said. 'Only the eldest son of an earl gets to be a lord with a courtesy title. Your brother is the Honourable Thomas Laurent Frost Graystone.'

'But Joanna is a lady,' Jamie persisted. 'And so is Susanna.'

They all looked to the other bedpost where Joanna was sitting, her new sister held very carefully. 'Lady Susanna Maria Frost Graystone,' she recited.

'That is the rule, I'm afraid,' Gaby said. 'There's no arguing with the College of Heralds. Even if it would be nice to have two matching sets of twins.'

Constantia, the new nurse, came in. 'Time for the little ones to sleep,' she said in her heavily accented English. 'And for their mama to sleep also.' She retrieved the babies competently, one in each arm. 'Come with me, children, and let your mama rest. Your grandmama is waiting for you.' The look she gave Gray was, Gaby thought, enough to rout most men. He took his son's place at the foot of the bed and just smiled until Constantia left, the children with her.

'Well, Lady Leybourne?' he asked, moving so he was sitting next to her, his legs up on the bed, his back against the pillows.

'Very well, Lord Leybourne.' Gaby rested her head on his shoulder. 'Tired, but so happy.' The shutters were half-drawn against the August sun and the filmy white curtains fluttered in the afternoon breeze that brought the scent of herbs and roses with it and, distantly, the sound of the river.

'Was it not clever of me to present you with twins?' he asked.

'And have me lumbering about like an elephant all through the summer heat?' She nuzzled her cheek against his shoulder. 'Yes, very clever. You have given me a ready-made family. Four children and we have only been married eight months.'

'Jamie and Joanna love you, you know.'

'I know. They explained very carefully the other day why they had begun calling me Mama. Their first mother was, obviously, Mother, which meant I was Mama. They are sweet, the pair of them. I just want to smother them in kisses sometimes. You know Jamie brought me a salamander last week?'

'If I bring you a salamander, will I get kisses?' Gray asked, his voice hopeful.

'You will get kisses whether you bring me sala-manders, diamonds or simply yourself. You will get kisses for ever.'

He slid down the bed and held her carefully against his chest. 'I'm amazed you can still love me after yesterday. All husbands should be chained to the foot of the bed when their wives give birth, then there would be no nonsense about who is the weaker sex. Sleep now, my love.'

'You sleep, too. And we will wake up and this will be no dream, but the reality of the rest of our lives.'

Gabrielle drifted off into sleep, Gray's murmured words mingling with the sound of the river, the sigh of the warm breeze, the beat of their hearts, and knew she would wake to a love that would last a lifetime.

* * * * *

LET'S TALK
Romance

For exclusive extracts, competitions
and special offers, find us online:

f facebook.com/millsandboon

⊙ @millsandboonuk

🐦 @millsandboon

Or get in touch on 0844 844 1351*

For all the latest titles coming soon,
visit millsandboon.co.uk/nextmonth

*Calls cost 7p per minute plus your phone company's price per
minute access charge